Ans	_____	M.L.	_____
ASH	_____	MLW	_____
Bev	_____	Mt.Pl	_____
C.C.	_____	NLM	_____
C.P.	_____	Ott	_____
Dick	_____	PC	1/07 _____
DRZ	_____	PH	_____
ECH	_____	P.P.	11/05 _____
ECS	_____	Pion.P.	_____
Gar	_____	Q.A.	_____
GRM	_____	Riv	_____
GSP	_____	RPP	_____
G.V.	_____	Ross	8/08 _____
Har	_____	S.C.	_____
JPCP	_____	St.A.	5/06 _____
KEN	_____	St.J	_____
K.L.	_____	St.Joa	_____
K.M.	_____	St.M.	_____
L.H.	_____	Sgt	_____
LO	_____	T.H.	_____
Lyn	_____	TLLO	_____
L.V.	1/09 _____	T.M.	_____
McC	_____	T.T.	6/07 _____
McG	_____	Ven	_____
McQ	_____	Vets	_____
MIL	_____	VP	_____
Heiland (2/07)	_____	Wat	_____
VanKerk n/m	_____	Wed	_____
	_____	WIL	_____
	_____	W.L.	_____
	_____		
	_____		_____
	_____		_____

Keepers of the Faith

*Also by Emilie Loring
in Large Print:*

Love Came Laughing By
The Solitary Horseman
When Hearts Are Light Again
With Banners
Uncharted Seas
There Is Always Love
Stars in Your Eyes
Rainbow at Dusk
My Dearest Love
Lighted Windows
I Hear Adventure Calling
High of Heart
Here Comes the Sun!
Give Me One Summer

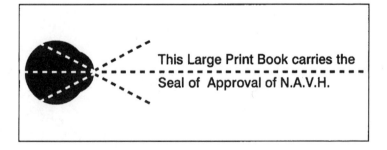

This Large Print Book carries the
Seal of Approval of N.A.V.H.

Keepers of the Faith

Emilie Loring

Thorndike Press • Waterville, Maine

Published in 2005 by arrangement with
Little, Brown and Company, Inc.

Thorndike Press® Large Print Candlelight.

The tree indicium is a trademark of Thorndike Press.

The text of this Large Print edition is unabridged.
Other aspects of the book may vary from the original edition.

Set in 16 pt. Plantin by Al Chase.

Printed in the United States on permanent paper.

Library of Congress Cataloging-in-Publication Data

Loring, Emilie Baker.
    Keepers of the faith / by Emilie Loring.
      p. cm. — (Thorndike Press large print Candlelight)
    ISBN 0-7862-7290-2 (lg. print : hc : alk. paper)
    1. World War, 1939–1945 — Washington (D.C.) —
Fiction. 2. Washington (D.C.) — Fiction. 3. Traitors —
Fiction. 4. Large type books. I. Title. II. Thorndike
Press large print Candlelight series.
PS3523.O645K44 2005
813′.52—dc22   2004025063

Keepers of the Faith

As the Founder/CEO of NAVH, the only national health agency solely devoted to those who, although not totally blind, have an eye disease which could lead to serious visual impairment, I am pleased to recognize Thorndike Press* as one of the leading publishers in the large print field.

Founded in 1954 in San Francisco to prepare large print textbooks for partially seeing children, NAVH became the pioneer and standard setting agency in the preparation of large type.

Today, those publishers who meet our standards carry the prestigious "Seal of Approval" indicating high quality large print. We are delighted that Thorndike Press is one of the publishers whose titles meet these standards. We are also pleased to recognize the significant contribution Thorndike Press is making in this important and growing field.

Lorraine H. Marchi, L.H.D.
Founder/CEO
NAVH

* Thorndike Press encompasses the following imprints: Thorndike, Wheeler, Walker and Large Print Press.

1

Nancy Barton approached home swinging a tennis racket. She glanced up at patches of blue sky between tree branches where recently there had been green leaves. Not many more out-of-door games with nurses on the hospital court . . . Birches had turned to gold. The maples were flames. The road was bordered by flares of goldenrod, purple plumes of asters and burning bushes of sumac. A scarlet leaf whirled and skipped ahead like a child gaily homeward bound from school. September had bowed out in a riot of color.

A crisp breeze tossed the waves of her short auburn hair, twitched at the sleeve of her moss green cardigan and her white skirt. Gorgeous air. She adored a New England autumn. Her enthusiasm cooled. Would she leave it next week for the South? She ought to be proud and happy that Ken wanted her to come to him, instead she was fiercely angry. Not an ideal frame of mind in which to start a marriage.

As she entered the hall of her sister's house a voice from the living room hailed her.

"Nan, come here."

The imperious command roused a hot wave of protest. Someday that same wave would burst the dam of her habit of taking it. Then what? She lingered on the threshold.

"I'm just off the tennis court, Di. I'll shower and come back."

"No. Read this first." The beautiful, tall woman in a Red Cross uniform, with cold blue eyes, smoothly lacquered hair the color of wheat, a determined mouth and a make-up that was a hundred per cent improvement on nature, held out a slip of yellow paper. Nan took it — read the message twice. The words were steadier the second time.

MARRIED TODAY. KEN

She sank to the blond mahogany bench before the fire and looked up at her sister standing in front of the mantel — her half-sister, she reminded herself; then at the colonial green walls and matching hangings of the charming living room, at the spiral of steam mounting from the spout of the silver kettle on the tea tray. She was awake. It wasn't a dream.

"Are you surprised?" Dianne Mitchell's question brought Nan's clear hazel eyes to meet the keen eyes watching her.

"Naturally, as I am wearing Ken's ring." She tried desperately to keep her voice under control. "Why wire you, Dianne? Hadn't he courage to break the news to me himself?"

"You put him off once too many times, Nan."

"If he had loved me as a man should love the girl he wants for a wife, he wouldn't have gone off the deep end with another woman because I postponed our marriage."

"You've a lot to learn about men, Nancy. I am disappointed in you."

"Why in *me?* You picked a naval officer — whom *you* liked immensely — as a husband for your sister. The fact that his family is tops socially helped, and little credit to that same sister that she allowed herself to be persuaded he was the man she wanted. You will be trustee of my property until I am twenty-five or marry. Instead of fighting for my freedom from your highhanded man-agement of my life, I, like a mouse, allowed myself to be argued into an engagement." She shredded the yellow paper and flung the scraps into the scarlet and orange flames weaving and dancing up the chimney like fire dervishes.

"I can take being jilted." She swallowed a sob and blinked back hot tears. "What I can't bear is that a man in whose fairness I believed would be such a heel as to wire *you* to tell me — not have the nerve to break the news to me himself. He didn't even mention my name. Great help he'll be to the U.S. Navy! If *he* would cheat, anyone would. I'm off men for good." She pulled a ring from the third finger of her left hand and watched the facets of the large diamond catch the firelight.

"I presume this should be returned by registered mail. Ken will need it for his blonde."

"How do you know he has married a blonde?" Dianne Mitchell's voice was sharp with suspicion.

"A gremlin whispered it."

Nan was proud of the flippancy of the reply. Why admit that yesterday — was it possible it was only yesterday? — she had received an ultimatum from Kenneth Rand warning her that unless she wrote him at once that she would join him on the fifteenth of the month at the base where he was stationed, he would marry someone else? At first she had thought it a joke, then had been so furious at the threat that she had waited to let her anger cool before answering. The fifteenth was a week ahead. He hadn't waited even twenty-four hours for her answer. His letter must have been a build-up for the jilt. Doubtless the blonde was a fast worker.

"I am glad you are taking it so sensibly that you can laugh, Nan." Why confess that the sound Dianne had heard had been a quickly swallowed sob? "Now that the decision to marry or not to marry has been made for you — we can go on from here."

"Not a chance." Nancy Barton thrust her hand with the ring in the palm hard into the pocket of her green cardigan. "From now on *I* make my plans. Do you know why I haven't been tempted to join one of the Women's Auxiliaries? Because most of my life I've served under your orders. 'Hup! Hup! Left! Right! Attention! March!' or words to that effect. No regimentation for me. It's time I stepped out on my own. You have charted my life to date, now I'll take over. I —"

"You'll have to admit it has been successfully charted," Dianne Mitchell interrupted. "You make society headlines wherever you go, you've had a sound education, with summers abroad to study languages, from the time you were a little girl until the war tore the world apart. Your singing and piano playing are far above average. You're an archery champion, a demon at tennis, you ride, skate, ski, dance, play an excellent game of cards and wear clothes like a professional model —"

"You check off my material qualifications as if I were being auctioned to the highest bidder who is not interested in my mind and spirit. You know nothing about the real me, that's why. You've left out two courses I took on myself: Nurses' Aide and secretarial."

"You interrupted before I had finished the inventory. You are beautiful with your heart-shaped face, naturally curly auburn hair, faultless skin, exquisite teeth, enormous hazel eyes set in jet-black lashes, and lovely hands."

"No credit to you, those items. They came from my mother."

"I've helped preserve and increase their attractiveness with care of your health, which is superb, haven't I? Someday you'll thank me for all this. I advised Kenneth Rand as a husband for you because I think him a coming man. A man with a future. You're the clinging-vine type, Nan. You need —"

"Someone to whom to cling? Not any

more. By the time this horrible war is over the dependent woman will be as extinct as the prairie hen. Had I married Ken, the blonde would have sailed into the offing sooner or later. That it happened sooner is a piece of luck, if you ask me. I believe in faithfulness to marriage vows. That's where you and I part company, Di."

I shouldn't have said that, I shouldn't, Nan reproached herself. Never before have I given the slightest hint that I thought Jerry Payne a trifle too devoted to his friend's wife.

"What do you mean by that crack?" Dianne's blue eyes were as hard as her voice.

"Nothing special. You'll have to admit that you have an extra man or two hanging round even in wartime. I meant a lot, though, when I declared that from now on I'm on my own. I'm grateful for what you've done for me. I know you've given me a grand foundation for life. I was sixteen when Mother died and left her small fortune in trust for me until I was twenty-five — or married — to be handled by your father and mine who, when he went, appointed you trustee in his place. If your training is worth anything I ought to be able to work out a design for living myself."

"Don't be silly, Nan. You're upset because of that news from Ken. There are other coming men in the world, though I think he is especially right for you. Let's forget him and dress. We're having supper with the Suttons tonight, remember."

"You may be. I'm not. I sent regrets."

"You're not going! To the *Suttons'*?"

"You couldn't have sounded more horrified if I had turned down a command dinner with the President."

"But they are newcomers here, socially desirable, and this is their first entertaining. They have *bought* — not leased — the adjoining place to ours; it isn't good neighborliness not to go. The supper is in honor of Mrs. Sutton's brother, invalided back from the Pacific after accomplishing thirty missions. He's a captain in the Marines and has been decorated. You must go. It's to be buffet. I'll phone her you've changed your mind —"

"If you do, I won't go. You're through managing me, Di. You're set to manage everything — clubs, community projects as well as every person who touches your life. Sam may be able to stand it, he can't escape, but I —"

"Hey, what goes on here? Do I smell gunpowder? Did I hear my name? What can't I

14

escape, Nancy B.?"

Nan forced a smile to meet the amused eyes, brown and friendly as those of a red setter, of the blond, thickset man standing on the threshold. "Nancy B." was his special name for her. He was tall except when standing beside his wife, who was half a head taller. She loved her sister's husband too much to hurt him. No brother could have been more considerate in the years she had lived in his house. Several times he had sided with her against his wife, and that had taken courage. Only once had she known him to make the same stand for himself. Di had interfered in his office routine and his fury had become one of the legends of the foundry. She had not attempted it again. Why didn't he assert himself at home? Not because of Di's money; he had a lot more than she. He was what was currently called a "big-shot industrialist."

"Just a touch of mutiny," his wife explained with a hint of the dictator addressing the populace in voice and manner. "Nan is threatening to fare forth on her own."

"If you ask me, it's high time." Back to the fire, Sam Mitchell lighted a cigarette.

"Thanks a million, Sam."

"Why thank him, Nan? He's practically

15

turning you out of his house."

"Nancy B. knows better than that, Dianne. She knows that I'll miss her like the devil, but I can't stand seeing a personality being smothered."

"You mean by *me?*"

"Sure by you. As a dictator you have World Enemy Number 1 licked to an appeaser. Who else in the house has anything to say? What caused this blowup?"

Nan couldn't believe her ears. Sam, the lazy, Sam the subservient husband, breaking out like this at home! What had happened to cause the change?

"A wire from Kenneth Rand announcing his marriage," Dianne answered lightly.

Sam Mitchell's incredulous eyes questioned his wife and then her sister.

"*Married!* Boy, I didn't know you'd broken your engagement, Nan."

"I hadn't. Ken wired Di the glad news."

"Di! Why didn't the heel inform you?"

"You'll have to ask him. He isn't so terribly to blame, Sam. He has been asking me to marry him and I have kept postponing it."

"This is one time your managing hand came a cropper, Di. You put that engagement across, didn't you?"

"Suppose I did. Nan wasn't forced into it, was she?"

Sam Mitchell ignored his wife's annoyed question. He crossed to Nan and tipped up her chin until he could look into her eyes.

"Pretty broken up about this, Nancy B.? I'm not. Gosh, how I've wished you'd tie a tin can to Lieutenant (j.g.) Kenneth Rand. Never liked him. Too smooth for my money. Mad enough for me to take the first plane southward bound and beat up the happy bridegroom?"

Nan shook her head.

"No, Sammy. I've had an escape. You know that one about the ill wind. It has given me a chance to start over. I'll hunt a real war job tomorrow morning."

"You'll do nothing of the kind, Nan. You are doing enough, with Civilian Defense, Nurses' Aide work and Officers' Club evenings. I forbid it," Dianne declared forcefully.

Nan glanced at Sam Mitchell. His arms were crossed on the tall, carved back of a chair. Would he come to her rescue? Evidently not. His eyes were half-covered by their lids in his usual lazy expression. It was up to her to fight for freedom.

"Watch me, that's all, just watch me, Di," she defied flippantly.

"If you do, I'll stop your allowance."

Sam Mitchell straightened and thrust his

17

hands hard into the pockets of his brown tweed coat.

"If you attempt that, Di, I'll walk out on you."

"Walk out! Sam Mitchell, have you gone crazy?"

His steady eyes met and held her incredulous blue ones. Color rose to her fair hair. Nan's heart shot to her throat and went into a nose dive. Did he know about Jerry Payne? she wondered in the instant of tense silence which followed Di's question. He lighted another cigarette, blew a smoke-ring before he answered.

"Could be. Perhaps I've just become sane. I meant what I said. Di has no legal right to stop your allowance, Nancy B. If she doesn't know that she'd better resign her trusteeship and have someone appointed who does. Go ahead. Try out any plan you want. I'll back you in anything."

"Sam Mitchell —" Dianne's eyes were blue fire in a face devoid of color under the rouge — "don't dare interfere between me and Nan, unless — unless you are in love with her." She watched the blood burn under his fair skin. "Good heavens, I believe you are!"

Nan looked from one to the other incredulously. Di's eyes were wide with unbelief, her husband's were murderous. What had started this horrid quarrel? Sam in love with his wife's sister? Di was crazy. Di was —

"Run along, Nancy B." Sam's voice was low and toneless. "This is no place for a little girl who still has star dust in her eyes."

Run! Nan didn't need to be told to make her escape. As she reached the threshold she heard his low, fierce voice: —

"You've started something now, Dianne."

2

Twelve. Nan counted the strokes of the tall clock on the stair landing. Midnight. She rose restlessly from a deep chair in her softly lighted bedroom. Why couldn't she settle down, sleep, and forget the last seven hours? Forget the wire from Ken, forget Dianne's furious "I believe you are in love with her" and Sam's fierce "You've started something now, Dianne"?

The mirror reflected her slim figure in lounge pajamas — aqua satin slacks, the pale gold and aqua plaid of her short-sleeved tunic and the copper sheen of her auburn hair — as she passed it on her way to the long open window. Star dust in her eyes, Sam had said. That was a joke. Did any girl of twenty-two have it now? There had been another fight with Di when she had persisted in her refusal to attend the Sutton supper. Just why had she declined the invitation in the first place?

Arms crossed on the railing of the iron

balcony outside her room, she looked down at the garden from which rose the faint scent of petunias. In the middle of it a swimming pool glimmered like an indigo mirror flecked with shimmering star-reflections, cold red stars, hot blue stars, hung against the indigo velvet of the sky.

Moonlight washed in a shadow-pattern under each tree. The stillness of autumn had descended on the countryside. Had the katydids been silenced by the first frost? There was no sound of their raucous night cries. From the distance drifted a baritone voice singing *"Speak low when you speak love."* The Sutton party on the adjoining estate must still be going strong. She had refused the invitation because she was fed up with attending social affairs when men were dying horribly, perhaps men she knew; when hearts were breaking on the home front and she was doing nothing to help — that was the answer.

"That's not fair to yourself," Nan reminded Nan. "You spend six hours a day at the hospital pinch-hitting for nurses and attendants; you're an Air Raid Warden. Of course you want a regular war job and of course you'll get one. Sam will back you."

"You've started something now, Dianne."

The memory of his fierce voice set her a-shiver. He wasn't in love with her, he was just devoted and tender as a brother would be. Darn Dianne. She had spoiled a beautiful friendship. In doing that she had opened a way of escape. She wouldn't want her half-sister in the house after this and her half-sister wouldn't stay.

"You've started something now, Dianne." Sam's words echoed through her mind again. What had he meant? What current of events had Di set in motion?

She must sidetrack that train of thought. Perhaps if she ran down to the garden for a few minutes, when she came back she would sleep.

She slipped on a beige wool greatcoat, opened her door and listened. No sound in the house save the ponderous ticking of the old clock on the landing. Sam and Dianne had returned an hour ago. She had heard the car in the drive. All clear.

She tiptoed down the stairs, holding her breath at every creak; ran across the terrace; down the garden path, beside which a few chrysanthemums and pink petunias, sturdy survivors of a frost, gleamed like pale stars. Gorgeous moonlight. No breeze. Night had tempered the day's crisp air. It was fairly warm.

Seated on a white bench she stared at the pool. Curious that the water should ripple on such a still night. She closed her eyes while she tried to pull some kind of order out of the chaos of the day's events. First had come the wire from Ken. Was she heartbroken? Definitely not. But, hurt, horribly hurt, that he had been such a coward as not to tell her. She hadn't loved him enough to marry him. She'd better face the fact she had shied away from before: that when he kissed her something within her rebelled. He must have sensed it. What man wouldn't want a girl to be more responsive?

Why had she become engaged to him? Better be honest with herself about that, too. It had been her cowardly desire to escape Dianne. Married, she would be free. It was a clear case of the pot calling the kettle black when she had called Ken a coward because he didn't wire her instead of her sister. Now that that point was cleared up, what next? A war job away from home and a long, long way. It would mean another fight with Dianne. Did Sam know enough of his wife's relations with Jerry Payne to threaten a walkout? It couldn't be true. Di was selfish, vain, a glutton for power and admiration, but she wouldn't —

"Lady." The voice at her feet brought her

up standing. A head appeared above the water. Two brown hands clutched the rim of the pool.

"If you'll turn your back, I'll retrieve my clothes behind that bench. A swimming pool in October is an icy place in which to spend the night."

Indignation routed fright. She looked down at an unshaven face. A hobo or a panhandler? How had he found his way to the Mitchell garden?

"You deserve to freeze. Who gave you permission to swim here? I've never seen you before."

The mouth beneath the slight mustache widened in a grin.

"You'll never see me again if you don't r-run away. I'm stiff with c-cold." The man's teeth chattered. "I've been f-floating, s-swimming under water waiting for you to l-leave. You wouldn't; and now, g-going, go-ing, g-gone!" With the last faint shivery word, head and hands disappeared with a splash.

"For Pete's sake!" Nan flung off the heavy coat, rolled up her slacks and stepped into the pool. The water was shallow near the edge. He couldn't drown, he mustn't. She groped on the bottom. Nothing there. Had he —

24

"As I suggested before — l-lady —"

The voice came from a few feet beyond.

"For heaven's sake, come out." She climbed out herself, pulled the legs of her slacks into place and picked up her coat. "I'll wait for you by the sundial. I'm an air-raid warden and I'm supposed to turn in any suspicious stranger who appears, and I'll never have a better chance." She flung the last half of her protest over her shoulder and walked away.

A splash! Had the stupid thing fallen in again? She listened. Sounded as if he were coming out. Would he try to escape? How long would it take him to dress? She would count up to fifty and if he hadn't spoken then she'd look for him. In these dangerous times one had to be suspicious. Sam's foundry was producing war goods. Perhaps this midnight visitor wasn't a tramp, perhaps he was an enemy paratrooper who had come down in the garden and, seeing the house pitch-black, had taken a chance at a swim. He might be one of the prisoners who escaped recently from Canada. In that case . . .

"Here I am, Warden."

She turned to look at the tall man who had spoken. His eyes, with fans of lines at the corners, were dull and feverish in a thin face tanned to the shade of bronzed leather under what appeared to be a two days' growth of beard. His teeth were amazingly white in contrast. A finely shaped hand held a plaid tweed topcoat together at the throat. Little rivulets trickled from his dark hair.

Nan's eyes traveled from his head, sleek as the coat of a wet seal, to the few inches of khaki-color pajamas visible between the bottom of his coat and his sandaled feet. Could he have landed from a parachute in that regalia? Looked more as if he had come out of bed.

"Explain why you were in our swimming pool," she commanded sternly. "I shan't let you go until I know who you are."

"You're offering an almost irresistible temptation to refuse. I like it — h-here." His smile vanished.

"Oh d-damn!" he muttered and gripped the side of the sundial. His body shook from head to foot. "I was so b-burning hot I thought a swim would c-cool me. Don't be f-frightened. It's jus-just a touch of mal-malaria," he explained through chattering teeth.

A touch! After the chill had passed he would burn with fever. He must have been delirious when he had thought of the pool.

26

No matter who he was she must try to help him.

"Come into the house. Quick! I'll mix something hot that will send that chill packing. I'm a nurse — of sorts."

"O-k-kay, Warden. I-it seems I'm your pr-prisoner."

She could feel his body shake as he walked up the garden path beside her. Once he stopped. She laid an encouraging hand on his arm.

"Come on. You can make it. It isn't far. 'One foot and then the other and the little dog reached Dover,' remember?"

The sound really was a laugh. She wondered how, ill as he was, he could see anything funny in the situation. A person could die from malaria. He must have read her mind.

"That little d-dog and D-Dover made me feel l-like a kid again. Are you a chi-children's nurse, by any — ch-chance?"

"Never mind what sort of nurse I am. Here we are at the terrace. Can you make the steps?"

"Sure, I —" The sentence ended in a shiver.

Lucky she had left the French window open when she went out. In the living room she kept one arm about the man's shoulders while she snapped on a lamp. She guided him to the long couch. He dropped to it heavily.

"Easy does it," she reminded. She lifted his feet. "Stretch out. That's better." She pulled off her coat and tucked it round his shoulders; smoothed back his wet dark hair. His forehead was burning. His lips below his mustache were dry and cracked. The chill had passed, the fever had begun. Would he be able to tell her where he came from? If not, she would phone the hospital and ask if they had room for him. If they hadn't, what should she do to stop —

"What goes on?"

Nan turned eagerly to the frowning man with a leather hunting-coat over his dinner jacket who stood on the threshold.

"Thank goodness you've come, Sammy."

"Why are you whispering? Why are your sandals wet? Is that a man on the couch or have I gone nuts?"

"It's a man."

She explained how he had come there, added: —

"Before he could tell who he was he began to shake like a dog shedding water after a swim. I brought him in with no questions answered. He looked so like a tramp I was suspicious of him. Watch him while I phone the hospital. I think he is a sick man who has escaped his nurse. If he rouses try to find out where he belongs. He's likely to be delirious and try to get away."

"Sure, I'll watch him." Sam Mitchell crossed to the couch. He looked down at the man lying there with eyes closed and crimson cheeks.

"Know him, Sam?"

"No. Poor duffer, looks mighty sick, doesn't he? Beat it to the phone. Be quick. He may die on our hands."

"Should we consult Di first?"

"About what? Good Lord, haven't you and I sense enough to get a sick man out of the house, Nancy B.? Scram!"

Sam's defiance of Dianne still endured, Nan thought, as in the telephone closet in the hall she waited for the call to go through.

Now that she had time to think of it, why had he been out walking after midnight? His usually ruddy face was almost pale. Why those heavy lines about his eyes? Was he worrying over that silly accusation of . . .

A voice from the hospital switched her train of thought. Hurriedly she told her story. Questions and answers . . . She cradled the phone and returned to the living room. Sam was sitting beside the couch.

"Still dead to the world," he reported in a low voice.

"Couldn't you make him talk?"

"No. He's in a sort of coma."

"They'll take him in at the hospital if we can get him there. All the ambulances are out."

"We'll get him there in ten minutes flat. I'll bring round the station wagon. It was so crisp today I had the robes put in. Had we better give him a shot of whisky before we move him?"

"I asked about that. The doctor said, 'No. Get him to the hospital as soon as possible.' He didn't want him to have anything until he had seen him. Didn't trust my diagnosis, I suspect."

"Not afraid to stay alone with the guy while I go for the car, are you?"

"Afraid of him? We'll be in luck if we can rouse him sufficiently to get him out of the house."

She watched her sister's husband leave by the window through which she had entered. Her gold sandals were drenched black. They oozed water each time she moved. Had she time to change? The man on the couch still slept. Better not. Di might hear her and insist on knowing why she was prowling round the house in the small hours. She would be furious if she knew that her husband and sister had carried on without benefit of her managerial ability. She laid her hand on the man's forehead. Still hot. Her touch roused him. He opened his eyes.

"Red! You — you double-crosser!" he whispered hoarsely.

Red! He must be thinking that she was an auburn-haired girl he knew and hated.

"I won't double-cross you this time. Trust me. Try to keep awake, please try. We want to get you home — or to the hospital."

"Haven't a home. The hospital!" With a supreme effort he swung his feet to the floor and sat up. "I can't go there. Orders —" He swayed, his eyes closed.

Nan knelt on the couch and with an arm about him drew his head to her shoulder to steady him.

"You won't have to stay there. Perhaps only overnight."

"Okay, nurse. I'll go with you even if you have red hair."

"That's the spirit. Please, please open your eyes and keep them open. I don't know how Sam and I will get you to the hospital if you don't."

"I'll try. The lids won't stay up. Who's Sam? Your husband?"

"Mine," Dianne Mitchell snapped.

Nan swallowed a groan of dismay, as her sister approached. Her turquoise satin housecoat with vertical black stripes accentuated her height. She loomed. Now what?

"Who is the man you are holding in your arms?"

"A lad I fished out of the swimming pool. Quite a prize, if you ask me." Nan was charmed with her light reply. Just went to show that she had forever thrown off her sister's domination. She had heard of a person being born again. Today registered her rebirth.

"What's the matter with him? Why doesn't he open his eyes? Did he fall into the pool? Is he tight?"

"No, he's sick, poor lamb." For theatrical effect Nan tenderly smoothed back the man's dark hair. To her dismay his eyes opened, met hers for an instant and closed. Had there been a conscious gleam in them? Was he faking? He couldn't be.

"Ready, Nancy B.," Sam Mitchell announced from the threshold.

Dianne wheeled to face her husband.

"So you're mixed up in this mystery too, Sam."

"Not much of a mystery. Nan finds the guy, lousy with malaria, in our pool, brings him here, phones the hospital for a room. We're taking him there. Out of the way." He brushed his wife aside as he approached the couch.

"Why not take him home?"

"He said he hadn't one." Nan stroked the wet head gently.

"I'll help him, Nancy B. Let's go, fella."

With a hand on Sam's arm the man pulled himself to his feet. He swayed and Nan steadied him.

"If he is as ill as he appears he can't walk. Get the stretcher in the gameroom, Sam," his wife commanded.

"Stand aside, Di. Nancy B. and I intend to do this on our own."

"She is not going with you at this time of night. She —"

The man, who had been hearing heavily against Sam, straightened. He stared at Dianne with vacant eyes.

"The gentleman is right. Red goes with us. It's a ticklish business to come between husband and wife, Madam. Ask Bill, he knows."

"Wife! He thinks Nan is his wife. Is the man drunk or crazy, Sam?"

"Hang it all, what difference does it make? He's sick. Here we go, boy. Put your arm round my neck. Okay. We'll make it.

Coming, Nancy B.?"

"Try to stop me." She attempted to choke back a hysterical chuckle. It would come. "Now that I've found a husband at long last, Sammy, 'I'll never desert Micawber'."

She caught up her beige coat before she followed her brother-in-law and the man he was half-lifting, half-steadying across the room. From the threshold she glanced back at her sister, who, for the first time since she had known her, looked utterly confounded.

" 'By, Di, I'll be seeing you," she called and ran across the hall.

3

There was a moment when Nan wondered if they could get their patient into the station wagon, he went so limp when they moved his arm, which was around Sam's neck.

"Let him rest a minute, he'll make it. Step up, will you, fella? He understands. Up you go." Sam boosted him as he raised a shaky foot. "He's on the seat. Quick, Nancy B., hold him on this side while I get behind the wheel. Wrap one of the robes round him."

The car shot forward. Nan laid her arm across the thin shoulders. She could feel the heat of his body through the robe. As they drove along the empty road whitened by the glow from the headlights, he muttered incessantly. Some of his ravings were intelligible.

"Gosh, delirious, isn't he, Nancy B.? Must have been through hell. Malaria would indicate the South Pacific Theater. He —"

"Sure, we'll come down, you — *Jap.*"

35

Nan held the man with all her strength as with the profane, shouted challenge he lunged forward. Sam laughed.

"That's telling them. Can you take it, Nancy B.?"

"Take it? Of course. It's horrible, but I wish every man in your foundry could hear him. You wouldn't have to fight slow-ups and absenteeism. After this, if ever I'm tempted to welsh on a job I'll think of this night and memory will stiffen my backbone. I thought at first he was a tramp. Instead he's a soldier. Air? Land? Sea or amphib? Sounds as if he had been a prisoner, doesn't it?"

"Yep. Strong fare he's handed out but good for us to hear or we may forget that the fighting in the Pacific is the most brutal war ever waged. Hunger. Torture. Disease. Fear. Hope. Escape. He has given us a line on all of them."

"Added to that from his muttering while you were getting the car I gathered that a redheaded woman had double-crossed him."

"Could be, though even with that growth of beard, he's the lean good-looking type women fall for. Wonder how he escaped? Perhaps we'll find out when he is better."

"Then you think he will get better? He

seems so terribly ill."

"Sure, unless that dip in the pool gives him double pneumonia. Malaria is constantly on the minds of men in the Surgeon General's department because it is the Number One Enemy of armies. The Doc will pump him full of something which will do the trick. Medicine marches on with time."

It was with a profound sense of relief that Nan saw their patient lifted into a wheel chair at the hospital by a white-robed intern. In the strong light his skin had a yellow tinge. Her eyes followed him along the white antiseptic-scented corridor. His incessant muttering drifted back.

"Come on, Nancy B.," Sam Mitchell urged. "We can't do anything more for him. He's in good hands."

She waited till the wheel chair had disappeared around a corner.

"I suppose we can't, Sam, but I feel as if I were deserting a lost child. He doesn't know where he is. Will they let us see our patient tomorrow? He is ours until someone claims him, isn't he?"

"Sure they'll let *you* see him." Sam chuckled. "Didn't the guy warn Di it was ticklish business to come between husband and wife? That crack tore full of holes your guess that a redhead had double-crossed him. 'Ask Bill, he knows,' he said. Perhaps 'Bill' had tried to barge in between a couple. It's being done. Wonder what gave him the cockeyed idea you belonged to him?" he added as he opened the great door.

"Probably has an auburn-haired wife. He called me 'Red,' " Nan explained as she went down the steps.

"Gorgeous night. The sky is silver-gilt with stars." She inhaled a long breath as they reached the station wagon. "The air is as full of prickly bubbles as champagne."

As the car shot forward Sam Mitchell said gruffly: —

"Don't let Di's crazy idea, that I'm in love with you, worry you, Nancy B."

Behind the wheel he stared straight ahead. She curbed an impulse to slip a reassuring hand under his arm, so near her — darn Dianne for making her self-conscious.

"Of course it won't, Sammy. She was fighting mad and lashed with the first words which came into her mind. Even as a young girl she was so beautiful she was allowed to get away with tantrums of anger. I've known her a lot longer than you have and I know the weapons she uses. She doesn't care how they hurt. Would she stand for the same thing handed her? Not for a minute. It's a pity we won't all accept the golden rule as a working formula for decent living, 'Would I like that said or done to me? No. Then I won't say or do it to the other fellow.' "

"You're envisioning Utopia, Nancy B. Did you mean it when you said you wanted a war job?"

"I did. I'll look for one tomorrow."

"You won't have to. I've found one for you."

"Sam, you angel! Where? When?"

"Don't grab my arm like that. You'll land us in a ditch."

"Sorry. I know better. I had a rush of excitement to the brain." She laughed. "Perhaps I haven't a brain, only a head. Tell me about it, quick."

"After you and Di had that set-to in the living room this afternoon — gosh, already it was yesterday — I went back to my office. Because of my war work I can get a clear line to Washington. Got in touch with my World War I buddy, Colonel Long, on the phone."

"You mean the officer who has a staff of interpreters under him in Washington?"

"That's the guy. His office is in the enormous Pentagon where the War Department functions."

"Washington! Go on, Sam, or I'll have a nervous breakdown from suspense. Did you get a job for me? An interpreter's job in *Washington?*"

"That's right. You've studied foreign languages almost from the time you said your first word. The Colonel's private translator-secretary is biting his nails in impatience to get to the fighting front. I told him if you took the job you would be there in two days. The sooner you make a break for freedom the better. Can you do it?"

"I can. My Christmas packages for the boys overseas went today. I'll have to notify the hospital to get someone to take my place as Nurses' Aide; ditto Civilian Defense to provide a substitute Air Raid Warden; tell the senior hostess that I won't be at any more officers' dances for the present, pack my bags and I'm off —"

"Tomorrow to fresh woods, and pastures new."

It never failed to surprise Nan when Sam quoted poetry, though she knew he loved it and that on his many business trips he carried a small book of one of his favorite poets in his pocket. He never quoted in Dianne's presence.

"To turn from poetry to prose, I have found a room for you, Nancy B."

"I'm beginning to cool off enough to think of that. I know that Washington is

40

crammed to the gun'ls.''

"And spilling over. After I talked with Long, I got in touch with an old friend, Amy Trask, the widow of a senator. She lives in a huge house in the middle of a garden on one of the broad avenues in the old secluded residential area. To help out she has taken four paying guests. She doesn't need the money. The Senator left her a super-comfortable fortune. She's sacrificing the privacy of her home as a contribution to winning the war.''

"She must be a grand person.''

"She is. When I told her that my sister was coming to Washington on a war job — you see I banked on your taking it — she came across with a room and bath she had been hoarding. I didn't want you starting out as a career woman in Girl Town at Arlington Farms with its 7500 females. You can get to that later if you find it will be more convenient.''

"Sam, you're the answer to this maiden's prayer.'' She tried to cover the emotion in her voice with a laugh but it didn't quite make the grade.

"Sure you want to go?'' he asked anxiously as he drove into the garage. "The job is Big League stuff. You'll be worked to a frazzle. I've sort of catapulted you into saying 'Yes.' ''

41

"I never was surer of anything. I feel as if a hand grenade had landed in the exact center of my daily life and blown it to smithereens. But I'll collect the pieces and start a new plan — of my own."

Two days later in a train, crowded with service men, with rain beating against the coach windows — no seat to be had in a Pullman — she thought of her sudden defiance of Dianne. Not so sudden. Unconsciously she must have been building up mental and emotional resistance to her for years. She remembered her cocksure assurance to Sam that she would start a new plan of life. Her courage dropped with the speed of a descending elevator out of control. Suppose she failed to make good on the job he had found for her?

It was late evening when she arrived in Washington. The Union Station was thronged with soldiers, sailors, Wacs and Waves, gold-braided officers, important-appearing businessmen with bulging brief cases. A feeling of utter desolation swept her as she crowded into a taxi with four other passengers.

"Squeeze hard, folks, and get together like you was sardines," the taxi driver called over his shoulder. He grinned and pushed his cap at a more raffish angle.

The rain came down harder. Somewhere in the distance thunder rumbled. When she ran up the steps of the Trask house clutching the handle of her week-end case, the wind snatched at her gabardine coat and blew it out like a balloon.

As she entered the spacious octagon hall, air from the open door set the pendants of a great crystal chandelier chiming like wildly shaken crystal bells. The reflection of its light set a sinister glare in the glass eyes of the head of the polar-bear rug at the foot of the beautiful winding stairway. Panic seized her. Could she make good in the important job?

The gray-haired colored butler in dark green livery lifted her raincoat from her shoulders.

"M's Amy's expectin' you, Miss Barton. She —"

A slim, black-haired youth in olive drab charged into the hall from a doorway at the right.

"I refuse to be a decoy any longer, Pat. I'm through," he angrily protested.

"*Sh-h!* The family'll hear you," warned the chestnut-haired girl in a pink frock who followed him.

"Can't hush-hush me, dope." He caught up a trench coat from the carved chest under the stairs, shrugged into it and clapped on a field cap with one gold bar. "And mark this, Smarty-pants, if I come across you necking with that French officer I'll give him a swift kick in the teeth. Goodby."

Without a glance at Nan and the butler the boy banged the massive front door behind him. The girl disappeared into the room they had left.

"Don' you mind them children, Miss, they's allers fightin'," the butler explained indulgently. "Now, don't you go an' feel lonesome. The rest of the family ain't like them. Youse a-goin' to like it fine here. Come this way. They's havin' a snack in the library. M's Amy said to bring you right along, you'd prob'ly be starvin'."

Nan gave thanks for her smartly tailored camel-beige wool suit in which to face "the family" as he led the way to an open door across the hall. She clutched her out-size green alligator-skin bag under her left arm, forcibly blinked back tears, tipped up her chin and followed, though she was uncomfortably aware of her damp hair curling out of bounds around her green beret and her nose shining from the mist of the outside world.

"M's Amy, Miss Nancy Barton," the

butler announced.

As she stood in the doorway, the room and its occupants were photographed indelibly on her memory. Book-lined walls. Softly shaded lamps. Orange and crimson flames dancing up a wide chimney . . . Firelight glinting on two tall silver vases, filled with scarlet glads. A large white-haired man in dinner clothes rising slowly from a chair. A fortyish man with a grave, sharp-featured face . . . Another short and ruddy man of about the same age . . . A slender, red-haired woman in filmy black with a glass in her hand, standing between them . . . The smoldering animosity in her green eyes lighted an answering spark in Nan's, which dried the tears. Had she met an enemy so soon?

"Hr-rump. Another redhead. 'Two stars keep not their motion in one sphere,' Amy," the large man quoted loudly.

And then a charming, brown-haired woman in an amethyst frock was coming forward with outstretched hand and smiling violet-blue eyes.

"So, you are Sam's Nancy B.? Welcome, my dear. You are very welcome."

"Tomorrow to fresh woods, and pastures new." The words echoed through the corridors of Nan's memory and swept away her spiritual and physical fatigue.

"Thank you, Mrs. Trask. I am happy to be here." In spite of the merry-pranks which the green eyes of the woman in black had set prickling along her nerves, she meant it. Her new life was off to an exciting start.

4

Nan picked up the morning paper and glanced at the date. The middle of November. The smooth surface of the mahogany desk in her office in the mammoth Pentagon was polished to such a degree that it reflected the copper sheen of her hair and the intricate design of the flat gold necklace that topped her beige jersey frock. She scanned the headlines.

Italy. Russia. France. Germany. The South Pacific. Death, destruction and devastation everywhere, and in the Capitol on the Hill domestic conflict. Would it never end? At least she was now doing her mite to help toward victory. She dropped the paper. Six weeks ago she had defied Di in her lovely living room, had announced her own little Declaration of Independence, and here she was in Washington, a city which the eyes of the whole world were watching, a city to which the ears of the whole world were listening. Sometimes she had to pinch herself to realize she was awake, with a honey of a job — Sam had been right, it was Big League stuff — and an entirely new outlook on life.

She thought of the first time she had stepped from the bus into a roadway under this huge five-sided building and she thought of how the glow from the scores of gay orange pillars in the main concourse had warmed her heart, cold with excitement, as she waited in a queue at a desk for her credentials. She remembered her confusion as she noticed the ramps leading to the different floors, identified by illuminated signs, and her despair of ever finding her way in and out of the maze.

It seemed years ago that she and Sam had left the sick man at the hospital. The next morning when she had inquired there for the patient she had been informed he had gone, that friends had come for him. No, they couldn't tell her his name. It was against the rules. That appeared to be the end of the episode. She would never know now who he was.

She swirled in her desk chair as the door opened. A thick-set, blond man with a visitor's badge on the lapel of his brown tweed coat smiled from the threshold.

"Sam! Sam! I was just thinking of you! I

was never so glad to see anyone in my life. It seems ages since I left home." She ran to him, both hands extended.

"That goes double for me, Nancy B. The M.P. in the concourse okayed my visitor's badge and turned me over to a guide. He beat it after depositing me at the office where I had an appointment. When he didn't return to continue the personally conducted tour I found my way here alone. It's claimed this is the largest office building in the world. They've said it: forty thousand occupants. Kept bumping into gold-braided admirals, generals and lesser big shots in uniform. Don't you get lost?"

"Not now. The first day I came I felt as if I were in a nightmare wandering along end-less corridors and ramps filled with people, all of whom, except myself, seemed to know where they were going. I had to fight the temptation to run home. The next two weeks I was threatened with a nervous breakdown for fear I would blunder into a restricted area and land in the guardhouse. I can make it now without a wrong turn. It's grand to see you, Sam."

"Your voice has tears in it. Not sorry you came, are you? Sit down again."

She shook her head vigorously and smiled at him tremulously. She hadn't realized until this minute how she had missed his comradeship, the friendly understanding in his brown eyes. He perched on the corner of the desk, clasped his hands, the backs covered with little spirals of hair like tiny gold springs, about his knees, and looked down at her.

"How goes the battle?"

"It isn't a battle, it's hard work and heartwarming interest, Sam. Even though I'm not on a combat front I have a thrilled sense of participation in winning the war. The translator-secretary who preceded me on this job has gone into active service and was he glad to go! When I appeared I thought for one hectic minute he would kiss me out of sheer gratitude. Do you realize that in this building the great game of war is planned?"

"Sure. It's the whole War Department of the U.S.A. I know many of the crowned heads here, if I can't find my way around. It's a madhouse, but an exciting town, Washington, isn't it?"

"You've said it, Sammy. At first, I had a smothering sense of crowds, a prickling awareness of antiaircraft guns visible on the tops of office buildings; of the yellow air-raid shelter signs; of raid drills halting traffic on the bridge. They gave me a breathless realization of danger. I felt I must hurry,

50

hurry, *hurry,* that there was no time to waste in sleep."

"That's not the way to tackle a job. You'll crack if you keep that up."

"I realized that days ago. Nancy Barton now has the situation well in hand, Mister. It's a minor miracle that you found war work that suits me so perfectly. I'm grateful to Mother and Father and Di for planning the summers abroad to study languages, and for the foreign governesses I had at home. I translate communications in French, Spanish, Italian, and German and interpret for my boss. The colorful foreign uniforms that come in and out of his office give me the thrills of my life."

"Long hours?"

"The lights in this building burn all night. If the boss stays his clerks and secretaries stay. I've never heard a complaint. Yesterday I was sent to Blair House, that's the Government guesthouse, to help two sheiks, their Royal Arabian Highnesses. Fortunately they spoke French. I have received heaps of invitations from your friends, but I haven't had a moment for social life or for using any of the accomplishments Di considered vital to my success. My work here allows time for two evenings a week as Nurses' Aide at a military hospital. One evening I devote to letters to the boys in the service. I'm never at a loss for something to write about in this wartime nerve-center."

"How did the living quarters I found for you turn out?"

"Couldn't be better. The house is adorable — perhaps that isn't the correct word for anything so huge — in the middle of a garden at present swathed in grotesque wrappings. You've seen it so you know how very special it is. I have a feeling it hasn't changed for decades. In comparison with the crowded city, the location seems positively countrified in spite of the fact that it is within five minutes' walk of a bus line. The food is super — served with a before-the-war perfection. I don't see how Mrs. Trask does it on what we pay. My room is large and comfortable."

"Sounds okay. Like Amy Trask?"

"Immensely. She's young — comparatively — but she mothers us all. She is up to her ears in war work, is a senior hostess at the Officers' Club dances. She enrolled me as a junior hostess the morning after my arrival. I haven't attended yet. I'm not used to mental concentration for such long hours; so, except for hospital and correspondence nights, I've been dropping into bed, dead to the world, directly after dinner. I'm getting adjusted, though."

"How about the seventeen-year-old daughter, Patricia?"

"She could be charming, she's a junior edition of her mother, pretty, smart, but at the dangerous age when a youngster thinks she knows it all. She has a lot to say about her right to live her own life. She defended a friend who had gone on a week end with a service man and a phony wedding ring, on the ground that a girl should make a sacrifice for a man who was fighting for her."

"Phooey! What are men fighting for, if not to keep the decent principles of life in the home? To protect our women from the sort of 'sacrifice' she's talking about? They are the keepers of the faith."

"I've told her that, Sam, but she is running round with a French captain — she says he is a Count — and turning down a charming second lieutenant, Randy Bond, stationed at Fort Myer, who apparently adores her."

"What's the matter with the French captain?"

"I've never seen him, but his ideas that Pat quotes give me the shivers. She comes into my room evenings. 'Mur-*der*' and 'Zowie' are her current exclamations. She spills her thoughts to me. It's a comfort she doesn't hide them. I feel like a grandmother as I listen and try to advise without antagonizing her. I never before realized that I had so many completely jelled convictions on the sort of conduct she defends."

"Like the other people in the house?"

"Yes. Pike, the butler, is a grand person. He rules us all with a rod of iron. We punch the time clock when we go out and come in. He keeps a record of our activities. There is a representative, Ralph Carew, who is taking his job solemnly. It's his first year. He is absorbed in postwar planning for peace. I'm all for that, too, but sometime when I know him better I'll suggest that he put up a fight to restore freedom to the individual in this country *now* — the right to work where, when and how he pleases."

"Hear! Hear! That goes double with me. What set you to thinking?"

"I've thought that ever since your foundry took on war work and you have had to fight interference with hiring and firing men for your jobs. Now that I'm a government girl I read the papers as I never read them before. I have time. I'm not on the social merry-go-round every minute."

"Perpetual motion is Di's design for living. Rushing here, there and everywhere with never a moment to read and think. Heading organizations and taking on new ones." He cleared his voice. "After all, it's her life she is spending. Why grouse about it? Go on about the Trasks' paying guests."

"There's a Foreign Broadcast radio bigwig, Oliver Stiles, 'Nolly' to the family, jolly, red-faced and redolent of cocktails. He has asked me to broadcast in French, sometime. I would love it."

"Don't promise so much that you'll have no time for fun."

"I don't *care* about fun, if only I can help toward victory. Mrs. Trask's uncle, Admiral Zeb Howe, retired, is one of our family. The kind you see on the screen, bushy white eyebrows, red skin, hook nose and a 'hr-rump' that rattles the window-panes. He's a dear, if he is a scold. His ideas are sound and he's so immaculate in dress and grooming it's a joy to look at him. Perhaps he has had as much to do with what you call my 'thinking' as the newspapers. Then there is Suzanne Dupree from one of the Carolinas. A widow with a drawl, green eyes and hair a little redder than mine. She writes a Washington gossip column which is syndicated in a number of Southern papers."

"Like her?"

"No, posi-*tive*-ly, no. The night I arrived

she looked at me with such animosity that I had an attack of heebie-jeebies in spite of the fact that I was pretty mad. Since then, she has 'honeyed' me — she's Southern — but plenty. She's out to get me. For what reason I can't imagine. Perhaps it is because Patricia shows I'm the object of her age-seventeen crush. Suzanne is striking-looking, and her clothes are something out of this world."

"Now that you are again in circulation are you recovering from the shock about Ken?"

"So fast that it frightens me when I think I might have married him. I wonder why I became engaged to him. I must have picked up the war-marriage germ. As a child I fell for every epidemic that came my way. He seemed to want me so terribly that I deceived myself into thinking I loved him. I'm a totally different person now that I am on my own. What makes a mouse a mouse, Sam?"

"In your case, years of living under Dianne's thumb. She has to be head man. She's so capable and domineering it takes a lot of fight to assert oneself, especially if one is half a head shorter. Ask me, I know."

"Spineless of me to be a Yes girl for so long. I'm terribly ashamed of it when I see Mrs. Trask carrying on so valiantly. Her heart must be in her mouth each time a communiqué as to the fighting in the Pacific Theater is released and the public is warned that there will be a tremendous sacrifice of life. But, she doesn't let friends or family know of her fears. She's an anchor to windward and an inspiration to us all. More and more I realize that it's a great world to the valiant, Sam."

"You've said it. Her son Tom, the Marine, is seven years older than Pat. Fine fella. I can see him going haywire if he knew of the ideas you say his young sister is picking up while he's fighting in those hell-holes in the Pacific."

"The Pacific! That reminds me. Sammy, have you heard what became of our patient? Ever find out whether he was land, air, sea or amphib?"

"Nope. Smoking allowed?" She pushed a glass ash-tray toward him. He applied a lighter to a cigarette.

"I've tried diplomacy, I've tried straight questioning at the hospital. No dice. Otherwise I have kept absolutely mum about his appearance in our pool. In short, zipped my lips. Afraid I might start something that the high-ups want kept off the record. I've a hunch he was an important person whom the government is keeping under its hat or the enemy has kidnaped."

"Oh Sam, not that last. I couldn't bear it."

"Did the guy make such a hit with you?"

"Good heavens, no, I wouldn't recognize him if I met him face to face. Couldn't even tell the color of his eyes. The light was dim at the pool and the living-room couch was in a dusky corner. He must have had a two days' growth of beard. I wonder if he would know us."

"Doubt it. We were just two faces in a fevered dream. How about a spot of dinner and bit of stepping tonight before my plane leaves, Nancy B.?"

"Sorry. It is my first evening at the Officers' Club, the dance is to be held at a historic tavern. Can't renege on that. Isn't Di with you?"

"No. I arrived this morning. Have a priority on the midnight plane. Too quick a hop for her. She misses you, though she won't acknowledge it. I'll call up Mrs. Trask and invite myself to dinner, then I'll take you to the Club."

"You won't have to do that. A bus picks up the girls who go to dance, but I'll love seeing you at dinner. Better allow plenty of time before for a talk with Mrs. Amy — and can she talk — she admires you enormously and Pat says you're an old dear."

"*Old.* Ooch! That hurts. Glad someone falls for my elderly charm," he growled, and closed the door behind him.

5

"There's a lot to be said for old-time elegance," Sam Mitchell thought as he entered the hall of Mrs. Trask's house. The glass eyes in the head of the polar-bearskin on the highly polished floor appeared to blink, the crystal pendants of the chandelier to chime a welcome. Did the wraiths of the Big Names who had gone up and down that stately stairway sometimes return at midnight? What put that cockeyed idea into his head?

"Good to see you, Mr. Sam."

The voice of the gray-haired colored man laid the ghosts of the past.

"Thanks, Pike, it's grand to be here again."

The butler deposited his topcoat and hat on the richly carved chest under the stairs.

"M's Amy, she say you go to her office, suh, jus' down the hall on the right. You knows the way. Used to be the Senator's smokin' room."

As he opened the door Amy Trask came

forward eagerly to greet him. Time and anxiety about her boy apparently hadn't touched her, he thought, as he noted the silver bow in her brown hair, to match her sandals, her violet crepe frock, which accentuated the smooth fairness of her skin and the purple tint in her blue eyes, the string of lustrous pearls. She caught his hands in hers.

"Sam, you're a dear to take time out in your busy life for me. You are heaven-sent. Sit here." She sank to a corner of the broad couch upholstered in faded yellow damask which matched the heavy hangings drawn across the long windows and patted the squashy cushion beside her. "I'm getting the jitters about one of my tenants. I need your advice."

"Another mystery man? You see too many movies, read too many crime stories, Amy."

"Don't laugh, Sam. I know I've gone haywire several times, but I figure it is better to be oversuspicious than under-, in these perilous times. If this is just another case of imagination on the loose you'll straighten me out. You owe me your help. Didn't you persuade me it was my duty to rent rooms in this ark of a house even when I don't need the money?"

"Why make me the goat? Didn't you agree with me that it would be one of your contributions toward winning the war? Pike said this was your 'office.' That huge desk looks like business but otherwise, it's deluxe for an office with its cabinet of silver boxes, big copper bowls of russet and yellow chrysanthemums and a dancing fire burning under the carved oak mantel. Are you making money?"

"Making money! That's a joke. When I discovered that my tenants weren't getting proper food I confiscated their ration books and began to feed them for what they would have to pay outside. One more interest to fill my time and mind so that Old Demon Fear won't get a foot inside the door of my imagination. Also, it's a challenge to my business sense and an outlet for my catering complex. My profit from the rooms goes into eats. Pike and I go to early market twice a week. I love to plan meals. I haven't entertained formally for two years, since the Senator — went."

"I remember your superb dinners and I thought of the Big Names who came to them as I looked at the stairway in the hall."

"That seems light-years ago, when you were a carefree bachelor and I could count on you when I needed an extra man. I hope it has been a happy marriage, Sam?"

"Has Nancy B. been telling you —" Good Lord, what a break. Equal to an admission that he wasn't happy.

"She hasn't talked about your home life, Sam."

"Nothing to talk about. I don't know why I burst out like that. To get back to your mystery man. Who is he?"

"It isn't a man. It's a girl. One of my Senator's Carolina friends asked me to take his war-widowed daughter, Suzanne Dupree. The family was wonderful to Tom, encouraged him to feel that their plantation was a second home when he was stationed at a near-by training post last year. I understand that news came of her husband's death after Tom's contingent had been ordered away."

"Suzanne Dupree. Nan spoke of her and her super-duper costumes."

"Glamorous as a descriptive word is out of date, Pat informs me, but I don't know of a better one for both. What could I do but invite her to come here after her parents had been so grand to my boy? She's been with us three months. Pike took an instant dislike to her. That fact may have contributed to my uneasiness. He has been with us so long that he feels a tremendous responsibility about the family — he includes my paying guests in that bracket. Lots of times he's an old meddler, at others he has uncanny intuition. I know he irritates Suzanne by the way he keeps tabs on her comings and goings."

"I hope he approves of Nancy B.?"

" 'A born lady,' he says. He doesn't realize that 'lady' as a word is even more out of date than 'glamorous.' Nan is a darling. Her laugh lifts the wings of my spirit. Pat is crazy about her. I could be a little jealous. I am sure that my daughter confides more in her than she does in me."

"Nancy B. is a safe confidante and a grand person. To return to this young woman you're worried about. What's the matter with her?"

"I can't tell you, Sam. She impresses me as being a woman with what is melodramatically known as a past. She wears black or white and has a convincing amount of wistfulness in eyes and smile for one fairly recently bereaved, but I don't trust her. I can't rid myself of the feeling that her line is good theater. She's pretty, she has red hair, a harsher red than Nan's brick-shade, she's smart and she has a lot of followers."

He was tempted to inquire why the girl didn't like Nan but decided it would be betraying Nancy B.'s confidence. Instead he asked: "Is the gal too gay with the boys?"

"N—o-o. Pat says she 'slays 'em,' but I've never seen any indication of anything questionable in her behavior."

"Has she a job?"

"She writes a Washington Society column which is syndicated in a number of Southern papers. She had that sort of a position at home. Oliver Stiles got her a chance to broadcast her gossip on his network. Nolly, short for Oliver, says she's got what it takes for both jobs. Through family connections she seems to have a lot of social pull. She gets bids to all the top functions."

"I don't see what in thunder you are worrying about."

"I don't know myself, I honestly don't know. The trouble is that I have invited her to dance at the Officers' Club and each time I see her there something in here —" she tapped her left temple — "rings a warning bell."

"Aha. Bells, not bats, in the belfry?"

"I'm glad if my foolishness can make you laugh. You look worn and worried. Labor trouble?"

"No more than usual. To return to the brick-head. Nothing against her but those temple bells?"

"Chuckle, Sam, I can take it. It may seem funny to you, but it is so serious to me that I carry Tom's letters in my bag when I go out and tuck them under my pillow when I sleep. Silly, when you think that he knew her in Carolina and may be writing to her. He is a Lieutenant in the Marine Air Force. He's serving somewhere in the South Pacific now. Today I had a phone call from an officer who had been in the same outfit with him for months. I invited him to come to the very special dance we are giving tonight at the Tavern. I doubt if he appears but he will be here tomorrow morning early with letters from my boy, he promised. I can't wait to see him."

"I think of you each time a communiqué is released, Amy. You're a grand sport."

A preliminary tap was followed by the opening of the door.

"Dinner is served, M's Amy," Pike announced. "Miss Pat, she just flew out the f'ont do', said, tell you she had a date for dinner an' would see you at the Tavern. I reckon 'tain't good for that young girl to be runnin' out like that. You an' I ought to do somethin' 'bout it, M's Amy. We sure had." He shook his head and shuffled off along the hall.

"Oh, dear," Amy Trask sighed, "I don't need Pike to remind me of that. I know she shouldn't run off without telling me where she's going. I try not to nag, but I can't let her run wild. She's only seventeen and still in school, Sam. She snubs her lifetime beau, Randy Bond, and apparently has lost her head — I hope not her heart — over a French officer Suzanne Dupree brought here. The reams of words published about the present juvenile delinquency terrify me."

"Take it easy, Amy. 'Never go out to meet trouble. If you just sit still, nine times out of ten someone will intercept it before it reaches you.' That isn't original. I read it somewhere and burned it into my memory. I need that sort of reminder myself."

"Thanks, Sam. You have a way of straightening out tangles with the philosophy you pick up. Do you still read poetry?" She tapped the pocket of his brown tweed coat and laughed. "A book as usual." She stopped on the threshold to plead, "Think over the Dupree matter. Don't dismiss it as one of 'Amy's spy-scares.' "

"I won't, cross my throat." He looked up at the girl coming down the stairs.

"Hi, Nancy B. It isn't fair to the armed forces to wear that lime green and silver dress. You're something out of this world." He was aware of the shaken warmth of his voice and laughed. "That's appreciation from a big brother, isn't it, Amy?"

"Appreciation straight from the heart, I'd say."

Later, on the way to the Tavern in the specially chartered bus, Nan remembered Amy Trask's quick agreement with Sam's remark about brotherly appreciation and her swift look at him. Did she suspect he might be — darn Dianne for putting that thought into her mind. Try as she would to keep it under, it kept bobbing to the top.

"All out!" shouted the driver.

She looked eagerly through the bus window. She had attended many dances for officers but never one against a historic background. The windows in the long, irregular façade of the Tavern, beautified by an elaborately wrought-iron balcony, peered into the moonlit night like blinking yellow eyes. Old-time carriage lamps at each side of the entrance lighted the steps. From inside drifted the scrape and tuning of fiddles.

"Exciting, isn't it? Aren't you thrilled?" Nan demanded of the dark-eyed, dark-haired girl in aqua frock and white rabbit coat with whom she shared the rear seat of the bus. Conversation had netted the information that her name was Gladys Grant, that she hailed from Iowa and was a G E

Jane, employed at the Pentagon.

"Old stuff to me." Gladys shrugged indifference. "One night you meet a man and fall hard for him. Biff! He's ordered off. So what? You never see him again. Oh, well! *C'est la guerre.* Dancing with 'em, even if it's nix on loving 'em, is something we can do to help win the war."

"And a pretty easy something when you think of what our men all over the world are doing," Nan reminded passionately.

"Sure, I'm not griping. I'm crazy to do more. I put in three evenings a week as Nurses' Aide at a military hospital. Boy, if the sights I see there wouldn't make a girl work her head off to help, nothing would. I have three brothers doing their bit. Got anyone special in the service?"

Nan thought of Ken Rand. He was no longer her special.

"No, but any number of friends in different branches who are continually in my thoughts" — and prayers. She added the last two words in her mind.

"Then you're not likely to have your heart torn up by the roots. From New England, aren't you?"

"Yes. How did you guess?"

"You enunciate so clearly, speak like a Boston girl who works in the same office with me. Like her, you're encased in a sort of shell of reserve. Boy, I felt it the minute I met you."

"I'm sorry, Gladys. I love to meet people but something in me holds back until I know them enough to really like them. Even if I get boiling mad, I'm all locked up inside. I can't seem to let myself go."

"With your hair!" Deep dimples dented Gladys' cheeks when she laughed. " 'Tain't possible. Someday when you're boiling mad the lid will fly off. You'll never get it on tight again. You'll be a different person."

"I hope so. I fight that reserve all the time."

"Why fight? Let nature take its course. Wait till you meet Mr. Right. You'll be surprised how you'll go all out for him. I've seen it happen with the Boston girl. She's so nutty about an ensign I wouldn't look at that I'm scared purple she'll do some crazy thing and mess up her life for fair."

"I don't want to be nuts about anyone. I'm here to work."

"Sure you are, but we've got to have some fun to keep us from becoming machines, haven't we? Look at Suzanne Dupree on the doorstep. No shell of reserve about that *femme*. Her eyework is something to write home about."

They were in the aisle of the bus now, slowly following the laughing, chattering girls ahead.

"Speaking of Suzanne, funny, isn't it, that Mrs. Trask should have two redheads in her especially selected group of junior hostesses," Gladys observed.

"Not so funny when you know that we both live at her house."

"Two in the same house! Gee, that's piling up TNT. I live in Girl Town, Arlington Farms. It's all right enough, nice chintzy rooms, many things free, from a grooming course to the use of sewing machines, but we're too far away to contact many men. Where to get them? That's the sixty-four-dollar question. Our turn to pile out."

The silver bow in Mrs. Trask's hair gleamed in the lamplight as she waited at the door for the two girls to join her. She laid a hand glittering with diamonds on the sleeve of Nan's white fox evening jacket as they entered the Tavern.

"I am delighted to have you with us, Nancy B. I'll adopt Sam's name for you. Gladys, you're a regular so you don't rate a special welcome."

"Nor special instructions, either, Mrs. Amy." The Iowa girl's twin dimples flashed.

71

"I know the musts and must nots." She ran ahead as Nan stopped in the hall with a soft croon of pleasure.

The place had a background of quiet charm. Huge logs burned in the open fireplaces. Beyond a doorway the flames of innumerable candles cast flickering reflections on the polished Georgian furniture of a large drawing room.

"The Tavern gives me the feeling that if the walls could speak they would tell thrilling tales."

"Pity they can't. George and Martha Washington danced here. I wonder what they would think of the present jitter-bugging. You told me you had attended dances for officers before, Nancy B."

Nan repressed a laugh. It was apparent from her voice that Mrs. Trask was a trifle anxious as to her qualifications as a member of what Gladys Grant had called her especially selected group.

"Many times and those for enlisted men, also."

"Then of course you know the rules?"

"I'm hoary with experience. I have a shockproof line. I admire the snapshots shown me; sympathize with the homesick; give advice to the lovelorn who suspects that the gal he left behind is double-crossing him; help the soldier who has discovered he doesn't love the charmer he swept into a whirlwind engagement just before he embarked, by composing a letter to her to that effect; memorize names and faces that I may be able to greet a man by name the next time I meet him — if I ever do. In short, go all out to help keep up the morale of the armed forces. Will I pass?"

"Top rating. There's a special Captain for whom I want you to 'go all out' tonight — if he comes. Something in my bones tells me he'll side-step. He was in the outfit with Tom for a while."

"Then you'll have real uncensored news from your boy. I am happy for you, Mrs. Trask."

"Call me Amy, Nancy B. Makes me feel young and in your class. In here, dearie, to leave your wrap. It's called the Female Strangers' Room because, legend has it, a mysterious lady languished and died in it. A creepy thought if you ask me."

The orchestra seated on a dais at an end of the long ballroom was playing "Pistol Packin' Mama" as Nan and Mrs. Trask approached the ballroom door.

"We'll wait till the music stops —"

"You're an ace saleswoman, even over the phone, Mrs. Trask," a man's voice behind them interrupted. "Here I am. Bill Jerrold to you. You sold me the party."

Something familiar in the voice. Nan turned. No. Never before had she seen the tall, lean, dark-haired officer with the gold oak leaf on the shoulder of his Marine uniform. He wore the blue ribbon with narrow red and white bands of the D.S.C. and the yellow, white, red and blue of the Asiatic-Pacific Theater, below a senior pilot's silver wings with a shield in the center surmounted by a star.

She looked up and met his keen questioning eyes. They struck a spark. Memory flamed. She *had* seen him. Where? He was looking at her hair. His lips set in a tense straight line. Apparently he didn't like —

"Red! You — you double-crosser."

The contemptuous words clanged through her memory. Little icy shivers pricked through her veins. No wonder his voice had been familiar. He was the man whom she and Sam had taken to the hospital.

6

"Nancy B." Mrs. Trask's voice roused her from the coma of surprise. "I want you to meet Captain —" she glanced at the insignia on his shoulder — "Major Jerrold. Bill, this is Nancy Barton, a member of my family."

She tried twice to retrieve her voice. It just wouldn't answer her whistle. His eyes on hers, the little line between Jerrold's brows deepened.

"Shall we dance, Miss Barton?"

The man would think she was a nodding mandarin. She couldn't speak. Excitement set her heart pounding as he put his arm around her. His was the same voice that had risen from the pool to remind, "As I suggested once before — lady." It was apparent that he didn't recognize her. Suppose she exclaimed theatrically, "Found at last!" Her excitement bubbled in a chuckle. He held her away from him and frowned down into her eyes.

75

"What's the joke? Am I such a rotten dancer?"

"Oh, no. *No,* you're marvelous." There was no trouble with her voice now, it gushed. "I — I just thought of something that happened on the way out and I —"

"Sorry I'm not sufficiently entertaining to keep your thoughts on me. Shall we return to Mrs. Trask?"

She tipped back her head and looked up at him.

"Don't beat me," she pleaded softly, "I can't help my red hair."

"How do you know I *hate* red hair?"

"*I'm* psychic." Now that the surprised excitement had passed, her heart was back on the job beating steadily. Her intelligence was picking up. This evening held entertaining possibilities.

"What say if we cut out to the lounge where we can hear ourselves talk to say nothing of hearing ourselves think, or would you rather dance?" he inquired as they came to a standstill securely wedged between three couples.

A lordly person, Major Bill Jerrold, a man accustomed to giving orders and having them obeyed.

"You don't call what we are doing dancing, or do you?" she asked.

In answer he dodged and danced their way to the door. In a candle-lighted alcove of the lounge he pushed two deep chairs before a gay little fire.

"Sit here. At least it's comparatively quiet. Smoke?"

She shook her head and he replaced the silver cigarette case in a pocket of his tunic.

"Drink?"

"Thanks, no. I can't stay long. Mrs. Trask expects each one of us to share our dances."

She studied his face as he rested his head against the crimson brocade back of a chair. Eyes dark as his hair, large, cleancut nose, stern mouth which went boyish when he smiled. A chin that could take it, indubitably. Had it been like that before the war or had his Pacific experience developed the look of iron-jawed determination?

It was evident the dance had tired him. His face was thin, its lines were deep, its bronze had paled. Malaria had taken toll in flesh and color. The leaping flames set the gold insignia on his shoulders and the silver wings glinting, gently touched the dark blue and yellow ribbons below them. Was it only this morning she had asked, "Ever find out whether our patient was land, air, sea or amphib, Sam?" Now she knew.

"A penny for your thoughts, Major

Jerrold, and not one of those pesky new ones that shine and fool us into mistaking it for a dime, either."

"Perhaps they are worth more than a penny, perhaps they rate a war bond. I was thinking that life apparently goes on in this country even more extravagantly than before December 7, 1941. Money to burn. Spending sprees. Strikes. Lobbying for special privileges. When a government high-up warns that we must brace ourselves to expect unprecedented casualties, when a ranking brass hat declares that strikes encourage the enemy, they are raked over the coals for their statements. And I was thinking that even a short stretch of service in the South Pacific might straighten out the critics' sense of values."

"I don't blame you for being bitter, Major, but remember, there are also millions of citizens who carry on loyally, who sacrifice eagerly, who think as you do."

"Right. Sorry I let myself go. Let's switch to another station and talk about you. There is something familiar about your voice and —" He looked hard at her eyes. She was used to that look. Translated it meant that he was wondering if her jetblack lashes were a natural.

"It isn't mascara, Major. My lashes are a

freak of nature. The real McCoy."

"You *are* a mind-reader, aren't you?" His face lighted and the worn lines vanished when he laughed.

"I ought to be on the subject of my lashes after twenty-two years of possession."

"Don't happen to be a nurse as well as a psychic, do you?"

It was evident from his voice that he was groping for an elusive memory. Did he partially remember his head against her shoulder, her hand smoothing his wet hair?

"I'm a government girl. Do you know a nurse named Barton?"

"That's the catch. When you speak, your voice reminds me of a girl who said she was a nurse. I have a vague impression I've seen lashes like yours before. Trouble is, I don't know whether it is real or part of delirium. Have you always lived in Washington?"

His quick frown indicated that he was still pursuing an elusive memory. She didn't want him to recognize her yet.

"I'm what is locally called a duration resident. I am also a junior hostess for the evening. While you and I are telling the story of our lives a lone officer may be longing for a partner. Shall we attempt to dance back through this mob?"

"That's up to you."

She remembered his pallor when they had stopped dancing.

"Then, let's walk."

Just before they reached Mrs. Trask, who was welcoming arriving officers in the corridor near the ballroom door, he demanded: —

"Why don't you want me to know who you are? Because I said I hated red hair? I don't wonder. No excuse for that mean crack."

She remembered his outburst against the enemy the night they had taken him to the hospital, remembered Sam's voice: —

"Hunger. Torture. Disease. Fear. Hope. Escape. He has given us a line on them all." He had every excuse for irritability.

"No hard feelings," she answered gaily. "I realize that my hair is an acquired taste."

"Then you will tell me where you come from?"

"Hush-hush! It's a military secret," she whispered and laughed.

"Okay, if that's the way you feel about it, that's the way it will be, Miss Barton. Here's Mrs. Trask. Good-by."

"Major Jerrold, who said you might come here?" Gladys Grant seized his arm as he turned away.

His smile brought back youth to his face.

"I'm not A.W.O.L. Doctor's okay," he said and turned to Nan. "Miss Grant is a crackajack nurse, she has been helping out at the hospital. Shall we do a little stepping, Glad? They're playing 'If You Please.' Can you resist that?"

"I can. Not one more step for you, m'lad. We'll sit out a dance. Miss Barton, Mrs. Trask has her beckoning eye on you. How did a male so good-looking as the French officer to whom she's talking escape the Hollywood net? Apparently he's Pat's beau. She's a knock-out in that pink crepe, isn't she?"

"I'll report to my boss at once." Nan laughed up at the keen, dark eyes watching her. "Here's hoping the Frenchman isn't allergic to the color of my hair, Major." She took a step toward Mrs. Trask, stopped, went forward eagerly.

"Carl!" She dropped her outstretched hands, her radiant smile faded as the blue eyes of the officer widened in surprise. He bowed from the waist.

"Sorry, but I'll have to regretfully admit you have made a mistake, Mademoiselle — ?" There was a trace of accent in his speech.

Nan held up a protesting hand.

"I'm the one who should apologize for

greeting you as a long-lost friend, for thinking you a boy grown-up with whom I played tennis one summer in — the White Mountains years ago. Now I see my mistake. His hair was light, yours is black. My apologies to you, too, Mrs. Trask. It isn't my habit to go about the world emoting over strangers."

"No apologies are necessary." There was a hint of amused indulgence in the Frenchman's voice. There was a coat of arms engraved on the ring on the little finger with which he smoothed a small, dark mustache. "My name is François Bouvoir. My heartfelt regrets that I am not the long-lost boy friend and entitled to such a tender greeting, Mademoiselle."

Nan shut her teeth hard in her lip to keep back a sharp reply to his sarcasm. Apparently he was accustomed to having the female of the species attempt to scrape acquaintance, had become expert in warding off a come-on from strange girls. Patricia was frowning annoyance.

"I've never been in your White Mountains, worse luck," his smooth voice went on. "I hope we meet again, Mademoiselle. Come, Chérie. Let us not miss this dance."

Four pairs of eyes watched the man and girl out of sight.

"He has a touch of the world-is-mine swagger, hasn't he?" Mrs. Trask observed. "He is a bona fide count, he dined with us several times before you came, Nancy B. He is Suzanne's friend. I've checked on him. He's attached to a group of the French Committee of National Liberation, who are here, like the United Nations Allies, to confer for the most effective employment of joint resources. Whom did you think he was?"

"A boy I met years ago. I've forgotten his last name." She held out her arm. A bit of torn silver-sequined lace dangled from the short sleeve. "Excuse me for a minute, Mrs. Amy, while I get this repaired?"

She didn't wait for an answer. In the Female Strangers' Room, she slipped on her white fox jacket, hung a lime satin poke bag over her arm and started for a door.

"That's the way to the garden, Miss," the smiling maid advised. The girl's brown face, white collar and pink frock reminded Nan of the coloring of a combination of ice cream, "Neapolitan Slice," that was served at parties in her childhood.

"I'm going out for a minute to cool off. It's frightfully hot in the ballroom," she explained and opened the door.

There was a seat at one end of the garden

in an arbor of tall box. Tucked away in a secluded corner she relived the last few minutes to the accompaniment of "Sunday, Monday and Always," drifting from the ballroom. In the instant her eyes had met the Frenchman's, she had mistaken him for Carl Brouner, a boy with whom she had played tennis one summer in Vienna, who had helped her with German while she reciprocated with lessons in English. She hadn't thought of him for years, and now she could visualize every one of their meetings, could even see him clap his hand to his mouth when she had accidentally struck him with her racket. It had taken three stitches to sew the cut, she remembered. She had admired him enormously, brazenly tagged after him, probably because they were so different. He was cocksure where she was timid. He would take desperate chances to win while she played a cautious, conservative game.

Curious when one taps a spring of memory which has been submerged for a long time how it gushes. How account for the hunch which, in the split second after she had exclaimed, "Carl!" had prompted, "Danger! Go slow!" had warned her to change the meeting place from Vienna to the White Mountains?

Of course she was mistaken, this man's hair was black, the hair of the boy she had known was fair. Perhaps it had been his intensely blue eyes which had reminded her of the boy in Vienna. It could —

"The lost is found." Bill Jerrold's voice shocked her from her reflections. He looked forbiddingly tall as he stood with his field overcoat slung across his shoulders. "Mrs. Trask missed you, was fearful that the sleeve mending was an excuse for faintness and asked Gladys Grant to check on you in the powder room. The maid told her you were here and I was ordered to find you."

"I'll report at once. You shouldn't be out in this cold air after your illness."

"You came here to think over what happened a few minutes ago in the corridor, didn't you?" he asked gravely. "Queer that you should have mistaken Count François Bouvoir for the boy, Carl, with whom you played in the mountains so many years ago. Ready to go in?"

"Yes. For a minute the heat and the crowd seemed unbearable, so I fled to the garden." She sniffed, "I love the scent of box."

"Okay now?" he asked as they walked side by side along the path.

"Quite okay. Gorgeous night." She looked up at the four bright stars which formed the Great Square. "That's Pegasus overhead, isn't it?"

"Yes. The winged horse of hope and dreams who sprang from the blood of hated and feared Medusa, slain by Perseus. Good springing from evil."

"Let's pray that a hundred years of peace will spring from the present horrible slaughter."

"Amen to that."

From the house drifted a man's voice singing "The Night Was Made for Love." At the foot of the garden steps Jerrold stopped.

"Just a minute, Miss Barton. We've met for the first time tonight though I have a hunch I've seen you before. You are troubled that you mistook Captain Bouvoir for an old acquaintance, aren't you? Can I help? I don't want to force your confidence. Perhaps it is a secret, then of course you can't tell me. A secret is no longer a secret when shared. I'll just remind you that so tense and in such danger is this country today, that even happenings that seem unimportant, fragmentary, may change the course of a life, of a battle, tragically."

His gravity sent little premonitory chills creeping along her veins. Did he mean that even a case of mistaken identity might have significant consequences? She confessed impulsively: —

"I didn't meet that boy in the mountains, Major Jerrold. I met him in Vienna. He was Carl Brouner, the son of an Austrian nobleman."

"Why did you switch the meeting place to the White Mountains?"

"Just one of those things. A voice inside warned, 'Don't say Vienna.' Not that it would have made any difference. I'm convinced he isn't the Carl I knew, but I'm sure I've met him before. Are you ever afflicted with an inner voice that noses into your affairs, Major?"

"You bet," he answered and laughed.

As they entered the house he lifted her coat from her shoulders.

"I'll give this to the maid in the powder room. You'd better report at once to —"

"Nan, honey, Mrs. Trask was about to send a crier —"

Jerrold wheeled to confront Suzanne Dupree who spoke behind him. Her face crimsoned, then whitened. Her hand went to her throat.

"*Bill!* Bill, where d-did you c-come

from?" she stammered.

"From the South Pacific. Surprised to see me here, Red?"

7

The next morning Nan incredulously regarded the man who opened her office door.

"Sam! I thought you left Washington on the midnight plane!"

He perched on the corner of her desk and lighted a cigarette.

"You look like a million in that silver gray outfit, Nancy B. I'm here because one can count on nothing except taxes that the government has a hand in. I had a priority but was bumped off by a buck private, a technician ordered on a hurry-up repair job. Dropped in for a minute to say 'Howdy' to the Colonel and to ask you how the dance came off. Have a good time?"

"Grand." She looked up at him eagerly. "I've found our patient."

"No kidding! Where?"

She told him, concluded: —

"Believe it or not, he is the officer who is a friend of Amy Trask's Tom. That's how he came to be at the dance at the Tavern. He's a Major in the Marines and wears a senior pilot's wings."

"What makes you so sure he is the guy we took to the hospital? Did he tell you he'd been there?"

"No. He asked if I were a nurse. Said my voice reminded him of someone, thought he had seen eyelashes like mine before, admitted he wasn't sure whether the impressions came from reality or from a feverish dream. When he said that, I knew that like the Northwest Mountie, in Major William Jerrold — Bill Jerrold for short — I had my man."

"Bill Jerrold! *Bill* Jerrold! Gosh, the human mind is a cockeyed thing. Major William Jerrold meant nothing to me, but Bill Jerrold crashed my memory. Now I know how he came to be in our pool. He's the brother for whom Betty Sutton, next door, was giving the buffet supper. He's a Devil Dog Marine. Judging from his sister's raves about him — I've heard it from others too — he's a hot pilot, a daring combat leader, a straight shooter and as fine a fella as they come."

"But her brother was a Captain. She didn't mention his surname. This man is a Major."

"Since then, probably, he's had a promotion as well as a medal for extraordinary valor. Leatherneck pilots and planes covered landings and stood off overwhelming Jap forces which were diving toward the beach to break up the attack on the islands. He wasn't at the supper. Mrs. Sutton got off a lot of stuff about a party in honor of a hero who hadn't arrived."

"Why didn't you tell me that night that the guest of honor was missing?"

"Forgot it. Had a lot on my mind. I'd been burning up the wires getting you this job. Kept wondering if you would take it. All the way home Di was in one of her fighting moods. By the time I had put up the car and walked off my mad I stumbled on you in the living room with the man you'd fished from the pool. You know what followed. I remember now that at the supper I wondered if the hero really hadn't come, or if for some military reason he didn't want his presence in town known and had neglected to get that fact across to his sister. Apparently neither guess was right. He was in bed shaking with chills and burning with fever. Poor devil. I've had malaria. I know."

"He must have stolen out of the house and wandered about half delirious until he found our pool. I can't understand why the hospital was so mysterious about his name and why he was whisked away."

"Probably I was right when I had a hunch that his presence at the Suttons' should have been kept a military secret. The brass hats doubtless did the whisking. Did you get a line on the reason he called you Red? Is he married?"

"I don't know. I wish you could have seen Suzanne Dupree's face when he and she met in the corridor of the Tavern last evening. Her eyes bulged like green glasses in her white face. 'Bill! Bill, where d-did you c-come from?' she stammered. You could hear ice tinkle in his answer, 'From the South Pacific. Surprised to see me here, Red?' "

Sam Mitchell whistled.

"Red! Remember how he stood up to Di? 'It's a ticklish business to come between husband and wife, Madam. Ask Bill, he knows.' Perhaps he came between this Suzanne and her husband or she's his wife and another leatherneck butted in. The situation offers as many dramatic possibilities as a soap opry. What happened after that?"

"I don't know. They walked along the corridor together. Perhaps he left early. I didn't see him again. I was dancing every moment."

"Did the dashing Suzanne disappear?"

"No. Each time I looked in her direction her unfriendly eyes were following me."

"Did Amy Trask witness her meeting with Bill Jerrold?"

"I think not. She was greeting a late arrival. Why?"

"Here's something to keep under your hat: Although the families are friends, Amy is a trifle disturbed about her. It would be queer if her doubts led into an answer to the reason of Bill Jerrold's delirious muttering. Did he try to date you?"

"No. He *hates* red hair."

"So what! Did he tell you that?"

"He did. Sammy, do you think I'm encased in a shell of reserve?"

"Grandma, what big eyes you've got." Gravity succeeded laughter. "Did the Major have the nerve to tell you that, too?"

"No. It wasn't he. It was a girl. What's the matter with me, Sam, that I can't warm up more when I meet a person?"

"There's nothing the matter with you, Nancy B. We can't all be extroverts. You're a grand kid." He cleared his husky voice and laughed. "Have you taken on a heartbeat who has set you wondering if you're chilly? I can tell there is something on your mind."

For an instant she was tempted to tell him of mistaking Captain François Bouvoir for

Carl Brouner. Why waste the short time he was here talking about a boy of whom he never had heard? She had told Major Jerrold, perhaps it would have been wiser if she hadn't confided in him.

"I hope I have something on my mind," she parried gaily. "If I haven't, I'll lose my job. I was thinking that the mistakes of my life have been many."

"My life has been reasonably full of them and that's a masterpiece of understatement. I know you well enough to know you're up against a problem. Wasn't that what set you thinking of mistakes? If at any time you need my help you'll find me at the same old stand. To return to Bill Jerrold. He asked if you were a nurse. Any other questions?"

"If I lived in Washington. I side-stepped that. Sam, if you see Mrs. Sutton don't tell her I have met her brother."

"What's the big idea?"

"It would be fun to keep him wondering if I'm a dreamgirl or a reality. I'll ask Mrs. Trask not to reveal from which part of the country I hail. Perhaps I'll never see him again. With Suzanne Dupree living at Mrs. Amy's he won't come there if his voice when he spoke to her is an indication of his feelings."

"If it's a showdown between a friend of

Tom's coming and Suzanne's staying, Amy will give the Dupree girl the gate."

He tamped out a cigarette and stood up.

"I'll shove along. Hope I haven't been bumped off this plane. Dianne misses you, Nancy B., though she'd die before she would admit it. Send her a line occasionally. You'll be coming home for Thanksgiving?"

"Sorry, I can't. I'm a working woman now, remember. We still have our Sundays free, but the President has suspended all holidays for Federal workers except Christmas and we are asked not to travel then. Space is needed for the service men going home. That's little enough to do for them."

"Right. I'll be seeing you. Good-by."

"I know you well enough to know you're up against a problem." The words recurred to Nan the next morning as she rested her arms in their forest green cardigan sleeves on the iron railing of the balcony outside her bedroom and looked down into the garden in its winter garb. It was this balcony so like hers at Di's that made her feel at home at Amy Trask's.

She drew a deep breath of the crisp air. Sunday. Buffet breakfast. The one morning in the week she didn't have to rush for a bus.

"Onward Christian Soldiers," chimed a

distant carillon. Skeleton branches of trees swayed as if in time to the martial music of the bells drifting by on a faint box-scented breeze. Little whirls of dust danced along the graveled paths. Heavenly day. The sky was robin's-egg blue between sailing fluffs of cloud with golden edges. The pink dogwoods in a corner of the garden below were a deep, mellow wine color. The sun was lavishly gilding everything visible as if to make up for the blackout Jack Frost had laid over the world last night.

She thrust her hands hard into the pockets of her cardigan. Sam thought she was up against a problem. Problem was too important a word to describe the haunting sense that somewhere she had seen François Bouvoir before. He wasn't Carl Brouner, that was settled, Carl had been blond. She could wipe him off the slate. Perhaps she had met the Count in France during one of the summers she had spent there. He knew they had met before, she was sure of it. What possible reason could he have for not admitting it?

He may have been the subject of a whispered scandal — perhaps political, maybe social — at the time they met and was afraid she might remember it. Could be. He was devoting himself to Patricia now and Patricia would inherit a fortune. There was something wrong or he wouldn't stick in her mind like a splinter. Could her distrust be "one of those fragmentary things which may change the course of a life or career tragically"?

Fragmentary! It might be a huge thing. She was bound to meet him again with Pat. Perhaps, though, if he had a scandalous past, as she suspected, he would avoid her. He might even try to put her out of the way if the scandal had been political. Cheering thought. Where had that come from? Something queer happened to the muscles of her stomach. Could it be fear? She unclenched her hands which had gone slightly clammy.

"You're hungry, goon, that's what's the matter with your stomach," she jeered at herself. "It's two hours later than your usual breakfast time. Scram!"

As she entered the mahogany-walled dining room the Admiral, retired, ensconced in a deep chair in the sunny, plant-filled bay, scowled at her above a newspaper and rose.

"What's the idea dashing into the room as if you were bursting though a paper hoop, Miss Nan? What you scared of?" he demanded in a voice which set the pair of green love-birds in a gilded cage above his head fluttering wildly.

The presence of the crusty Admiral and love-birds in the same bay was an incongruity that tickled her sense of humor. She picked up a plate from the buffet.

"I suddenly remembered that this was popover morning and dashed in to make sure I wouldn't be too late to get one. That radio man, Nolly Stiles, and Patricia are gluttons for popovers. Loud cheers. There are six on the plate."

From a crystal pitcher she filled a glass with orange juice, peeked under the silver covers of two chafing-dishes, helped herself to creamy scrambled eggs and crisp bacon, poured steaming, fragrant coffee into a cup and carried her tray to the large table. Seated, she smiled at the man who, settled back in his chair again, was regarding her from beneath white eyebrows heavy as able-bodied mustaches.

"What's wrong with the world this morning, Admiral Howe?" I shouldn't have said that, she told herself contritely, his heart is raw because he can't get into the fight and he eases the ache by finding fault with everyone who is in it. "Or is it with me?" she demanded in the hope of diverting his mind from her first question. "Don't you like me in green?"

"I wasn't thinking of you, Miss Nan. I was thinking that at last —" he chirruped at the birds and scowled at his paper — "they've *done* it."

Nan savored the crisp perfection of a popover liberally spread with orange marmalade.

"Who have done what, Admiral?"

"Those chaps in Moscow have come out with what, on the surface, looks like a sane plan for real unity of the United Nations. BIG FOUR PLEDGED TO WORLD ORDER. Please God it works." He *hr-rumped* the emotion from his voice and whistled to the love-birds.

"Oh, there you are, Amy," he growled as Mrs. Trask entered. "What you got your hat on for? Where you going?"

His niece glanced into one of the pair of bronze-framed mirrors that flanked the buffet before she filled a glass with orange juice.

"To church later, Uncle Zeb. Has Pat been down for breakfast?"

"Not yet. You spoil that girl, Amy, allowing her to stay out all hours."

"Only Friday and Saturday evenings, Uncle Zeb. I'll admit I'm troubled about Captain Bouvoir. She had him or he had her in tow at the officers' dance. He's too old to be playing round with a youngster like Pat. Do you like this purple turban, Nancy B.?"

"High Style, I calls it. It is perfect with your gray suit. I'll change and go to church with you, if you don't mind."

"I'd love it. Tom's friend is coming for breakfast." She flung a challenging glance at the man in the bay who countered with his characteristic snort.

"That's just like a woman, sentiment. Sentiment and no sense. He talked with you for half an hour yesterday morning, showed you pictures and letters and you invite him to breakfast. Surprised you didn't ask him to live here."

"That's an idea, Uncle Zeb. He could have Tom's rooms."

"How do you know he isn't a damfake, Amy? What proof have you he didn't steal that stuff from the real friend of Tom's, perhaps knocked him off to get it?"

"You wouldn't doubt him if you had met him, Uncle Zeb." Mrs. Trask appeared unperturbed by his grisly suggestions. "Your arthritis must be very bad this morning. I saw you crunching a chocolate bar after dinner last night. You know you shouldn't eat it. Oh, well, boys will be boys."

"I'm allowed one a day," the Admiral growled. He returned to his grievance.

"When are you going to produce that new crush of yours? What's your confounded Captain's name?"

"His name?" Amy Trask cocked her head at the angle of a bird listening. "Here he is now." She went to the door. "Come in and have breakfast and meet the family, those that are here," she added as Major Bill Jerrold stepped into the room.

"You don't know a damthing about the Service, do you, Amy? That gold leaf on your new guest's shoulder means a Major, not a Captain," scolded the Admiral.

"Mrs. Trask knew me from Tom's letters as a Captain, sir. I didn't get the gold leaf until a few days ago. My hostess suggested breakfast and am I starving!"

Amy Trask's eyes were thick with tears as she looked up at him. She tucked her hand under his arm and led him to the buffet.

"I would think Tom was back. He — he was always in a chronic state of starvation." She steadied her lips before she added: —

"It — it's wonderful to have a hungry boy in the house again, Bill."

The Admiral cleared his throat with a force that set the love-birds a-flutter and rubbed fingers impatiently across his eyes as if they stung.

"It's wonderful to be here, Mrs. Trask."

Bill Jerrold helped himself to coffee, eggs and bacon and pulled up a chair beside Nan.

"I hope you are pleased too, Miss Barton?"

"Only time can answer that question, Major. Perhaps you'll prove to be the answer to this gal's prayer — and perhaps —"

"I won't." He shook his head. "Unfortunately I'm allergic to red hair."

"How thoughtful of you to warn me." Nan rose. "I'll take mine out of sight at once," she said and left the room.

8

Major Bill Jerrold certainly had flashed a KEEP OFF warning yesterday when he had announced he was allergic to red hair, Nan reflected as she rode to work in the bus. Why think of him this glorious day? She felt on top of the world when she wore her Gordon plaid skirt, matching Scotch cap and short beaver jacket. Clothes might not make the man but they were a morale booster for a girl.

Early as it was sailors were paddling canoes on the Potomac and bicyclists by the score pedaled along the avenues. Flower vendors at street corners were doing a thriving business with chrysanthemums, white, yellow, pink, crimson and bronze. The girl seated beside her was humming "Oh, What a Beautiful Morning." It was that kind of a day.

As she hung up her jacket in the office her thoughts returned to Bill Jerrold. Why had she shown him by her hasty departure from the dining room yesterday that she cared what he thought? She wrinkled her nose at the girl looking back at her from the mirror.

"He might fare farther and do worse, my dear, though I say it who shouldn't," she told her reflection.

At a window she looked out at the bridge crowded with traffic, at the river sparkling in the sunshine, at the white shaft of the Washington Monument. Beyond another window the Navy's new Arlington Annex loomed on a rise overlooking the Pentagon. The Marines filled a large section of the sprawling, three-story building. Had Bill Jerrold been assigned to work there? She'd better push him out of her thoughts pronto and settle down at her desk.

The chief's buzzer. He was commencing early. She picked up her notebook, settled the silver necklace which topped her dark green blouse and crossed to his door humming "Oh, What a Beautiful Morning."

The stocky man in olive drab uniform with a silver eagle on his shoulder, his black eyebrows arched by nature in an expression of perpetual surprise, vouchsafed her a gruff "Good morning."

"Captain Bouvoir is in need of an interpreter and was sent here, Miss Barton," he explained.

Nan's heart stood still as she looked at the

smiling dark-haired man with a visitor's badge on his blue tunic, who had risen as she entered.

"I met Mademoiselle Barton the other evening at a dance for officers at Gadsby's Tavern, Colonel Long. She mistook me for a long-lost boy friend. Couldn't we pretend I am the lad and start from there, Mademoiselle?"

"Sorry, we can't because now that I see you for the second time I am wondering how I could have made such a mistake. What does Captain Bouvoir want us to do for him, Colonel Long?"

Her chief tapped a letter open on his desk.

"A translation of this. Don't you read or speak German, Captain?"

"No, sir. I was educated in England. My family had such an intense hatred of the Germans — our country home was devastated in the last war — that I had no desire to study the language. I wouldn't have troubled you with this if I hadn't suspected that it might contain something the authorities should see. Didn't want to cry 'Wolf' until I was sure."

"How soon can you make the translation, Miss Barton?"

"I haven't finished work on the two letters you turned over to me late yesterday, Colonel, but, I'll have this ready before you go to lunch."

Bouvoir hastened to open the door for her, said over his shoulder: —

"I'll be back in a few hours, sir," and followed her into her office.

Now what? Nan thought as she dropped the letter to her desk. Was there anything more than the translation behind this visit?

"How did you happen to come to us, Captain Bouvoir? There are so many other bureaus for this sort of work," she reminded as he sat on the arm of the chair across the desk from hers.

"After your case of mistaken identity the other evening, I asked Patricia for whom you worked. One assumes that every woman in the city under eighty is here to work. She thinks you are an angel, Mademoiselle. She has spoken of you often as 'Nan, who lives with us.' We're great friends, Chérie and I. I had to see you again; used to that, aren't you? Used to having victims succumb after the first look at those sensational lashes?" The warmth of his voice and eyes sent a little shiver along Nan's nerves. "With the letter as an excuse, here I am. Can't we make my resemblance to your small boy friend a basis for our friendship?"

Why not? Perhaps if she saw him occasionally, someday her subconscious would flash the time and place of a previous meeting on the screen of memory. She couldn't rid herself of the feeling that it was significant, that that same memory might save Pat from unhappiness.

"The word friendship means a lot to me, Captain Bouvoir. Suppose we call it a trial acquaintance?"

"Better a half loaf than nothing." He was standing now, looking down at her. "Will you dine and dance with me some night?"

"Thank you, yes."

"It's a date. Suppose we decide on it now?"

Nan shook her head.

"My social engagement book is at home. I'll have to consult that."

"What time do you get back to Mrs. Trask's? I'll telephone tonight."

"I'm in my room between six and seven, if I don't stay late to work." She glanced at the letter on her desk. "If you want this translation —"

"I'm already on the way." He paused to ask, "Do I still remind you of the small boy with whom you played in the White Mountains?"

"No. So little that I wondered while you

have been talking how I could have made the mistake. Must have been that the wavering candlelight at the Tavern disinterred the memory of the flickering candlelight at the inn where I met the boy of whom I haven't thought for years. As I suggested —"

"Until six-thirty tonight," he reminded. Her eyes followed him as he crossed the office. "A touch of the world-is-mine swagger," Mrs. Trask had said. She was one hundred per cent right.

As the door closed behind him Nan picked up the letter. Had it been used as an excuse to see her, to test the truth of her statement at the officers' dance that she had been mistaken when for an instant she had thought him the boy grown-up with whom she had played? He wasn't of course, because that boy would have been able to read German, but if he hadn't met her somewhere would he have cared enough to come? He had learned her name from Pat before they met last night. He hadn't been taken by surprise as she had been. He was prepared coolly to ignore acquaintance. If it were not for his slight accent he could easily be taken for an American; he was proficient in the use of current lingo.

Later, she laid the original letter and the

translation on Colonel Long's desk, reported: —

"A letter from a brother in the enemy country, to a sister in the United States. No subversive material in it, unless it is in cipher. It is full of family references, apparently nothing more."

The Colonel tipped back in his chair and ran stubby fingers through salt-and-pepper hair. His eyebrows registered their perpetual surprise.

"I'll turn it over to our code expert. Bouvoir is attached to one of the French groups here. Contact man, he would be called in business. I checked on him after he left the office. When he comes for the letter I'll tell him you were delayed by emergency work, that we'll have it for him tomorrow. Say nothing about the cipher test. Wonder why he came to us? Did you tell where and what your job is when you met him?"

The quick shift of his eyes to hers set blood burning in her cheeks.

"No, sir."

"Don't look as if you would tell the story of your life at a first meeting, but you never can tell how a woman will react to an officer with a line like his. What did he mean when he said you mistook him for someone else?"

She explained.

"Quite sure he isn't the person you thought him?"

"Quite sure, Colonel. That boy's hair was fair. Curious I should have made such a mistake. I've always thought myself tops at remembering faces. Sam calls me 'The Memory.' "

"Your brother-in-law dropped in before he left town Saturday, to inquire if you were making good."

His grin was the nicest thing about him, Nan thought before he added: —

"Don't look so worried. I let you down easy, but I didn't tell him that you are the most efficient translator-secretary I've ever had in my office. Sam's a grand person. To look at him and hear him laugh you wouldn't think he carried such tremendous responsibility. We were buddies in World War I, drove camions filled with ammunition to the front, evacuated Hill 67 together. We both left college in our freshman year to join the Field Service, later became second looeys in the U.S. Army. Now I'm holding down a desk job here and he's fighting absenteeism and slowdowns."

"And is he fighting!" It wasn't all the memory of Sam's foundry troubles that shook Nan's voice: Di made life terribly hard for him.

"There is a lot to be said for the chance to fight, Miss Barton. Put these letters in the follow-up file. I will take care of them when I return." He rose. "I won't be gone more than fifteen minutes. Don't go to lunch till I get back."

As if she ever went to lunch when he was away, Nan thought as she returned to her office. It was apparent that he liked Sam immensely. Who didn't? He was such a dear. Why wasn't Dianne nicer to him? Why did she —

"Anyone at home?" a voice inquired behind her.

She turned to face the door to the corridor. Major William Jerrold, tall and imposing in the green uniform of the Marines with insignia and ribbons, stood on the threshold. She had time to think that some of the lines had smoothed out which had furrowed his face, that his eyes which she had thought dark like his hair were a shining deep blue, before he asserted: —

"I'm a brave man 'to beard the lion in his den, the Douglas in his hall.' Lifted word for word from *Marmion* by a certain Sir Walter Scott, in case you've forgotten. Still mad?"

"Mad?"

"Your puzzled frown is a masterpiece of

its kind, but it doesn't get across. You know what I mean. Don't stall."

"I'm beginning to see light. You think I'm 'mad' because you don't like my hair? You wouldn't be a little egotistical, would you, thinking that I care? It has its public."

The hint of amusement in her voice sent a tinge of red under his bronze, set a glint in his eyes.

"I didn't say I didn't like *your* hair," he contradicted gruffly and closed the door.

"With your permission," he said, and drew a chair to the opposite side of the desk and sat down. "I've come to ask you some questions."

His grave voice sent Nan's pulses into a quickstep. Had he suddenly realized she was the girl who had found him in the pool? So what? Even that wouldn't account for the third-degree hint in his manner. Or would it, if he thought she might tell of his presence at the Suttons'? She tapped a paper on her desk.

"I'm really very busy. Could you call again later?"

"I could *not*. I want an answer to this question now. Are you engaged?"

She felt the color warm her face. What did he mean? Could he have heard about Ken?

"I *hope* this job is permanent. Are you

looking for a translator-secretary, Major?"

"You're a convincing actress. You know I meant engaged to be married. Are you?"

"I can't see that it is any of your business, but I am not."

"Were you ever engaged to Bouvoir?"

"To *Bouvoir?* You mean to Captain — the Count François Bouvoir we met the other evening? Have you forgotten that I told you I realized he wasn't the man I thought him? Didn't you hear him say he never had seen me before?"

"I did, but for some obscure reason I felt he was putting on an act. Exit the Count — for good, I hope. I didn't like him. Is there anyone else?" His question brought lovely soft color to her face.

"N-*No!* Just why this burning interest in my love life?"

"Would you consider taking me on as head man for a while?"

"You mean, *you* and — and —"

Amazement stopped her voice. Was this a recurrence of delirium? She managed a sound which would pass for a laugh, dropped her lashes in assumed confusion before they swept up.

"*Are* my ears burning. *Really,* Major, this is so — sudden."

"Quit fooling, Nancy Barton. I'm in dead

earnest. Will you play round with me?"

"I believe you really *mean* it. I thought you were having a return of malarial delirium."

"What do you know about my malaria?"

His eyes were like blue steel points boring into hers. Close call. More than ever now she didn't want him to discover that she was the girl who had found him in the pool.

"Gladys Grant referred to it the night of the officers' dance at the Tavern, didn't she?"

"Right. How about it? Will you take me on as a steady?"

"You don't mean as a fiancé?"

"Not at present, though it may come to that."

"I thought you were married."

"Who, me? Where did you pick up that crazy idea?"

"Doubtless from the same source from which you picked up my one-time engagement to the Count — Captain Bouvoir."

"I'm not married. Never have been. Will you accept my proposal?"

"Tell me one reason why I should. You don't like me. I don't like you.

"I do not love thee, Doctor Fell,
The reason why I cannot tell.

Lifted word for word from a certain Tom Brown in case you've forgotten."

"I haven't asked you to love me." His correction was gruff. "I ask you to go out with me as often as you can. I know it sounds cockeyed. I can't tell you why, except that our being seen together may help a ticklish situation."

"You're not putting me between you and Suzanne Dupree, are you? It wasn't necessary to be a mind-reader to know that you and she had met before the officers' dance."

"Thanks for your high opinion of me. I'm not in the habit of hiding behind a woman's skirts. I'll say once more, it is terribly important that you allow me to stick around. It's nothing you can't handle. I'll be ordered away soon, then the thing will drop. Will you do it?"

"Did you think this up all by yourself?"

"I did not. It is a request, not an order, from a higher-up."

"Won't you tell why the finger has been put on me? I'm always tremendously interested in the motive behind a person's action."

"Can't. Am I to be head man in your stag line? Yes or no?"

"Even in this maddest of worlds that

seems a crazy proposition. Are you sure it is necessary?"

"If you must know, it is your patriotic duty. It may save lives."

Her troubled eyes sought his steady ones.

"Judging from his sister's raves about him — I've heard it from others too — Bill Jerrold's a straight shooter, and as fine a fella as they come."

Sam's words echoed through her mind. She heard them as plainly as if her brother-in-law were speaking in the room. Uncanny. She drew a long breath.

"I don't know why I believe you, but I do. If it means as much as that it is 'Yes.' "

She sensed his intense relief. It was as if every taut nerve in his body relaxed.

"Thanks. You're on the beam. You won't welsh when you get home and think it over, will you?"

Flash-back. She saw herself in the station wagon on the way to the hospital, heard her own voice: —

"If ever I'm tempted to welsh on a job I'll think of this night and memory will stiffen my backbone." She had made a promise to herself. She would keep it.

"No."

"Now I'll let you get back to work. I hope you'll play up to the part, pretend that I'm

116

the Marine who puts stars in your eyes." He laughed. "You'll be surprised to find what a Grade A actor I am. I'm a movie director's dream. We'll break in by dinner and dance at a night spot this evening. Be ready at seven."

"Make it eight. I'll go tonight, but after this only on Saturday. I can't indulge in late evenings and be Little Bright Eyes at this desk in the morning and I'm here to help win this horrible war."

"You're helping when you go out with me, remember. Saturdays sold to Bill Jerrold. I'll have to see you on other days or it won't seem as if we are really that way about each other."

"That sounds as if I'd have to give *all* my fun time to you."

"I can tell by your voice you don't like it. If you think I do, you're mistaken. At eight," he reminded and closed the door.

9

Bill Jerrold strode along a corridor of the Pentagon crowded with uniformed men and women, A.T.S. girls, Waafs, Wrens here from England to assist the British Army staff with office work. He frowned as he reviewed the last ten minutes. Nan Barton was a good sport to consent to his proposition. She must trust him if she didn't like him. Thank the Lord for that. When the plan had been outlined to him by the General to whose staff he had been assigned, he had protested that he had got off on the wrong foot with her, that she wouldn't consent, it was absurd to think she would; that already she must have a special man in her life who should take over the job. His superior officer had reminded: —

"The information you ferreted out in the prison camp and during your escape through the jungle has been of inestimable value, Major Jerrold. My orders are to hold you in Washington, to give you a job in this Intelligence Department, to keep you contented while your knowledge of South Pacific conditions can be tapped for use in the campaign ahead. You were a lawyer before you were a Marine. You have been trained to compute human values. If the suspicion you have just outlined to me is fact, following up that will keep you on your toes. What's more, unraveling that mystery — if there is one — may take as much daring as covering a landing attack." That was that.

He had returned to the United States under orders to report to Washington immediately. He must have been woozy from malaria when he had stopped over at his sister's house. Nothing else would explain his delay in getting to Washington. Why think of it? He had been forgiven and decorated.

It was part of his present job to keep his eyes, ears and senses peeled to detect even happenings that seemed unimportant, fragmentary. When Captain Bouvoir had denied having met Nan Barton before, he had had a hunch there was something there which would bear watching and had reported the episode to the General. The plan for him to apply for top-man rating in Nan Barton's life had followed. To his amazement he had put it across.

"The job may take as much daring as covering a landing party," the General had predicted. That was some daring. His thoughts went back to the Carolina post where he and Tom Trask had trained for those same landings. Piloting a diving plane, parachuting, were not all he had learned there. He had learned to distrust a woman with red hair. Queer that Suzanne Dupree, out of all the houses in Washington, should live at Mrs. Trask's. Not so queer though, when one thought it out. Tom Trask and he, as his friend, had been made royally welcome at her parents' Carolina plantation because of the friendship between the elders of the families. He visualized Suzanne sitting on the top step of the porch, her hair flaming in the light from a window behind her, surrounded by eager young officers, laughing with all, promising one with her eyes.

Why in thunder return to the past? Hadn't he problems enough now? He forced his thoughts back to the present. Nan Barton had denied having been engaged to Captain François Bouvoir. She was lovely enough to have had a dozen men after her. She had thought his proposition due to the return of an attack of malaria. She had something there. His proposal, almost insistence, when he knew that she didn't like him, was cockeyed enough to be part of the delirium which had overtaken him when he collapsed at his sister's home.

The short time he had been there was obscured in a fog. He remembered warning Betty that his presence at her house must not be suspected and he remembered waking at the small-town hospital and the few sane moments which followed when he told the doctor who he was, that no one must know he was there, that he was on an important mission, that he must get to Washington at once and secretly.

After that, it was as if a thick smoke screen smothered him. The next time he wakened he was in the Walter Reed Hospital. How had his transportation from New England been accomplished? Magic was the word for it and only medical magic could account for his return to almost normal health after his experience in the Pacific.

Memory dimmed out his surroundings and in their place projected a picture with sound effects. The stillness of a moonlit South Sea night shattered by the guttering roar of landing boats. Bombers waiting out of sight. Dark lines of small boats. White wakes. Roar of big naval guns. Red tracers streaking toward shore. Crash of palms. Columns of smoke. Black fountains of debris. Flash signals for bombs. Boats creeping toward the white beach. Machine guns. Burning plane. A jump. Prison camp. Enemy plans detected. Information to be passed on. Desperation. Escape. Nights creeping through the hideous jungle.

He brushed his hand across his eyes. Would time never blot out the horror? He must thrust it from his mind. He resolutely visualized the face of Nancy Barton. That was an antidote for nightmare. Since the officers' dance at the Tavern he had been certain he had seen her jet black lashes before, had heard her charming voice.

He couldn't forget her expression when he had made the extraordinary proposition this morning. She looked as if he had gone suddenly haywire. It must seem a crazy plan to her, though as the General had explained to him, there was a good and sufficient reason for putting it through. He was to be her escort on every possible occasion. Would the presence of Suzanne Dupree in the same house with her complicate matters? What would she say when she heard that Nancy Barton and Bill Jerrold were stepping out together? Something malicious, of course. He must watch out for that. Hadn't he reason to hate and distrust her?

"Shift the wave length, Bill," he reminded himself fiercely. "Don't let her get into the bloodstream of your memory again."

"How about a bite of lunch together, Major Jerrold?"

The smooth voice with its hint of accent dammed the stream of consciousness. It took an instant for him to coordinate his thoughts and vision, to realize that Captain François Bouvoir had stopped him in a corridor of the Pentagon. Why spend a moment with him? The first time he had seen him, he had disliked the man's cockiness, the suave sarcasm with which he had replied to Nan Barton's embarrassed explanation of her greeting. He opened his lips to refuse, instead heard himself saying: —

"Sounds like a good idea if we can find one in this maze."

"There is an excellent café at the end of the ramp."

"Then let's go."

He listened with one ear to the Frenchman's voice going on and on, with the other he was hearing a girl's exclamation, "Carl!" With the eyes of memory he was seeing her radiant face, her hands outstretched in greeting, the officer's eyes widening in surprise. Curious that she should have mistaken for a friend a man whom she had not seen before — or had she? To find the answer to that question was his present assignment.

"Here we are."

Bouvoir's announcement snapped his mind to attention. As he picked up a tray and selected food he wondered if the Captain had the same scene in mind and was eager to offer an explanation.

With their luncheons set out on a table for two Bouvoir eyed the bowl of steaming stew before him with gustatory anticipation.

"This city has the finest oysters I've met in my travels, and I've covered a good part of the globe. I see you like yours raw. I can't swallow them that way, they shiver in my throat."

"That's an appetizing thought." Bill Jerrold replaced the oyster on his fork in its shell and lifted another. "Here's hoping this one has more self-control."

"I admit that was not a tactful suggestion, Major. Are you located in this mammoth building?"

"Dropped in on business. You ought to recognize a visitor. You're wearing a badge yourself."

"Right. One becomes so accustomed to seeing the labels that one ceases to notice them. You were coming out of Mademoiselle Barton's office as I passed. Charming girl. At this moment she is making a translation of a letter —"

"Better not mention it here. These places

have a thousand ears." With a slight movement of his head Jerrold indicated a man in civilian clothes at the next table whose face was as brown and immobile as a bronze Buddha. It was apparent that he had stopped eating to listen.

Bouvoir shrugged his Gallic shrug.

"Pourquoi non? It is not that kind of a letter, but we will let it go. Amusing that Mademoiselle Barton mistook me for an old friend, the other evening, *n'est-ce pas?"*

Here it is. I was right. He's building up to an explanation, Bill Jerrold told himself.

"A case of mistaken identity isn't unusual, especially when years go by between meetings, Captain. I judged from what she said that she was a very small girl when you and she — when she *thought* you and she played games together."

Bouvoir's smile was that of an indulgent teacher correcting a rather stupid pupil.

"As I told Mademoiselle I have never seen your White Mountains. I came to this country for the first time in January 1943."

"How did you manage to escape from France at that hectic time?"

"It is enough to say I came; if I told more it might mean reprisals, death to many. When the Nazis seized the vast estates of my family we scattered. Some are in England.

Others in Switzerland. I am the only one in America."

"Tough luck to lose your home. Like it here?" Jerrold asked, not because he especially cared, but because he could think of nothing else to say.

" 'Like' is too tame a word. You Americans are so kind in this city. I have met many members of Congress and their wives. My engagement book is filled with what Mademoiselle Patricia calls 'dates.' "

"Don't you do any *work?*"

"*Tiens!* I take care of the social duties. Would you not call an unending round of cocktail parties, teas, dinners and cards, work?"

"I would and how. I take it that it's your job to cement friendship between the part of the French nation you represent and my countrymen. Right?"

"Right. Often one can accomplish more over a tea or dinner table or at a bar than across an office desk. But I have much paper work mornings. Now, a little about yourself. A Marine Major, the Pacific Theater, a pilot and decorated, I can see that. Tough life, fighting in the South Seas, is it not?"

"Tough — but plenty. Heat. Suffocating moisture. Bugs. Snakes. Mud. Mosquitoes as deadly as the enemy."

"That's a terrifying summing up. Did the Japs nick you?"

"No. The mosquitoes and the jungle did and did they do a job! Malaria."

"I thought atabrine had licked that."

"Every man is expected to take one tablet a day as a protection, but foxhole fighting and jungle living leave little thought for a daily routine."

"I can understand that, too. Have you been always a soldier?"

"Good Lord, no. In my law practice I handled the legal business of a large automobile corporation — inherited the client, with many others, from my father. Now the huge plant is converted to war work."

Captain François Bouvoir leaned slightly forward.

"You Americans are so adaptable. One minute an *avocat,* the next a soldier. What is your plant — you called it — making in place of motor cars?"

"I've been so long in Service I've forgotten."

Bouvoir shrugged, glanced at the man at the adjoining table and nodded.

"*Vous avez raison.*" He consulted his wrist watch and rose hastily.

"I am late for an engagement. It has been pleasant to have this chat with you, Major.

We will meet again soon?"

"Sounds good to me."

Bill Jerrold's eyes followed him until he disappeared. What's it all about? he asked himself.

He repeated the question later in an office in the Marines section of the near-by Navy Annex, to a small, thin, stern-faced man, with a sharp, wedge-shaped chin, sleek platinum hair, one star on the shoulder of his uniform.

The Brigadier General drummed the tips of bony fingers on his desk.

"What is it all about? That's what we expect you to find out, Major. We've looked him up. He is the person he claims to be. Absolutely no flaw in his dossier. But — you started this ball rolling when you reported the meeting between Miss Barton and Bouvoir. It can't be stopped. Wherever the said ball rolls we will see that the girl's name never appears. How did you get along with your — your — shall we call it proposal?"

Bill Jerrold resented the twinkle in the keen black eyes regarding him.

"She accepted, though the Lord only knows why she did. She made no bones about saying she didn't like me."

"You put it on patriotic grounds?"

"Yes, sir. There's a lot of foolishness

being put across under the name of patriotism, General. I don't like this type of it. I want to get back to the front. It has been proved that a bridgehead cannot be secured on a hostile shore without almost complete air-cover. The greatest air battles in history are just ahead. There's a red-hot time coming, the most horrible scrap the United States ever has been in. Every pilot we have will be needed to cover the 'Ducks,' 'Buffaloes' and those betracked 'Alligators' as they plow up the beaches in landing operations."

"I've been instructed to inform you that you are not going back into the fight, Major Jerrold."

"Not going back! Why? What have I done?"

"Made yourself a top-ranking Marine flyer. You're of immense value as a pilot, but your instructorable ability is immeasurable. Men like you are needed to 'read the Bible' to the youngsters here. Your orders are to remain in Washington attached to Intelligence for that indefinite period known as the present."

"Stay here! I can't do it. I want to get back into the thick of the fight."

"Do you think I like sitting at this desk, Major? I haven't reached retiring age but I was told that I, also, am needed here 'at present.' " He cleared his voice of bitterness. "Remember the oath you took when you joined the Marines?"

"Yes, sir."

"This job is your present responsibility. You may remember, also, that Prime Minister Churchill recently observed that 'the price of greatness is responsibility.' "

"I'm not looking for greatness, I'm looking for a fight."

"You may get one when you least expect it. Meanwhile, carry on. It ought not to be difficult. She's a beautiful girl." He answered the surprise in Jerrold's eyes. "I've seen her. You don't think I'd send one of my officers into a situation I was afraid to face myself, do you? If only I were a little younger and a trifle plumper — That will be all for the present, Major."

10

Bill Jerrold had to force their way through a crowd to the table he had reserved at the supper club. The orchestra in cherry red uniforms that matched the music stands were shifting scores.

"That was a battle," he declared as he seated himself opposite Nan. "There was one horrible moment when I thought we wouldn't make it. Did you come through without damage to that snappy black frock and that sequin-and-veil apology for a hat?"

"Yes. My gorgeous spray of yellow orchids is intact, also." She touched the flowers at her shoulder. "You mustn't send me a corsage every time we go out. It's —" The hard beating of her heart got in the way of her voice. What was there in this situation to start a shivery premonition of trouble? "I'm like the old woman in *Mother Goose*, wondering if I be really I — here with you?"

On the bandstand, which glowed with the color of a midsummer sunset, piano, trumpet, trombone, saxophone, clarinet, guitar, bass, drums, commenced to beat out with flawless rhythm "People Will Say We're In Love." She leaned a little toward him.

"Is that part of it? Will they?" she asked.

"Not if you look as troubled as you look at the present moment. 'People' will think I'm heckling you. Couldn't you smile for the guy, lady?"

"I can and will if only you'll tell me what it's all about. I feel as if I had lost my way in the dark."

"Try to think of yourself as being under military orders."

"I do and remind myself that you don't like being 'tied up,' either."

"Did I say that? I must have lost my manners in the jungle. Forget it; just remember we're on a binge. I ordered dinner ahead without consulting you to make sure we would have something to eat. These night clubs are so popular. Washington is dancing mad."

"It is a desperate effort to forget and get away from it all, isn't it? Escape from reports and war business and the tragic news on the radio. There are more officers than civilian men on the floor tonight."

"It's the American way of life to dance

when the clouds are heaviest. While we are waiting for service, let's step. The orchestra has switched to 'Speak Low.' That's a fox trot, isn't it? Shall we try it?"

They made the round of the room, bumping into couples who were singing the words of the song into each other's ears. Nan stopped when they reached their table.

"Too much of a crowd. Dancing through it is more of a fight than battling for a bus seat between four and six P.M., when the terminal sounds like the Union Station and is that something! The starter shouts like a foghorn train caller as he announces destinations."

"Even under difficulties you fox trot like a dream. Don't keep trying to cover up the adhesive plaster on your left arm with that huge emerald green chiffon handkerchief tied around your wrist. The patch is one of the current American badges of honor on the civilian front."

"Maybe, but I don't care to flaunt it at a supper club. It might appear to suggest a 'holier than thou' complex. There is a Blood Donor Center at the Pentagon. I wouldn't have arranged a date there today if I had known we had a party on tonight."

"From now on you'll never know in the

morning what may happen before the next. What will you have to drink?"

"Sparkling white grape juice. I hope that won't spoil your fun?"

"On the contrary, it helps me resist temptation. Doctor's orders. I'm on the wagon. As far as that goes I have been from the day I began to fly. Alcohol and a plane-stick don't mix."

He gave an order to the waiter who had set oysters roasted in the shell before them. The man hurried away.

"These oysters remind me, Captain — Count to you — François Bouvoir and I lunched together."

"Did — he — did he speak of my mistake in thinking him a boy with whom I once played tennis?"

"He referred to it briefly when he said you were doing a translation job for him. He was all set to tell me about a letter he had taken to your office when I headed him off. If he's been in this country since January, 1943 he should have learned not to mention personal business in a crowded cafeteria — café to him. Did he speak of your mistaking him for someone else?"

"Briefly — that's your word. He invited me to dine and dance with him."

"Speedy work at the second meeting,

though you must be used to a quick conquest."

"At least he didn't ask to be head man in my life."

"He may at the third." His eyes were alight with laughter. "Could be. Did you say you would?"

"Would what?"

"Go out with him?"

"Yes. I'm determined to find out of whom he reminds me without letting him know that I still feel I've met him somewhere. Of course the impression may be a hangover from a previous incarnation."

"I like your dash and sparkle."

"That 'dash and sparkle' is of comparatively recent vintage. But thereby hangs a tale which wouldn't interest you. To keep laughter in one's life keeps one sane in these tragic times, doesn't it?"

"You've said it. While you are turning the thumbscrews of investigation on the Captain, don't forget that I have first claim on your time."

"I didn't know when I said 'Yes' to François Bouvoir's invitation that I was shortly to be swept into the present imitation romance." Because she didn't want him to answer she turned her head to look at the stage. "She has a lovely voice, hasn't she?"

The floor was clear now: the dancers had returned to the tables to listen to a dark-haired, willowy girl in a rose-red frock glittering with gold sequins singing "You'll Never Know."

Nan leaned forward.

"Won't I ever know, Major?" she coaxed softly and experimented with what Gladys Grant had dubbed Suzanne Dupree's eye-work. She saw the color mount under his dark skin and felt her own rise in response.

"Play fair, Nan," he warned, "if you expect me to."

"What was the matter with that? Didn't you tell me that I must appear as if we were 'that way' about each other? Isn't it natural that I would want to know why I have been plunged into this grotesque situation?"

"It isn't what you said, but the way you said it. I recognized Suzanne Dupree's technique, though I've never seen it worked through an eye-veil. Makes it even more deadly. Don't try that on me or I'll renege on my part of the arrangement."

"That's telling me. You don't think for a minute that I wouldn't be glad to be free of this absurd —"

"Nan!"

Startled, she looked up incredulously at the officer in navy uniform who had stopped at the table. Her breath caught in a little gasp.

"Ken! Where did you come from? I thought you were —" She was aware that Bill Jerrold had risen and was looking at her expectantly. It took her an instant to retrieve her voice.

"Lieutenant Rand, Major Jerrold. I thought you were in Texas, Ken."

"Had a leave. Wired Sam to ask where you were. He answered, 'None of your darn business.' Pretty crazy about you, isn't he? Then I tried my backer, Di. She came across. I phoned Mrs. Trask's. The butler said you were here."

"He may seem to be a butler but he doubles as a guardian angel. I always tell Pike where I am going in case my boss wants to find me. You'd be surprised at what curious hours I work, Ken." She was aware she was chattering but it served to cover her surprise.

"Let's dance before that 'boss' catches up with you." The orchestra was playing the "Merry Widow Waltz" dreamily, invitingly.

"Sure. Go ahead," Bill Jerrold answered Nan's questioning eyes. "Don't make it too long, though, or I shall cut in, Lieutenant. Miss Barton and I are celebrating a contract."

The hint of possession in his voice sent the color to Nan's face. She flashed an indignant glance at him as she rose.

Kenneth Rand's arm tightened round her as they glided into step. "What sort of contract are you and Major Whosis celebrating, Nan?"

"Something very special. It's hush-hush. A military secret."

"Kidding me, aren't you? The Major is in love with you, isn't he?"

"Could be. Why not? *'Somebody loves me,'*" she hummed. "Why not he? You didn't think I'd be mourning in sackcloth and ashes for you, Jaygee, or did you?"

"I've *got* to make you understand. Let's get out of this."

Why not? It would be interesting to know how the fast-working blonde had landed her man so quickly. Where was the bride? Had the fortunes of war parted them so soon?

There was a tiger-skin banquette before a fake window, draped in old blue damask hangings, in the lounge.

"Sit here," Rand said. Seated beside her he leaned forward in a manner that screened her from the room. She remembered that pose. It had preceded, usually, a declaration of devotion.

"What have you *got* to make me understand, Ken? Better begin. Time marches on and my Major is a man of his word. He doesn't pull his punches."

"That's telling me. You've changed a lot, sweet." He laid his hand over hers.

"Don't do that!" He was putting on his old act. "Why shouldn't I change? I'm a career woman now. By the way, what's your reaction to a career woman, Ken?"

"Don't like it. Loved you as you were. I'm still terribly in love with you."

"Really! What has become of the girl you married? You did marry her, didn't you, or was that wire you sent Di a bluff to break our engagement?"

"Don't be peeved. I'm trying to make you understand. I was infatuated with a —"

"Blonde."

"How did you know?" His surprise was genuine.

"I'm psychic." She thought of the time she had made that statement before in answer to a man's bitter, "I *hate* red hair."

"Go on, you were infatuated —"

"We were all set to be married. I sent the wire to Di on my way to the chapel. I thought it only fair to let you know."

"Fair! Let *me* know? That's precious. You didn't mention me. Go on. I take it the bride left you waiting at the church?" To herself she added fervently, "I *hope* she did." The light was not too dim for her to see his pale blue eyes darken with anger.

"You are psychic, aren't you?" His light tone was a triumph of will over fury. "She eloped with another man."

"And you decided to look up your former fiancée as a playmate for your leave? It's a true-and-tried plot formula."

"Don't make a joke of it. After the wire had gone I realized my mistake, knew that you were the only girl I wanted. Marry me tomorrow, will you, sweet?"

She twisted free from the arm he laid over her shoulders and stood with her back to the room.

"Same old technique, Ken. You really ought to cultivate a new line."

"Why won't you be serious, Nan? I love you." He caught her hands hard in his. "Marry me."

"Sorry, no can do." Faintly from the dining room drifted the music of the U.S. Marines' Song: *From the halls of Monte-zuma, to the shores of Tripoli.* It provided a cue. "You see, I happen to be desperately in love with my Major."

"I warned you if you made it too long I'd cut in, Lieutenant."

Nan turned. Bill Jerrold stood behind her.

Had he heard her impassioned declaration? She had given it all she had.

Her thoughts were in a turmoil as she danced back to the table with him. She couldn't remember what Ken had said as he bowed and turned away; she had a vague remembrance that it was something about seeing her again when he returned.

"I'm afraid your squab chicken is cold," Bill Jerrold regretted as he drew out her chair. "I didn't dare have the waiter take it back for fear we'd never get another, there is such a mob here."

"This is fine." She kept her eyes on her plate while she wondered if he would refer to the sentence he must have overheard.

"Is Rand an old friend or an old enemy?" he inquired. "I sense tension in your every nerve and muscle."

"If you call several years of friendship old. I — we were engaged." Too late she realized the touch of defiance in her voice.

"So you have been engaged? I merely picked the wrong man. It's the Navy. Were you in love with this Rand?"

"Is it likely I would be engaged to him if I weren't?"

His laughing eyes met hers.

"Wouldn't you?"

"You know perfectly well what I mean."

Her voice prickled with exasperation. "You are not comparing this wacky arrangement — to an engagement, are you? Allah be praised, that your higher-up didn't require that — last."

"Hold everything. If we quarrel in public we'll upset the Intelligence kettle of fish. Why didn't you marry that Lieutenant (j.g.)?"

Should she tell the truth? Why admit she had been jilted? Why not improvise?

"When I heard he had been ordered on foreign service, I couldn't take it. I sent back his ring."

"Not being able to take that tough break doesn't seem like you."

"What do you know about me?"

"Nothing — much, but I get an impression of any girl I meet. As you don't care to dance in this crowd let's get acquainted. To carry on this 'wacky arrangement' convincingly, we ought to be posted on one another's past. Willing now to tell me where you came from?"

Perversely, she still didn't want him to know she was the girl who had found him in the pool next door to his sister's home.

"It's a difficult question to answer. Before this horrible war much of my life was spent abroad." That was the truth.

"Still side-stepping. Okay. I might have asked our 'boss' — he'd know — but I prefer to have you tell me. How did you happen to pick Washington for your war job?"

She told him of her training in languages, concluded: —

"I heard that Colonel Long needed an interpreter. For reasons you wouldn't understand I didn't join the Wacs or the Waves. What I have done adds up to the same thing. I have released a man for active service. Any other questions?"

"That's just the entering wedge."

He asked if she had many friends in the service. What she thought of the "Draft Daddy Bill"? Did she approve of a fourth term for a President of the United States? Did she like her music hot or sweet? How did she feel about hasty war marriages? Had she followed the campaign in Sicily and the advance of the Eighth and Fifth Armies in Italy? The slow but sure forward campaign among the islands in the South Pacific? Did she realize that the fighting there spread over millions of square miles?

"You should have warned me in advance that there would be an 'Information Please' quiz," she protested. "I would have boned up for it."

"You're making the grade. Ever thought what kind of a world you want after the war?"

Dessert came with that question. Frozen pudding in tall, thin glasses, *petits fours* and small cups of fragrant, hot black coffee.

"I can answer *that* one. I want a world in which people will *really* have the right to life, liberty and the pursuit of happiness. A world in which the golden rule will have prove itself a practical working formula for individuals and for countries." She tempered her eager voice.

"When I told that to Sam, he said, 'You're envisioning Utopia, Nancy B.' Do *you* think the world I want is impossible?"

"I agree with you that it would be almost an earthly heaven."

"Neatly side-stepped. Isn't it time to dismiss this class?"

"Have I worn you out? I'm sorry. I had to know something of what the girl thinks to whom I'm assigned."

"The girl has grown older in the process. You've discovered a lot I never knew I thought. Suppose you tell me something about yourself, now."

"I? I'm a frustrated fighter. That's why I'm so grouchy. I want to be doing something for which I'm not fit. More details later."

"Perhaps someday you will tell me a little of what happened before you came home." Without giving him time to answer she reminded: —

"It is getting late. This isn't Saturday. I'm a working woman who has to rise practically at dawn to catch a bus."

As he held her jacket he asked: —

"Why didn't you get quarters in one of the dorms in Girl Town at Arlington Farms? It would have been much nearer your job."

"Sam wanted me to live at Mrs. Trask's."

"The Sam whom you just quoted? Who is 'crazy' about you?"

She resented his tone.

"Not so crazy about me as I am about him. Let's go."

11

When Nan entered her room Patricia Trask, in a quilted rose-color satin house coat and silver mules, was huddled in the wing chair done in green-and-gold striped cotton. Nan closed the door quickly behind her and drew the green curtains on their matching poles across the long windows.

"Pat, what are you doing here at this time of night? School tomorrow, remember."

"Why are you so late? You have to get up at dawn, too. Been stepping out with the Captain?"

Nan sighed as she slipped her beaver jacket on a hanger. She didn't feel equal to Patricia and her combative mood tonight. She had a mental muddle to straighten out. What was behind Bill Jerrold's extraordinary request? She carefully laid the yellow orchids in water in a shallow dish. While she considered her reply to the girl's question she stepped out of her shimmering black frock.

"Which Captain?" she asked lightly. "You'd be surprised at the number I've met. The Pentagon swarms with them. Quote: From this giant War Department Head-quarters, a staff as large as the population of Hagerstown, Maryland, directs the United States Army on the fighting fronts and in training. Unquote. Not that I have an inkling of the size of the population of said town, but I can believe it, whatever it is. The ramps and corridors glimmer with silver and gold insignia."

Patricia impatiently brushed back the strand of chestnut hair that dangled over her left eye as she watched Nan belt a pale blue faille house coat.

"Don't stall. You know perfectly well I mean Captain François Bouvoir — he won't let me speak of him as Count. Have you noticed the coat of arms on his ring? It's simply colossal. I suppose he sent you those snazzy orchids. He says it to me with gardenias."

Perched on the bench before the dressing table, Nan drew off a high-heeled black pump and flexed her toes in a filmy stocking.

"Ooch! Are my feet battered! There was such a crowd dancing they were stepped on fore and aft."

"I think you're poisonous to steal my beau, Nancy Barton."

147

Nan looked up impatiently from her absorption in her tired feet. She shut her lips hard to keep back an indignant retort as she saw that the girl's violet-blue eyes, so like her mother's, were glittering with tears. Life could seem heartbreakingly tragic at seventeen, she remembered, and tempered her reply.

"Just whom do you mean by *your* 'beau', Pat?"

"Mur–der! You ask that when you know I'm keen about Captain Bouvoir and — and that he is about me." The second statement lacked the assurance of the first.

"If you are so sure of that why accuse me of stealing him? If it is true I couldn't, even if I wanted to."

"Suzanne Dupree told me he phoned you for a date before you got back from work."

"How did she know?"

"She answered the extension phone on this floor and said she delivered the message to you."

"This is the first I have heard of the call."

"It isn't fair of him to ask another girl out on the nights I can't go. That pesky school. Mother keeps me at that when she knows I want a war job."

Nan, who had been brushing her hair till it glowed into a copper gold frame for her face, turned from the mirror.

"Cross-your-throat-and-hope-to-die, Pat, do you want to leave school to help win the war or to be free to go out any night you want to go? If the last, I warn you now that a war job is a harder master than school. You've got to be on the alert in the morning or out you go."

"You sound like Mother. Why haven't I a right to live my own life?"

"Phooey, on that 'right-to-live-my-own-life' stuff. Perhaps you have, if living it doesn't harm anyone else. You are rehearsing 'The Merchant of Venice' at school, aren't you? Remember that the Judge conceded Shylock one pound of Antonio's flesh, that was all, not an extra jot of blood could be shed. That's the catch in the I've-a-right-to-live-my-own-life argument, Pat. Granted the right to live as we like, in the process we haven't the right to hurt those who love us by slipping off the decency beam. Get what I mean?"

"Mother, I suppose."

"For one. How about your Uncle Zeb who thinks the sun rises and sets in your shoes? How about your brother?"

"Tom wouldn't be hurt, he'd beat me up if I did something that gave him a headache. I'm keen about him." Her voice was thick with tears. "If anything should happen to Tom —"

"He's in horrible danger, Pat, but nothing, nothing could hurt him so much as to have his kid sister mortgage her future by the particular brand of right-to-live-my-own-life experiment your girl friend tried out."

Patricia sniffed but not too contemptuously.

"Zowie, you're Miss New England, all right."

"Where did you pick up the idea that New England has a corner on high standards of human behavior, Pat? Cover the country, and you'll discover that, by and large, it's the American Way. You don't get around much, do you, kid?"

"That slaps me down." Patricia giggled. "I *might* have called you 'Our Puritan.' You should hear the twist Suzanne gives the word when she refers to you."

Nan relaxed. The crisis was passed for the present. Pat was smiling. She patted her mouth to conceal an able-bodied yawn.

"Miss New England begs to inform Miss Washington, D.C. that she is rapidly becoming dead to the world and would like to retire."

"So what?"

"So she will remind her that the bus will pass the end of the avenue on the scheduled minute in the morning come hell or highwater. Scram."

"Okay." Patricia uncurled and rose. "You haven't said you weren't out with my Captain."

"If you mean François Bouvoir for heaven's sake stop calling him '*my* Captain.' " Nan's patience was fraying at the edges. Beginning with the self-same Bouvoir's call, followed by Bill Jerrold's startling proposition, it had been quite a day. "Can't you realize that the man has a dozen girls? That what he is handing you is his regular Frenchman's line?"

"I don't believe it. It is too utterly sweet and personal." Patricia put her hand over her heart and drew a long ecstatic breath. "Love is so *bea*-u-tiful, Nan." The theatrical outburst would have been funny if it hadn't been terrifying.

"Beautiful, but remember, Pat, that love is also loyalty, respect, tenderness *and* protection. No man will hurt the girl he *really* loves. Poor child, you'll have to learn the hard way." She hated her patronizing tone, but it might help. "You are too young, too inexperienced, to judge character, aren't you?"

That did it. Patricia flamed with resentment.

"Too young! Everyone says I appear years older than my age."

"Then prove it by not allowing yourself to be fooled. If you will be happier to know it, I went out with Major Jerrold tonight. He sent the orchids. I didn't even see Captain Bouvoir."

"With Major Jerrold, not with François?" The girl's radiance frightened Nan. It dimmed as quickly as it flashed.

"I know Bill's a great pal of Tom's, but it's my turn to warn 'Watch your step.' Suzanne knew him at home. He was stationed near her plantation. She hinted that he had a hectic affair with a married woman, that her husband beat him up."

In the manner of a movie trick shot the memory-film flipped over and presented the picture of the man with whom Nan had spent the evening. She couldn't see him being beaten up by anyone.

"Thanks for the warning, Pat. You watch your step and I'll watch mine." She patted back a yawn. "Time and that bus wait for no woman."

"I'm going." The girl swooped and kissed Nan's cheek. "That's a lush house coat you're wearing. You're a sweet kid. Lots younger than I am, if you ask me. *I* don't think you're chilly," she flung over her shoulder and departed.

"Are you chilly?" Nan demanded of the looking-glass girl as before the mirror she pinned her hair into a curly topknot. She wrinkled her nose at her reflection. "I'll take the matter up with you, gal, after I've had some sleep. At the present moment I don't care —"

Who would knock at this time of night? She cautiously opened the door. Mrs. Trask, in a Chinese-mandarin coat, its purple satin heavily embroidered in green-and-gold dragons, stood there.

"Mrs. Amy! Come in. What's happened? Not bad news about — about your — Tom?"

"No, Nancy B. Not that, thank God. I knew Patricia had been here. I watched her come out and go into her room. I'm worried to death about that child. If only her father were here. Every growing-up girl needs a father. I had to talk to someone. If I try to speak seriously to her she tells me to 'collapse,' meaning sit down, and to stop being 'hysterical.' "

"Sit here." Nan drew forward the wing chair. "Honestly, I don't think you need worry. She's talking a lot of stuff, but I'm sure in her heart she's sound and sweet." She seated herself in a low slipper chair as Mrs. Trask, with a long sigh, rested her head against the back of the tall one opposite.

"I hope so. It's that French Count, the Captain whom you thought you'd seen before, the child has on her mind, isn't it?" As Nan didn't answer, she added: "You won't be betraying her confidence if you say 'Yes,' she intimated as much to me. Her teachers sent for me to report that her marks are poor, that she is inattentive. She wants to leave school. Sometimes I think I will let her and find the hardest job possible for her."

"Oh no, Mrs. Amy. She's brilliant. Her education will mean so much more later than the work she can do now. Besides, she's helping in the Red Cross Motor Corps and is a Junior Volunteer at the hospital. Don't worry about François Bouvoir. He won't harm Patricia. He wouldn't dare, it would wash him up completely. I suspect he is out for what he can get socially. Her infatuation for him will pass. I know, I was desperately in love with my English teacher at seventeen, all the girls adored him, fought for his attention. I doubt if one of us can remember his name now."

"Times are different, Nancy B. There is an emotional lawlessness rampant camouflaged in the guise of patriotism. The ADVICE TO THE WORRIED columns show the trend. Where a few years ago the burning question was 'Should I allow a boy to kiss me?' it is now 'Is it okay for me to go on a week end with a soldier?' If only Pat hadn't antagonized Randy Bond. He doesn't come near her. I would trust her anywhere with him."

"It hurts me unbearably to have you worried about Pat when your heart is aching for your boy, Mrs. Amy."

"You're a grand person. That's why I came here tonight — it's almost morning, isn't it — to ask a favor. Will you try to lure Captain Bouvoir from Pat? You can do it."

"I — I don't like him. I — I would be glad to help you — but —"

"Please. Justify it to your conscience as your Girl Scout deed. That's all I came for." She rose. "Don't answer now. Think it over."

Nan frowned at the door Mrs. Amy had closed behind her. She liked Pat, was fond of her, wanted to protect the girl, but what complications might arise if she accepted François Bouvoir's invitations? She had intended to dine and dance with him occa-

155

sionally, but that was before she had said "Yes" to Bill Jerrold's breath-snatching proposition. She had realized this morning in her office that the French Captain with even slight encouragement would drop at her feet like a ripe apple. Nothing permanent, but a diversion for him. And if he knew they had met before and was afraid of what she might tell, anything could happen. She shivered. Was that the chill of a tragic event casting its shadow?

She reached to snap out the light on the dressing table. It illumined the spray of yellow orchids in the crystal dish. What would the Major say if she carried out Amy Trask's plan to save Pat?

"Suzanne Dupree knew him at home. She hinted that he had a hectic affair with a married woman. Watch your step," Patricia had warned.

Seated on the side of the bed Nan kicked off blue satin mules. "A hectic affair with a married woman," she repeated under her breath. Had he been referring to that when in the living room at home he had said in his delirium: —

"It's a ticklish business to come between husband and wife, Madam. Ask Bill, he knows."

"Something tells me I'm caught in a blitz

with no air-raid shelter in sight," she reflected aloud. "Was it only earlier today I was humming 'Oh, What a Beautiful Morning'?" In retrospect it doesn't look so beautiful, she thought. Something warns me there's a catch in it.

"What's the answer, Major Bill Jerrold, and just where do we go from here?" she demanded impatiently and turned off the bedside lamp.

12

Sunday again. Her one free day in the week with time in which to straighten out the confused what-to-do tangle in her mind, Nancy Barton reflected. Seated on the only vacant bench she looked across the rippling blue Tidal Basin which reflected the white marble reproduction of the Roman Pantheon, the Jefferson Memorial.

She glanced at the tiny watch set in diamonds on her wrist. Almost time for Bill Jerrold, if he were coming. The day after their evening at the supper club, he had sent a note saying he would be away a few days, but would see her Sunday, to be sure and reserve the afternoon for him. Before she left the house an hour ago she had told Pike to tell Major Jerrold, when, or if, he came, where to find her. Would he come? Perhaps she had dreamed that ten minutes in her office with him. It certainly was of the stuff from which dreams are made.

A squirrel chattered noisily at her feet. A

man on the next bench, whose expression-less face reminded her of a bronze mask, and gave her an uneasy feeling that she had seen him before, scattered a few peanuts and the creature loped toward him. As if he felt her scrutiny his sharp black eyes challenged hers with an intentness which set her a-shiver.

"Bill Jerrold coming up," announced a voice. The Major dropped to the seat beside her. His cap with eagle, globe and anchor insignia was tilted at a cocky angle, his over-coat was a masterpiece of fine tailoring.

"I spotted your beaver jacket and green beret several minutes ago, dodged and dashed among strolling servicemen and their girls for fear someone would get this seat before I did."

The man on the next bench thrust the bag of peanuts into his pocket and walked away. Two sharp lines cut between Jerrold's eyes as they followed him before they returned to Nan.

"Now that we are alone why the SOS?" he asked.

"Did it sound that serious? It isn't. I've come to a crossroads and need advice. You have only yourself to blame if, figuratively speaking, I sob out my troubles on your shoulder."

"My shoulder is broad and if I say it who

shouldn't, pretty darn comfy." He grinned.
"So I have been informed. What's on your mind? Shoot."

She told him of Mrs. Trask's plea to her to divert Captain Bouvoir's attention from Patricia. Concluded: —

"I want to help Mrs. Amy, but —"

"Why didn't you tell her you were giving another man the come-on and wouldn't double-cross him?"

"Because it didn't seem possible that I was."

"You've had several days since we made the agreement in which to get used to the idea."

"You were away and I — I — hoped that perhaps when you returned the reason for what you call an agreement would have disappeared. Situations change with miraculous suddenness these days."

"That one hasn't."

"O—kay."

"I don't like your sigh of resignation."

"Did you expect a chortle of joy?"

"Let's get back to the Bouvoir angle. I'll tell Mrs. Trask that I'm that way about you and I can't allow my girl to 'lure' — that was her word, wasn't it — the dashing Captain even to help her, that we'll find another way to save Pat."

"I have the solution!" Her eyes were brilliant, her voice provocatively gay.

"I like you when you sparkle, Nan."

"That's a break, Major."

"Go on with the solution," he ordered gruffly.

"Fall in love with her yourself. Instead of me getting the Captain away from her, you get her away from the Captain. It would be an ideal arrangement and I'll wager a war stamp she couldn't help falling in love with you."

"Is that conclusion based on your own reaction?"

She remembered her impassioned declaration to Ken Rand: "You see, I happen to be desperately in love with my Major." Could he be referring to that?

"It is not. You certainly are quick on the comeback. What do you think of my plan?"

"No dice. First, I'm committed to you — provisionally, of course. Second, I don't try to attract youngsters, I'm too old. Third, I'm in love, unprovisionally."

"Sorry, I remember now."

"Remember what?"

"Don't bite. Patricia told me."

"What did Patricia tell you?"

"That you — you had had —" She swallowed "a hectic affair with a married woman" and substituted lamely — "that you were in — in love."

"Something tells me that isn't all she told you, but I've just admitted I'm in love, haven't I?"

"Right. This isn't getting us anywhere. How can we ease Mrs. Amy's mind about Patricia?"

"We'll work it out. Meanwhile, don't take any stock in the yarns Suzanne Dupree tells Pat. I happen to be familiar with the Dupree method. What say to tea somewhere? I feel like celebrating my return to — my girl. Where would you like to go?"

"Where there is music and a chance to see some of the Big Names of the Capital."

"Let's take a chance at the Mayflower. Come on. We'll pick up a taxi."

The man who had fed the squirrel was talking with the driver of a cab. As they approached he turned away and walked east. Nan stopped and looked after him.

"Did you notice his eyes? They were steel points in an expressionless face. They gave me the shivers. I have the queerest feeling I have seen him before. I felt that way about Captain Bouvoir. You don't suppose my mind is getting a we-have-met-before twist, or do you?"

162

"I do not. Remember I told you I blocked Bouvoir when he began to tell me in the cafeteria of the letter you were translating for him? This man was at the next table. If he wasn't listening to our conversation he was giving a grand imitation. Hop in. To the Mayflower," he directed the driver.

They passed guarded 1600 Pennsylvania Avenue. Both streets paralleling the side entrances were barred.

"The White House looks grim," Nan deplored. "Gone are the days when citizens from all over the country could roam through the reception rooms and children roll eggs on the lawn. War is just what Sherman said it was — plus."

"And he only knew the war of '61. Each one grows more hideous, more deadly. Let's forget it for a little while."

After they were seated at a candle-lighted table in the tearoom far enough from the music to make conversation audible and had ordered, Nan said: —

"It doesn't seem fair, after all you went through in the Pacific, that an affair of wartime strategy should be thrust between you and the girl you love. Can't you explain to her?"

"No. If my heartthrob is what's on your mind, skip it. I shall till I get this assignment off my hands."

"Meaning me, I presume, Major?"

"Who else?"

She poured fragrant tea, added sugar and lemon in response to his assenting nod, passed the cup to him and filled one for herself.

"You have beautiful hands."

"Corsages and compliments are not necessarily included in our pact," she reminded. She held up her right hand and regarded the broken nail on the forefinger. It was conspicuous because of the rosy perfection of the others.

"Hospital work plays the dickens with hands. So what, if they can help, and mine do."

"They look capable as well as beautiful. Like rings?"

"Mad about them. Big splashy ones that are out of place on my job."

"Lovely hands pouring tea were a recurring delusion when I was fighting through the jungle. Mother's, in the firelighted living room at home," he added gruffly.

"Don't answer if you resent the question, Major. Have you ever been afraid?" she asked earnestly.

"Horribly. The first time I stepped out from a plane hundreds of feet above the earth I was so paralyzed with fright I was sure I couldn't make the jump, to say nothing of pulling my rip-cord. The fact that my chute opened and I landed safely cured me of that particular brand of jitters. There were times after that — and plenty going into combat — when I was scared stiff."

"It helps to hear you admit it. I — I haven't a lot of physical courage."

"You'll measure up all right if ever the test comes, the time when there is only one way to go. Ahead. The certainty of that will pull you together, will help you march straight up to the firing line. You'll be on your own. You will know there is no one to help, know that you've *got* to make good — or else."

He cleared his husky voice and laughed.

"We are getting too serious. This is supposed to be a party. Let's sign off. See that iron-jawed man being seated near the door by the major-domo? He's a headliner on the Hill at the moment. He's one of the opponents of the 'Draft Daddy Bill.' "

"He looks like a fighter. Lovely woman with him. His wife?"

"I wouldn't know. To return to our 'pact': the situation is no tougher for me than for you. This 'Sam' about whom, by your own admission, you're 'crazy,' may take it hard."

Nan disciplined a laugh and substituted a deep sigh.

"He'll understand." She placed her hand over her heart and drew a long, ecstatic breath. "Love is so bea-u-tiful, Bill," she declared in a perfect imitation of Patricia's gesture and intonation.

"Unh-huh. Kidding me, aren't you? I'm beginning to wonder if the light of your life is Sam or that Navy man to whom you were engaged. Look who's at the third table at your right. Count François Bouvoir with Suzanne Dupree and a Brigadier General. Can't see his face. What's she got up her sleeve?"

"Does she have to have something?"

"It is safer to assume she has. She reminds me of an experience that made me so fighting mad — let's skip it. Does the Captain still remind you of the boy with whom you played —" he lowered his voice — "in Vienna?"

"I haven't seen him but once since the evening at the Inn. He came to our office on business. I know he isn't the person I thought him, but his resemblance to someone I have met worries me."

"Sorry I brought up that. Like your job?

In my quiz at the Supper Club I neglected to inquire."

When he smiled one forgot the fine lines about his eyes and the deep creases between his nose and mouth which his war experience had etched.

"Love it. Nolly Stiles has asked me to substitute in the Foreign Broadcast Service of his network when a commentator in French or Italian gives out. I'm bursting with pride that he thinks me capable. I may have to cut some of my dates with you if the workers in his studio drop out from the flu as they are doing at the Pentagon. They are absent in droves."

"Don't forget that keeping dates with me is an important job, also."

"I won't — but I wish I could know why."

"Remember what happened to Bluebeard's wife?"

She nodded in response to his boyish grin.

"Was there a redhead among those hung in that mysterious closet?"

"History doesn't state and I *wish* you wouldn't call your hair red. The Dupree hair is red. Yours is coppery." He rose. "How are you, Bouvoir?"

Nan's startled eyes met the blue eyes of the officer in French uniform looking down at her. Their expression sent a tiny trickle of ice water down her spine. For Pete's sake, why should it, she demanded of herself impatiently.

"I have been most unfortunate in missing you on the telephone, Mademoiselle Barton. Are you never at home between six and seven? That was the hour you gave me to call, right?"

"Right." Nan resented Bill Jerrold's steady regard. "I'm sorry, but I've taken on two more stretches at the hospital and sometimes it is eleven before I get home."

"I shall not give up hope. I am a *very* persistent man, Mademoiselle. *Au revoir.*"

Bill Jerrold followed Bouvoir's straight military figure with his eyes before he resumed his seat.

"Have you taken on more evenings at the hospital, Nan?" he inquired.

"No. I crossed my fingers under the table when I said that. All's fair in love and war, and I consider my chance to fill in as a foreign broadcaster at Nolly Stiles's studio whenever he needs me War with a Capital W. An evening with Captain Bouvoir may prove to be a lot of fun, but he'll have to wait for it. His patronizing, godlike smile gets under my skin."

"That's telling him. What's the girl at the piano singing?"

" 'None but the Lonely Heart.' That song

reminds me of the hearts and lives being broken and trampled in this horrible war — and tightens my throat till —" She swallowed hard and smiled at him through tears. "I'm sorry to inflict you with an emotional breakdown."

"All right with me. I've come to the conclusion that in spite of —"

"If you say New England chilliness, patriotism or no patriotism — what you call our arrangement is definitely off."

"Hold back the *ack-ack* till I finish. I was about to say that hazel eyes framed in drenched wet lashes do something to *my* heart. If you've finished your tea let's go before I make any more statements that are proscribed by our pact."

As they entered the lounge Susanne Dupree and Captain Bouvoir were talking with the short man in the uniform of a Brigadier General of Marines who had been at their table. The officer looked casually at Nan and Jerrold before he turned to answer what appeared to be Suzanne's laughing challenge.

When they reached the sidewalk Nan inquired: —

"Don't you know the General whom Suzanne was going all-out to charm? He is a Marine."

"Sure, I know him."

"He glanced at you and away as if he never had seen you before."

"Shall we walk or ride?"

"Walk. The air is gorgeous." She looked up at his grave face. "Did I make a military blunder when I inquired if you knew Suzanne's General? You seem to have withdrawn behind a dark, dark cloud."

The two lines between his brows deepened.

"It isn't your question that is running me ragged. It is wondering why he was there — with them. He's the higher-up under whose orders you and I are working."

13

It had been a curious Thanksgiving. Nan had worked at the office all day and so late that she had had to rush dressing to make the dinner table on time. Now, she couldn't shake off the feeling that she was talking, laughing, eating in a dream. Amy Trask, in an amethyst velvet frock, lustrous pearls, and a few spectacular diamonds, seated at the head of the long candle-lighted table; the yellow chrysanthemums, rich lace, choice china, shining silver and sparkling crystal between her and the Admiral in full-dress navy blues at the opposite end, and Pike, serving dinner, were as unreal as the setting.

She glanced at the members of what the mistress of the house affectionately called her "family." Bill Jerrold sat at her right. Suzanne Dupree, her black-sequined frock cut to display to advantage her lovely shoulders, was seated between Oliver Stiles and Captain François Bouvoir. She was concentrating on the Frenchman to the evident annoyance of Patricia — seated at the Admiral's left — who, in contrast to Suzanne, looked young and sweet in her simple white frock. At the girl's other side Randy Bond glowered like a thunder god about to hurl destruction. Why did she snub the boy and show her hurt for Suzanne to gloat over? At least it was proof that the sophistication of which she boasted didn't go very deep. Bouvoir answered a question of his hostess.

"Yes, Madame Trask. In France women are taking a leading part in the underground movement. No matter what her age, schoolgirl or grandmother, each has definite duties to perform in French resistance."

He spoke with such conviction and authority that everyone stopped talking to listen. Mrs. Trask answered and the give-and-take of conversation flowed on again.

Nan saw her side of the table reflected in the wall mirror beside the buffet. The emerald green of the sparkling butterfly in her hair was repeated in the necklace about her throat. Her gold lamé frock, soft as tissue, was a colorful contrast to the black dinner jacket of Ralph Carew at her right and the Admiral's blue at her left.

She felt like a buffer between the two men, who commenced a heated argument as to whether the absentee-soldier vote was a matter for State or Federal control.

In the mirror she met the eyes of Gladys Grant, seated on the other side of Carew. The girl raised her black brows, flashed twin dimples, before she touched the arm of the Congressman.

"You ought to save that eloquence for the Hill, when the subject comes up for debate in the House, Mr. Carew," she suggested, and followed with a question which would take time and direct attention to her to answer.

Nan suppressed a smile. Gladys had complained: —

"Everything but men in Girl Town. Where to get them? That's the sixty-four-dollar question." This man wouldn't be ordered off to war. Had she decided to secure him? He was attractive, if he wasn't a ball of fire.

"I beg pardon, Admiral. Did you ask me a question?"

"I did. You seemed miles away. I offered you a penny for your thoughts."

"They are worth a dollar war stamp, but they are yours for nothing. I was thinking that a — a man I know isn't a ball of fire and then I thought, who would want to live with a ball of fire, anyway."

"Hr-rump! You picked a streak of fire

when you took on a Marine, a do-or-die fighter, as a beau. I've seen you going out together. Why did you do it? You look like a girl who'd have too much sense to rush into marriage. Met Jerrold in this very room for the first time a few weeks ago, didn't you?"

"Sh-h, soft-pedal please, Admiral. He may hear you. I'd met him before that." She thought of the man in the pool. "Several weeks before, we are quite old friends. Besides, I haven't the slightest intention of marrying."

"Picked up the career-woman bug, have you?"

"No, Admiral, no career for me. I want a home, a husband and babies sometime and from my observation the two are not an all-out success as working partners. I don't intend to marry for a long, long time."

"Then look out that Jerrold doesn't rush you. Those Marines are daredevils. They —"

"Don't tell me that like sailors, they have a girl in every port, Admiral."

"You're a saucy, disrespectful young woman, but I like you. I . . ."

He stopped and glared at Pike, who entered with a yellow envelope in his white-gloved hand. As if a spell had been cast on the room, conversation ceased. Sentences hung half-finished. All movement was suspended as each one stared at the butler. Were they thinking, as she was, that the message might mean tragedy for the woman at the head of the table?

Amy Trask sprang to her feet. The men rose like a varicolored wave. Bill Jerrold laid his arm across her shoulders. She steadied her mouth, a slash of red in the stark whiteness of her face, before she stammered: —

"Is — is it for me, Pike?"

"No, Ma'am, no, *Ma'am*, 'tain't for you, M's Amy." The colored man's voice was as tender as that of a parent soothing a frightened child. "It's for Miss Nancy Barton, that's who it's for."

As he handed the envelope to Nan, Amy Trask sank back into her chair.

"Sit down everybody, please. Sorry I made a scene. I — I thought it might be —"

"Hr-rump!" The Admiral's explosion filled the gap left by her failing voice. "Who's burning up the wires sending a message to you, Miss Nan? Another beau? Understood the Western Union wouldn't forward I LOVE YOU messages."

Nan crumpled the paper she had read and tucked it into the V of her golden frock.

"And I understand it will if it is from a soldier. This one imagined I might be homesick and sent his love."

"Are you homesick, Nancy B.?" Mrs. Trask asked in a valiant effort to restore her jangled nerves to normal.

"No, Mrs. Amy. I love being here with you." She was aware that François Bouvoir was listening, though apparently he was absorbed in what Suzanne was whispering. She turned to serve herself from the tray Pike's beige-frocked, white-capped niece was offering.

"Pumpkin pie! I didn't know it was served outside New England."

While the Admiral related to the table at large the colorful and slightly Bacchanalian details of the many times and places in which he had enjoyed the festive pumpkin, Nan was thinking of the message tucked in the front of her frock.

BACK SATURDAY. HAVE LICENSE.
DON'T MAKE SPITE MARRIAGE.
I LOVE YOU. ORDERS. KEN.

A spite marriage, She wasn't making any kind of marriage, certainly not one with Kenneth Rand. She looked up suddenly from the plate on which she was absent-mindedly forking the pie into infinitesimal pieces. François Bouvoir was regarding her intently. Always when he was near she felt under surveillance, as if he were waiting for a chance to trip her on the boy-in-the-White-Mountains story. Was he wondering now if she had told the truth about the telegram? Two weeks had passed since she had translated the letter for him. The cipher expert had found no subversive material in it. That fact confirmed her suspicion that he had used it as an excuse to see her.

The Admiral rose with wine glass in hand.

"To the lady of our home and hearts, Amy Trask," he proposed.

Standing, they raised their glasses to the woman seated at the head of the table. Nan's throat tightened. Amy was such a valiant soul. Never before tonight by word or look had she betrayed the fear for the safety of her son which must be like a steel hand squeezing her heart.

"And now to the United Nations," pledged the Admiral in a voice which roused the sleeping love-birds and set them chirping.

On her feet Amy Trask drank the toast and raised her glass again.

"To the men in the service. May they — and those who love them — be granted faith and strength to carry on till Victory."

In the emotion-charged silence which followed she furtively drew a finger across her wet lashes.

"Coffee is served in the lib'ry, M's Amy," Pike's deep, rich voice suggested beside her.

"That takes us right back to daily living." She had recovered her gay courage. "Shall we adjourn?"

Voices were unusually high, there was considerable unnecessary laughter, as they left the dining room. Nan recognized it as an outlet for emotion caused by Amy Trask's fervent words "and those who love them."

A crackling fire was shooting scarlet flames up the broad chimney of the book-lined room, with its crimson hangings drawn across the long windows and its deep inviting chairs covered with the same brocade. Patricia turned on the radio.

"I hear you cried last night." The baritone voice singing the tender words sent to Nan's eyes the tears she had been choking back in her throat since Amy Trask's toast. She stared at a shelf of books till she could get her emotion under control. "And those who love them," Amy had said.

She thought of the brides, wives with young children, mothers and fathers, who, like Amy Trask, turned rigid with fear at sight of a yellow envelope, of those whose hearts already had been pulled up by the roots by one of the messages. The women who are the keepers of the faith, as Sam had said. She felt a maddening sense of futility. If only she, who had no one near for whom to be terrified, could do more to help.

"Did *you?*"

She turned to find François Bouvoir behind her.

"Did I what?" she demanded, as she took the silver-framed porcelain coffee cup he offered.

"Cry last night. Weren't you listening to the song?"

She shook her head and perched on the broad arm of the sofa.

"I was admiring the set of Scott behind us. A Cadell Edition beautifully bound in half morocco. Books so choice don't cross my path every day."

"Are you a collector?"

What was behind the question? The intentness of his blue eyes belied the lightness of his voice.

"It's a complex. I collect everything. If I have a speciality it's silver boxes with —"

"Men running a close second?"

"I hate innuendo." Her indignation brought a slight increase of color to his face. "Say what you mean."

He opened his left hand and dropped a crumpled yellow paper into her lap.

"This fell as you left the dining room."

"And you read it?"

"Naturally. How else could I know to whom to return it? Jerrold's gone off the deep end about you — I have become adept in American lingo, you'll notice. Is this Ken right? Is it to be a spite marriage?"

"I really wouldn't know, Captain. You might contact 'Ken' and ask him, or, better still, ask the Major his intentions. Patricia is looking in your direction. Suppose you postpone the quiz until some other time."

"You don't like me, do you? You won't go out with me because of Jerrold. He has set you against me, *n'est-ce pas?* Do you know where he was late this afternoon? He was entertaining a lovely lady at the Mayflower." He caught her right wrist lightly. "What do you say to that, Mademoiselle?" He was smiling but there was a hint of cruelty in his eyes.

She steadied the cup with her left hand.

"That I intend to dine and dance with you next time you ask me and that I won't like you if you spill this coffee on my brand-new frock." She freed her wrist. "Now that the Squander-bug has arrived in our midst, it's the last I shall buy till Victory."

"Sorry. Shall we make a date for next Monday?"

"I don't like to go out evenings during the first of the week, but I'll make an exception this once."

"*Merci, Mademoiselle.*" He glanced at Bill Jerrold, who had entered the room.

"The Major appears to be the white-haired boy around here," he observed caustically.

"He spent months in the same outfit with Tom Trask, as you must know. To Mrs. Amy, having him here is next best to having her boy."

"What's his job now? He's doing something more than convalescing."

"I don't know any more than I know what yours is."

"Mine is —"

"*Don't* tell me. If I don't know I can't be accused of telling."

"Nothing secret about mine. I am —"

"Break it up! Break it up!" Nolly Stiles interrupted in his loud-speaker voice. "The next feature on the program will be cards, kiddies of the radio audience. Captain, you are needed in the line-up."

With an impatient shrug Bouvoir obeyed the summons. Bill Jerrold took his place.

"Was he annoying you?" he demanded.

Nan carefully set down the coffee cup on a near-by table.

"Not especially. I have agreed to dine and dance with him Monday."

"I'll bet he told you he saw me this afternoon with a woman at the Mayflower. He was with a group of his compatriots. I saw him watching us."

Nan laughed.

"You're positively tragic, Major. Why shouldn't you entertain a woman? After all, ours is nothing but an arrangement of convenience."

"In case you are interested, the woman with me at the Mayflower is my sister. She and I spent the day together. Mrs. Trask invited her to dine here but she had another engagement. We had quite a gossip fest."

"Mrs. Sut—"

"Yes, Mrs. Sutton who lives in the next place to the Sam Mitchells, the Sam Mitchells whose charming sister works in Washington. Ever heard of them? They have a pool in their garden."

"And do I know it. No hard feelings because I sidestepped telling the story of my life, Major?"

"I'll take that up with you later. I'd like to know how much I remember is dream-stuff and how much is reality. I understand now that the Sam you are 'crazy' about is your brother-in-law. That leaves me up against the Navy for competition. I understand, also, that your sister Dianne is a determined person, that her neighbors are betting among themselves that your engagement to Lieutenant Rand will be on again."

Nan's laugh was a mixture of incredulity and exasperation.

"I'll say you had a gossip fest — definitely. Anything more about me?"

"Much, much more, but it will keep. Is that a telegram you're clutching? What's happened? Anything serious?"

Should she tell him? Why not? It would prove that she was not taking the "arrangement" with him seriously. She smoothed out the slip of yellow paper and offered it.

"Depends upon the point of view. Read it. It is from the aforementioned Lieutenant Rand."

He glanced over the typewritten words and returned the message.

"Seems rather sure of you, doesn't he? Will you do it? The Mitchell neighbors appear to believe you will. What does he mean by 'spite marriage'?"

Nan ignored the last question.

"I have almost forty-eight hours in which

to think it over. This is Thursday, he comes Saturday."

"What about this little assignment you've taken on with me? Don't decide anything till I have talked with you again. We'll have dinner together tomorrow night. Don't say 'No.' It's a date. Mrs. Trask is beckoning. Good Lord, are you and I always to be under orders?"

She laughed.

"Two months ago I made a break for freedom. Just between you and me, Major, I'm beginning to believe there ain't no such animal. 'Tention company, forward march — to the card table."

14

The yellow envelope propped against the inkwell on the flat mahogany desk was the first thing Nan saw when she entered her office in the Pentagon the next morning. Without stopping to shed her beaver jacket she ripped it open.

COME AT ONCE. SAM IN ACCIDENT.
DIANNE.

She stared incredulously at the typed words. Sam hurt? Unbelievable. He was so sturdy, so strong, so ruddy, so clear-eyed, nothing serious could happen to him. It must be serious or Di wouldn't have sent for her. Could she get to him in time? Time for what? Why waste that same time imagining tragedy? Too early for Colonel Long. She must go ahead on the chance that he would let her go.

She dialed the airport. Watched the hands of the wall clock as she waited. The official at the other end of the line was adamant. It made no difference if she were called home on account of an accident to her brother, there wouldn't be a seat on a plane going north for two days — if then.

That meant the train. While she waited for her call to the Union Station to be answered she thought of the work ahead for the day. She could —

"Information," a voice sing-songed in her ear. She made notes of the answers to her questions. As she cradled the phone she heard Colonel Long enter his office. She was at his desk before he had pulled out his chair.

"What's happened, Miss Barton? You're white."

"It's Sam." She held out the telegram. "It was on my desk when I came in. A train leaves in forty minutes. It will get me home in the early evening if you can spare me. I cleared my desk yesterday. Nothing has come in this morn—"

"Don't stop to talk. Will you have to go back to the house for a bag?"

"No, sir. I have plenty of clothes at home."

"Then beat it. Give my best to Sam. Tell him to 'Remember Hill 67.' That was our slogan." He cleared his husky voice.

"Having come through that hell safely, we told ourselves we could pull through anything. Need money?"

"No, sir."

"Scram."

She stepped into a cab in the covered roadway under the main concourse.

"Union Station. Make it fast, driver. It's terribly important. Don't, don't stop to take another passenger, *please*." she begged as a man beckoned and shouted: —

"Hi! Taxi."

The cab shot forward with a speed that shook her Scotch cap of Gordon plaid over her left eye. Perched on the very edge of the seat, muscles tensing at each stop, she kept her eyes on her wrist watch. If only time would stand still.

The gate at the track clanged behind her. Heads topped with cocky service caps stuck out of coach windows. Boyish voices cheered as she raced along beside the train whose wheels had begun to move.

A Negro porter, who had been beckoning frantically, shouting, "Hurry! Hurry!" fairly boosted her to the rear step of a Pullman and with a wave of his hand to someone ahead swung up after her. Miracles did happen. She'd made it.

"Is — is there a ch-chance for a s-seat?"

she panted as the train picked up speed.

"Are you Miss Nancy Barton?"

"Yes."

"Then you's got a seat. A Colonel up at the Pentagon telephoned the ticket office you'd get here the last minute an' we must hold the train and find a seat for you. You was goin' to someone who was dyin'. We does what we can to fill War Department orders. This way, Miss."

Dying. The word blew through her mind like an icy wind as, swaying from the motion of the train, she followed him forward between two rows of occupied chairs. Dying. The word picked up the rhythm of the wheels. It couldn't apply to Sam, it couldn't. Men like him were needed on the home front, terribly needed.

"Here you are, Miss." The porter indicated a seat in a corner in the forward end of the Pullman. "It may be a little crowded, but you ain't got no bags —"

"I don't mind being crowded if only I can get there — be— before —" Her tight throat shut off the sentence. She handed him the silver she had clutched since paying the cab driver. He touched his cap.

"Thanks, Miss. If there is anything I can do, ring. I doesn't have much chance to help just plain passengers, though."

A man who took his job seriously. His strained voice showed that. For the first time she really looked at him. His naturally dark face was a light buckskin in color, his eyes were heavy with fatigue.

"These crowded trains must be hard for you, porter," she sympathized.

"Hard. Yo's don't know the half, Miss. But, I likes my job. Shovin' the soldiers from place to place helps win the war, don't it? Comin'. Comin'," he shouted in answer to a yelled "George. *George!*"

"That's what I call split-second timing, Miss, the way you made this train. Ticket." The stout genial man in dark blue smiled down at her and held out his hand.

"That split-second timing didn't allow even a dash to the ticket window, conductor." She opened her green alligator bag. "How much is the fare?"

With the pink ticket which denoted her paid-up passage on the window ledge, Nan sank into the chair, pulled off her cap, closed her eyes and leaned her head back against the white cover. On her way at last. Her heart was quieting. Days of office work had unfitted her for the race from taxi to Pullman and had it been a race! Why think of it? She had made it.

Was it only last evening she had told Bill

Jerrold she didn't believe there was such a thing as freedom? And he had said — Her lids flew open. He had said they would dine together tomorrow — that was today — She must get word to him.

She pulled a memorandum pad from her bag. Pencil poised she considered. Better send the wire to Marine Headquarters at Arlington Annex. A message would surely reach him there before evening. She wrote: —

Called home. Sam seriously hurt.

NAN

She rang for the porter. He assured her he would send the wire at the next stop.

"Will there be a chance for lunch on the train?" she asked.

He removed his cap and scratched his once crisp black hair, now streaked with white.

"I reckon our best bet will be to get off when we stop at noon an' try for a san'wich at the eatin' place, the dinin' car'll be jammed all the way. You'll know it when we get there."

She knew it when they got there by the crowds that spilled from the Pullmans and coaches. After a few futile struggles among civilians and servicemen, also fighting for a sandwich, she purchased a morning paper and a magazine and returned to her seat. Food for the mind would have to suffice till she reached home. It looked as if the government's and the railroads' plea not to travel unless necessary had fallen on deaf ears. Perhaps, though, these people were being summoned home as she was, because someone they loved had been hurt.

SAM IN ACCIDENT. A curious message. With her eyes on the shining tracks parallel with the train, running on and on endlessly and never meeting, her thoughts trooped along. If only Di had been a little more explicit. Perhaps she couldn't be, perhaps the accident had occurred at the foundry, perhaps — she shivered. Not that. Sam's workers might slow up, be absent without real need, but they wouldn't harm him.

In an effort to blunt her anxiety she picked up the newspaper.

The British Eighth Army battles its way across the swollen Sangro River, thus cracking the so-called winter line of the Nazis. Marines and soldiers storm and capture Tarawa and Makin Islands. The most costly U.S. victory to date.

She dropped the paper and thought of Bill Jerrold's record and of his dejection when he had confided to her that he would not be sent back to the front lines; of his extraordinary request verging on command that she accept him as temporary head man in her life. Curious that the officer whom he had called their boss should have appeared so friendly with Suzanne and Captain Bouvoir that afternoon at the Mayflower.

Lucky she was not romantically interested in someone else, her thoughts carried on. Ken had wired he would be with her Saturday. That would be tomorrow. Could he believe really that she would marry him? He would contact the Trask house and she wouldn't be there. She had forgotten Mrs. Amy. She would phone her when she reached home. It would be cruel to impose one more task on the already overburdened "George."

"Praise the Lord and pass the ammunition." From the rear of the Pullman men's voices rose in the martial music of the song.

As she listened she wondered if the singers knew to which theater of war they were bound? If deep in their hearts they were "horribly" afraid? If they dreamed of returning home to receive the D.S.C. for "extraordinary heroism"? If they had a premonition that they would not come back at all?

The newspaper slid to the floor as she rested her head against the chairback and watched the panorama of sky and earth slide by the window to the monotonous accompaniment of the *click, clack, click, clack* of iron wheels on steel rails. This interminable day was drawing to a close. A great red sun had slipped halfway below the horizon and left the western sky aflame with crimson, scarlet and brazen orange. The gorgeous colors melted into lemon and pale green where they touched the still, blue heaven. Small ponds were lacquered copper by the glow. Giant trees, stripped to skeletons, were etched against it.

Smoke was spiraling from little country houses cuddling in valleys or nestling against the side of a hill. Lights sprung on in windows. Farmers plodded from long red barns with heavy milk pails, a shaggy dog at heel. Boggy edges of meadows were rimmed with rosy ice. The sun dropped from sight. Violet dusk blurred the outlines of hills and houses. Slowly, one by one, blossomed the stars to shimmer at their posts, to watch the world till dawn.

Pegasus, the Great Square, had risen when Nan raced up the path of her sister's house. Would she be too late? She didn't stop to ring. Opened the door. How still. How terrifyingly still. She waited for her tight throat to release her voice before she stole on tiptoe across the hall. The lovely green living room was softly lighted. Flames weaving and shooting up the chimney cast grotesque shadows on the walls and on the figure of a man in brown tweeds seated on the arm of a rose brocade chair, staring into the fire. It couldn't — she brushed her hand across her eyes and looked again.

"S-Sam," she said unsteadily, "Sam, you're not —" A sob finished the sentence.

He sprang to his feet. His left arm was in a sling.

"Nancy B.!" Sam Mitchell's voice cracked from amazement. "What in thunder brought you back? Hey, wait a minute. You're groggy." He threw his right arm about her shoulders as the sudden release from fear for him took the stiffening from her knees. She pressed her head against his chest with a long, shuddering sob. He patted her head anxiously.

"What's the matter, Nancy B.? Tell your old brother all about it. What's happened?"

She lifted her head and stepped back.

"N-Nothing to me." She fumbled in her green bag for a handkerchief and dabbed at her eyes. "It — it was you, S-Sammy. Di wired me that you had been in an accident, to come at once and I thought —"

"That I had passed out? Nothing to it. A crazy fool at the foundry who'd been worked on by outsiders nicked me on the arm with a bullet as I was coming from the office yesterday. You say *Dianne* wired you to come?"

"Yes." Her voice still caught in her throat. She brushed her hand across her eyes. Being here in Di's house seemed to have no connection with reality.

"Uh-uh, I sniff a plot. Come on. They are in the library."

"Who are? What plot?" she queried as they crossed the hall.

In answer he threw open the door of a book-lined room. At first Nan saw only a gay little fire, then the glitter of gold braid on a navy blue sleeve. Her eyes traveled up to the face of the man in uniform standing before the mantel.

"Ken!" she whispered. *"Ken!"*

"Oh, you've come, Nan."

It was Dianne speaking. Dianne in filmy light blue, smiling and rising from a chair. She laughed and spoke to the man who had thrown his cigarette into the red coals.

"Our conspiracy worked, Lieutenant."

15

In the tingling silence which followed Dianne's exultant exclamation, Nan thought, this is like a movie and melodrama at that. Four actors on a screen staring at each other. Sam's accident had been used as an excuse to trick her into coming. Fury surging within her threatened to break loose.

"Well, I'll be dam—"

"Just what did you mean, Di, by 'Our conspiracy worked'?" Nan's question interrupted Sam Mitchell's explosive protest.

"Explain, Kenneth." Dianne lightly turned over the situation to Lieutenant Rand, standing before the fire with his hands clasped behind him. "I got her here. It's up to you to carry on."

"You're right, Di. Come into the living room, sweet, where I can explain without an audience," he suggested in a voice which had lost its usual assurance.

"You'll explain right here, Rand," Sam Mitchell announced. "Have you gone screwy? You wire Di you are married. Today you blow in here and say you're not. Which is it?"

"I'm *not*."

"Sure of that? Let's have a look at the message Di sent you, Nancy B."

She drew the yellow slip from her bag.

"I — thought something terrible had happened to you, Sammy," she said as she handed it to him.

"COME AT ONCE. SAM IN ACCIDENT. DIANNE," he read aloud.

"What was the big idea, Di? You knew the doctor said the flesh wound would heal in a few days."

"I don't know why you put *me* on the carpet, Sam." His wife's protest was tinged with martyrdom. "Ken had a few days before being sent heaven knows where. He saw Nan in Washington a while ago and was convinced that she still loved him. He admitted that the affair with the other woman was nothing more than an acute brainstorm and asked me to help him get Nan back. We decided that as he had such a short leave it would be better for them to be married here —"

"Apparently the bride wasn't to be consulted." Nan steadied her shaken voice. "You knew you couldn't get me here for that reason, so you tricked me into coming. Smart work, Di. After this, keep out of my life and I mean keep out."

Kenneth Rand laughed.

"Perhaps we didn't play fair, sweet, but the trick is worth it if only to see you blaze. Gosh, you're beautiful. Your eyes are something out of this world. I didn't know you had it in you."

"You'd be surprised at the things you don't know about me, Ken. Sam, a bus leaves for the city in about twenty minutes. Call a taxi to take me to the village, please. I can easily make the night train for Washington and be at my desk tomorrow."

"Don't phone for that taxi, Sam." Dianne laughed. "I'm unnecessarily excited. You couldn't with one hand. Calm down, Nan. You're not going back tonight or tomorrow."

"No?" The girl she used to be could have let her sister get away with that, but not this one. "Oh, yes I am. I'll dial for that taxi myself."

Ken Rand caught her arm.

"Not until you hear what I have to say, sweet."

She stood rigid under his touch and looked up at him with burning intensity.

"For the first time in my life, Ken, I wish I

were a man with the power to knock another man down and that man is Lieutenant (j.g.) Rand. Take your hand from my arm and — quick."

He looked as stunned as he might have if a pet dog had snarled at him. Nan choked back a gurgle of laughter. The sound frightened her. Was this unbelievable day to end in hysterics as well as histrionics?

"Nancy B." Sam Mitchell stopped her on the way to the telephone. "I know how you feel but I wish you would wait till tomorrow. You've had a nerve-racking trip. It's dollars to doughnuts you'd either have to perch on the arm of another person's seat or stand all the way to Washington. I can't begin to tell you what it means to me to know you care so much for your old brother-in-law —"

"Which passion he reciprocates," Dianne cut in.

The bitterness of her voice, the smoldering anger in Sam's eyes at her interruption, revealed the lack of mental and spiritual rapport between the man and woman who had been husband and wife for a decade. The realization of their utter incompatibility hurt Nan intolerably. Sam was such a grand person. He deserved the best.

"You will stay, won't you?" He had taken

her thoughtful silence for consent.

"I can't, Sammy. It would be unfair to Colonel Long. I left my job to fly to the side of my dying —"

"Cut the sarcasm, Nancy B. We've had enough of that here." Sam Mitchell's voice held the ring of steel on steel. "It's just a piece of luck that I'm not dead instead of dying. Call the taxi. While you're waiting better have something to eat."

"I'll get something in the city." As she twirled the dial with a pencil, she resisted the angry urge to add, "I'll never eat in Dianne's house again as long as I live." Why hurt Sam who was such a dear? She answered a voice on the phone. . . .

"What! The bus taken off *yes*terday? *Why?* Yes, I've heard there is a war on. How does one get to the city? The walking is good? Thanks for the suggestion." She cradled the phone.

"The village comic says there is no bus, Sam. I —" She caught the pleased smirk on her sister's lips. "You knew that, Di?"

"Certainly I knew it. Stop this nonsense about going back tonight, settle down and listen to Ken. You won't leave this hou—"

A ringing slap on her cheek shattered the word and set her eyes blinking like a crossroads traffic warning.

"One word more and I'll do it again. I told you to keep out of my life," Nan reminded breathlessly.

"She's right, I'll do the talking from now on, Dianne," Rand intervened hastily. "I sold myself to her once before, I can do it again if I have to promise to drive her back to Washington tonight myself."

"That won't be necessary, Lieutenant. I'm here to take over."

Sam Mitchell stared at the tall man in trench coat and cap tilted at a cocky angle in the doorway.

"Bill," Nan whispered under her breath. *"Bill."*

"It's you again, Major. Here to celebrate another contract with Miss Barton?" Rand demanded furiously. Hands clenched into fists he took a step forward, his blue eyes burning black in his white face. Dianne, whose left cheek glowed red as a stoplight, caught his arm and held him.

"To what do we owe this pleasure — Mr. — ?" Her frosty voice shattered the charged silence.

"Jerrold, Bill Jerrold, Mrs. Mitchell." He removed his cap and tucked it under his left arm. "The front door was unlatched and as my ring was unanswered I walked in. You were so deeply engaged in — shall we call it conversation or battle? — that you didn't hear me. Do you want to return to Washington, Nan?"

"Do I? I'm going tonight if have to hitchhike."

"You won't have to do that, I promise. Let's get started."

"Just a minute, Jerrold." Sam's gravity sent little chills creeping along Nan's nerves. "My sister doesn't leave this house until I know your plan for getting her to Washington."

"Right, Mr. Mitchell. When I received Nan's wire that she was on her way to you because you were seriously hurt, I had a hunch there was something phony in the air." He glanced at Rand before he added, "The War Department checked with your foundry. You're an important person, I discovered. When I learned that the injury was slight I knew something was wrong, got a lift in an army plane coming this way on government business. I've requisitioned the Sutton convertible — my sister's in case you care to check on me, Mrs. Mitchell — to drive to the airport where I have two priorities on a returning plane. Now that my cards are all on the table — Coming Nan?"

"I am. May I have five minutes to get a coat I left behind me?"

"Ten if you need them."

"Come into the living room, Jerrold. I want to talk to you," Nan heard Sam Mitchell say.

Ken Rand caught up with her at the foot of the stairs.

"Sweet, you can't do this to me."

"Can't I? Watch me, that's all. Just watch me," she challenged.

"Make it snappy, Nan," Bill Jerrold reminded from the living-room threshold.

Her room seemed ghostly when she entered it, haunted by memories of the person she used to be. She didn't of course believe in ghosts but she had a curious feeling that her double walked beside her. Coming back here gave her a sense of power, as if the timidity and indecision which had hobbled that other girl had been swept away, leaving this one with the strength and compulsion to fight, and die if need be, for what she knew was right. Doubtless later she would burn with shame that she had struck her sister. At the present moment she experienced only exultation that for once Dianne got what was coming to her. Some of the strength in that stinging slap had been for Sam. Gladys Grant had said: —

"Someday when you're boiling mad the lid will fly off your temper. You'll never get it on tight again. You'll be a different person." The lid had flown off — and plenty. She hurriedly took from the closet a long black coat with a sable collar she had left at home under the mistaken impression that Washington would be warm in winter.

"From this date you'll never know in the morning what may happen before the next," Bill Jerrold had said. He was two hundred per cent right, she agreed, as she started down the stairs. Sam and he were waiting in the hall — alone. That helped. She wouldn't care if she never saw Dianne or Ken Rand again. She saluted.

"Sir, the parade is formed. Sammy, take care of yourself." She laid her hand gently on his bandaged arm. "You know —" she swallowed hard — "you know a big part of my world would be blacked out if — if — I didn't have you."

"Take her away, Jerrold, quick, before I cry." The pain in Sam Mitchell's eyes belied the lightness of his voice. He touched her cheek with his lips before he opened the front door with a flourish.

"It's a grand night. I wish I were going." He followed them to the porch. "On your way, Nancy B. Good flying, Major."

His voice set tears thick in Nan's eyes. When she reached the gray convertible with the top thrown back, she turned and called: —

"Remember Hill 67, Sammy."

"Why Hill 67?" Jerrold inquired as the car picked up speed.

She told him the story back of Colonel Long's message to Sam Mitchell.

"I reminded Sam of it because I knew he was desperately unhappy. I thought if he remembered how he had pulled through that war peril it might encourage him to believe there was a solution to his home problem."

"You don't like his wife, I take it."

"Dianne is my half-sister, she had the care and responsibility of me from the time I was a small girl. I'm grateful for that. She is super-efficient with a fixation to manage other people's lives as she tried to manage mine today. She threw me completely off balance by almost breaking my heart with anxiety for Sam. Prepare for a shock. Hold tight to the wheel, Major. Shortly before you came I — I slapped her face."

She loved his laugh and in that same second knew she loved him. Could it happen as quick as that? Was that why when he had spoken from the threshold back at Sam's it had seemed as if the sun had broken through thick clouds of fear and anger?

205

"Miss Nancy Barton giving emotion its head. You are such a self-contained young person it's hard to believe at this moment that you are really you." He chuckled. "You were very small girl in your confession. I take it from your tone of self-horror that you have never slapped anyone before. Nice going. I still don't know the whole story of your mad dash from Washington."

He made no comment as she explained. Was he listening? She stopped talking.

"Go on," he prodded. "Rand claimed he had sold himself to you once, could again. What next?"

"Enter Major William Jerrold. I haven't recovered yet from the shock of your appearance. Why did you come?"

"I suspected something phony about that wire, remembered the message you received from Rand yesterday, remembered that my sister had told me that the Mitchell neighbors were betting that Mrs. would have you engaged again to the Lieutenant. Those two items fitted together like scraps of a picture puzzle. Result, here I am. One of my present jobs is to keep an eye on you. Sorry you had such a scare about your brother-in-law. Admitting that your sister played a dirty trick, have you ever tried taking what you call her 'interference' philosophically? Saying to your-self, 'That's only Dianne' and going on from there?"

She shook her head vigorously.

"Major, you don't know her. It wouldn't work. Let's switch to another station. This trip of yours isn't a total loss if you saw your sister."

"It wouldn't be a total loss if I hadn't seen her. Why isn't this the perfect time to tell how you happened to discover me in the Mitchell pool?"

She told of trying to straighten out certain mental tangles as she sat on the bench in the garden, of hearing his voice, of helping him to the house.

"Was one of the tangles the broken en-gagement to Rand?"

"Yes. Now, perhaps it had better be told. He saw another girl and left me flat. Also, I had reached the humiliating realization that I had been a mouse for years while I al-lowed Dianne to manage my life. I was for-mulating my personal Declaration of Independence, going terribly dramatic about it in my mind, when a voice at my feet said, 'Lady —' and brought me up standing."

"After I was in the house did you put your arm around me, draw my head to your shoulder, smooth my hair?"

"Could be. It's part of my nursing technique."

"On the crest of the wave again, aren't you? The sparkle is back in your voice. Even though I was given only routine attention, I'm glad to know that that memory isn't a part of my delirium. Are you warm enough? Rather have the top up?"

"No. I love driving like this. The air is so crisp and cold. I feel as if I could reach up and pull down a cluster of stars to stick in my hair. . . . Friend Pegasus is brilliant tonight." She nodded toward the constellation. "With all the beauty of the world itself, why, oh why, do nations fight and destroy it? For that matter, why do a man and woman wreck the life they have vowed to live together? I'm sorry. I didn't mean to bore you with my views on matrimony."

"You are thinking of your brother-in-law and his wife, aren't you? Divorce would solve the problem. Perhaps you don't believe in that solution?"

"There are cases where it is the only one to save the wreckage of two, perhaps more, lives, but I hope and pray that it never will come my way."

"Amen to that. See that faint light sweeping the sky? It is from the airport for which we are headed. We'll have a bite to eat —"

"Major, you've said something. I haven't eaten since breakfast. Crowded train. Too boiling mad to think of it at the Mitchells'. Now I'm ravenous."

"Your spirits have been rising steadily as the distance between the roadster and the Mitchells' increases. Would you say that you are now emotionally normal?"

She straightened in her seat and looked up at him.

"You have had something unpleasant to tell me, haven't you, while I have been chattering? That's why you flew from Washington to find me, isn't it?"

"Don't be panicky. NO, in upper-case letters, to both questions. I came to find you because I was infernally uneasy about you. You may think what I have to report is exceedingly agreeable."

"Hurry, tell me."

"Relax. Sit back in your seat and take it easy. Our one-star boss agrees with Amy Trask that it will be an excellent idea for you to interfere in Bouvoir's little flirtation with Patricia."

"Does he know that we saw him at the Mayflower with Suzanne and the Captain?"

"I haven't referred to it, neither has he."

"The plot thickens. Does he mean that I am to accept the Captain's invitations? Tell 'our boss' that I have a date with him for Monday."

The same queer sensation tightened the muscles of her stomach that on the Sunday morning after she had met him had followed the thought that François Bouvoir might try to put her out of the way. Fear?

"You shivered. How come? Are you afraid of Bouvoir, Nan?"

"Of course I'm not a-afraid." She hoped her assurance was more convincing to him than it was to herself. "Does this new arrangement cancel the one between you and me?"

"It does *not*. It merely means that I'll have to share your playtime with him. I shall be on the side-lines, so watch your step, lady."

She sat erect, glanced into the windshield mirror and straightened her Scotch cap.

"Sounds terribly exciting." Her eyes laughed at him from between fringes of black lashes. "Maybe I shall find the Captain-Count so entertaining I won't have time for you."

"Maybe," he replied laconically and, to her disappointment, let it go at that.

16

Bill Jerrold stopped to read the headlines in an EXTRA displayed under the dim light on a newsstand.

The United States Sixth Army had pushed its way one mile deeper into New Britain. Japanese equipment, including big guns, was captured.

He dropped pennies into a box. Stuck the paper in the pocket of his field overcoat.

"I wasn't stealing a free read," he explained to the youthful proprietor, whose brilliant black eyes in a thickly freckled face were gazing at him adoringly.

The boy touched his cap.

"You were welcome to it, Marine. I've got two brothers in your outfit. I think it's tops."

"So do I, fella. Put it there." He held out his hand. The boy gripped it. "Good luck to the brothers and hard fighting," he said and walked on.

He looked up. Spectacular sky. A million

stars shimmered and twinkled. It was like the night three weeks ago when he and Nan had flown to Washington. Under her gaiety he had sensed the emotional strain of the day just passed. Her laughter had been very near tears. Had the go-ahead in regard to Bouvoir been responsible for her gaiety with its undertone of excitement? Why not? The Frenchman was past-master in the art of making a girl think she was the one love of his life.

He lingered to watch the skaters on the Reflecting Pool. Lights glinting on skate blades, the reds and greens, blues and yellows of the women's costumes gave the effect of a technicolor movie. There were men in the moist heat of the jungle who would be thinking, perhaps at this minute, of the ice between the Monument and the Memorial where they had skated in the past.

There was a ring in a white velvet case in a wreath-hung window. He stopped to look at it and remembered Nan's confessed penchant for "splashy" rings. An outsize square diamond was set in a narrow border of emeralds, they in turn were surrounded by baguettes of diamonds. It would be interesting to know how much a ring like that would set one back.

Inside the store customers were lined up

before the show-cases, except the one at which he stopped. The eager salesman produced the ring from the window and went into his sales talk.

The center stone had the new multi-facet cut. The emeralds were small but a perfect color. The baguettes were fine stones. The price was moderate for the quality. Sure, the tax boosted it, but the tax would double April first.

"Sold," Jerrold interrupted. As he wrote a check he thought, "Thanks to Father — and my own practice — I can shoot the works, occasionally." He handed the slip of pink paper to the salesman.

"You'll want to verify this. I'll call for the ring tomorrow. Where are the cigarette cases?"

As he walked toward the other end of the store he saw Suzanne Dupree. No mistaking her hair. A salesman was fastening the bracelet of a watch to her wrist. He caught a twinkle of diamonds. As if she felt his eyes she glanced over her shoulder.

"Bill Jerrold! What are you doing here? Wait a minute." She turned to the salesman.

"You are sure it has been sufficiently regulated?"

"It may need adjusting after you have

worn it a short time. Bring it in. I hope you enjoy it, Madam."

The watch was new. It looked expensive. Must be a bull market on gossip, he had time to think before she joined him.

"Glad to get my watch back," she said. "They've kept it for ages. Been selecting a present for the woman in your life, Bill?" she inquired archly.

A dot of black velvet crowned her red hair. Through a filmy veil which reached the tip of her nose her eyes shone green as emeralds. The bulk of the silver fox jacket she hugged around her was in striking contrast to the slim knee-length black skirt and gauzy beige stockings and high-heeled black pumps below it. He hadn't seen her since the Thanksgiving dinner, then he had avoided her. Perhaps this was a heaven-sent opportunity to find out, if possible, the significance of her friendship with Captain Bouvoir.

"I'm after a cigarette case for my sister's Christmas. I'll duck it tonight. Customers are standing two deep at the show-case where they are. I'm through here."

"So am I."

When they reached the street she slipped her hand under his arm.

"Let's walk. You and I have a lot to talk over, Bill."

"How about dropping in somewhere, hearing some music and having a bite to eat? I haven't dined yet. My day has been packed full of conferences. They say a quarter of a million newcomers have flocked to Washington. I believe it. They are all on the streets tonight. Why are the shops open?"

"They keep open Thursday evening that working women may do their Christmas shopping as I have been doing. I'm terribly late with it, but I have a pilot friend who is scheduled to fly to my home town Christmas eve. He's promised to take my gifts along. If you really want to eat there's a place where I pick up a lot of items for my column. The music is not too loud and there is a new kind of revue, unless you want to dance."

"I don't. Come on."

It was evident that Suzanne did know the place and that the place knew her, Jerrold decided as the obsequious major-domo led them to a ringside table in a room done in turquoise blue and gold. A tall, colored tap stepper was giving his all as they took their seats.

"I doubt if Bill Robinson could beat that exhibition," Jerrold said. "What will you have, Suzanne?"

She ordered a cocktail.

"They serve a delectable crab Newburg. How would you like that with a green salad, a sweet and coffee?"

"Okay with me." He gave the order to a hovering waiter.

"Didn't have a chance to speak to you, Suzanne, the afternoon at the Mayflower when you were entertaining a General and a Captain. Did you successfully bridge the gap in rank?"

"I did. The General is a friend of Dad's. Captain Bouvoir has been anxious to meet him so I arranged a cocktail party."

"Born diplomat, aren't you? Did they hit it off?"

"Like the two blades of a pair of shears."

"Been running round with Bouvoir quite a lot, haven't you?"

"I've been out with him several times. He knows oodles of social headliners and I get stuff for my column and radio. I have family friends here who count, whom he wants to know. Reciprocity. Purely business." She drew a long unsteady breath. "I'm not running round with anyone since Garry went down in that hell in the Pacific."

"Don't make me laugh, Suzanne. That mourning-widow stuff won't get across with me, after I sat by and saw you, while your husband was alive, lead Tom Trask to the point of infatuation where he was ready to forget you had a husband."

"*You* kept him from forgetting." Her voice and eyes were vindictive.

"Sure, I did. He was my pal at Marine Barracks for months. Do you think I would stand by and see him ruin his life and wash up his career for a woman who had no faithfulness in her?"

"You're hard as nails, Bill, because you don't know what love is."

"According to the yarn you handed Patricia Trask, I was or am in love."

"That was just — just a warning to her not to fall for your charm. Do you mean to tell Mrs. Amy about — Tom?"

"It depends upon your behavior. Why did you go to her house of all others in Washington?"

"I had to get away from the plantation. Tom had told us that his mother intended to rent some of the rooms in her big house as a war service, so I got Dad to trade on their friendship to get me in. Please don't tell Mrs. Amy, honey. Evidently Tom has not written her about me. Ah do need ma job and a decent place in which to live now that ah've left the home where ah was raised."

"Skip the Southern touch with me, Su-

217

zanne. Your accent has worn thin. As to telling Mrs. Amy, you're safe unless I find that you are hurting her or Patricia. With that subject nicely washed up let's listen to the show. The girl in glittery light blue on the stage is sure putting on an act. She's playing a solo vox with her right hand and doing a fast boogie-woogie with her left. Some stunt."

The program was long. Twice Jerrold suggested that perhaps Suzanne had had enough and each time he noticed she glanced at her sparkling wrist watch before she shook her head.

"It's fun. Let's stay a little longer."

She was twirling the water glass thought-fully. Was she preparing to spring the real reason for this interview, planned the in-stant she had seen him, he was convinced?

"You — you are a lawyer, aren't you, Bill?"

Law! What's up? he asked himself.

"Ex-lawyer. I'm a Marine."

"Bill, please take me seriously. I want advice."

She leaned a little forward. If she were anyone but Suzanne Dupree he would have believed that her green eyes registered a hint of fright. Couldn't be. She was too hard-boiled.

"If it's legal advice, consult a Washington lawyer."

"It isn't that kind. I'm — I'm asking for a friend who doesn't dare inquire herself for fear she may start something."

"Question."

"Don't snap, Bill. This friend of mine has been helping a person —"

"Receiving money for it?" Did the "help" tie up with the purchase of the wrist watch? He remembered the salesman's "I hope you enjoy it, Madam," and her casual "Glad to get my watch back. They've kept it for ages." The two remarks didn't hang together.

"Y-yes. She commenced because it was interesting — now — she's tired of it and the person she helped —"

"Worked for. Stick to facts, Suzanne."

"You make it seem terribly commercial, Bill — won't allow her to stop. Threatens to make public what she has done."

"If it was not crooked, let him rip."

"But don't you see, Bill, she has taken money from him and people will think it was for — for another reason."

"Looks like a jam. Afraid I can't advise you — your friend, Suzanne. If the man were threatening to hold up your friend for money, it would be blackmail and the court would step in. Then there would be publicity to burn. Let's go."

As they walked home, while she chattered, he wondered if she had been selling information. She was selfish, shallow, predatory, but he had thought her on the level when it came to patriotism.

As they stepped into the hall at Mrs. Trask's, Nan Barton in her blue and white Nurses' Aide uniform came from the office. She stopped when she saw them and held out a green cardigan.

"The next time you borrow this, Suzanne, I'll be tremendously obliged if you will put it back and not leave it on the floor in Mrs. Amy's office."

She was a little ashamed of her furious outburst as she regarded the two standing just inside the massive oak door. Bill Jerrold looked as dazed as if a block-buster had exploded at his feet, as if he had never seen a thoroughly angry girl before. Suzanne's face had gone red, then white. Her green eyes were wary. She crossed to a table and appeared to be looking for a card or mail.

"I was expecting a call. What's all the shootin' about when we came in, honey?" she inquired with injured sweetness. "What harm if I did borrow your cardigan? So long since I've worn color I wanted to see how I would look in it. How did you know it was I who had it?"

Why explain that Patricia had seen her with it? Why drag Pat into an unpleasant situation? After all, what difference did it make? Nan asked herself. She wouldn't have indulged in that angry flare-up if her heart hadn't been aching intolerably. A new consignment of wounded had arrived at the hospital. Their valor and their helplessness had strained her emotions to the breaking-point. She had gone from one to another untiringly, easing pain where she could. Her sense of inadequacy doubtless accounted for her burst of rage. Why not be honest with herself and admit that it wasn't entirely the borrowed cardigan that had roused her anger? Seeing Suzanne come in with Bill Jerrold as if they had spent the evening to-gether had been the spark which had set off the explosion. She loved him. As Glad had prophesied, she'd met Mr. Right and gone all out for him and he was in love with an-other girl. Retribution good and plenty for becoming engaged to Ken Rand whom she didn't love. Just the same, hadn't Bill sense enough to realize that Suzanne was a woman on the prowl?

"M's Dupree," Pike spoke from the threshold of the dining room. "A gent'man phoned you. Two gent'men. Very important, one says. I wrote down his name an' left it on the desk in your room."

"Important! I'll attend to it at once," Suzanne assured hurriedly. "Good night, Bill. Had a wonderful evening. I'd forgotten you could be such a *dear*. Here's where I speed the parting guest." She laid her hand on the knob of the front door.

"Postpone the parting for an instant, please," Nan pleaded. "I'm going to the pantry for a bite and —"

"There's some Trask Specials I made ready for you, Miss Nan."

"You're an angel, Pike. You know I'm ravenous when I return from the hospital."

As the butler disappeared into the dining room, she paused on the threshold.

"Don't make the parting too long and tender, Suzanne. Mrs. Amy is out. She may return any minute to break it up."

In the pantry, as large and as white as the Mitchell kitchen, Nan removed two plates of sandwiches from the icebox and placed them on a table. Who were the two men who were so anxious to contact Suzanne? she wondered. She was tricky and vindictive. She had been hateful herself when she had warned about Mrs. Amy. From a mouse you're developing into a cat with nasty sharp claws, she accused herself. Just because it infuriated you to see Bill Jerrold stand there without speaking, as if his breath had been knocked out of him, was no reason for you to dash off and leave him at the mercy of that man snatcher.

Man snatcher. And that, my dear, is the joke of the week. As if Major William Jerrold, D.S.C., couldn't take care of himself, in any situation. I wonder where they went for their "wonderful evening"? Why should I care?

She filled a clear glass goblet with creamy milk, placed it with a plate and fork on the white enamel table, perched on a stool and helped herself to a sandwich.

Paper-thin slices of tongue — that must have taken points — with lettuce and mayonnaise. She inspected the second plate. Crab meat filling. Luscious. Pike certainly went all out for me tonight, she thought.

"Enough for two?" a voice inquired.

17

With a portion of sandwich poised midway between plate and mouth Nan unbelievingly regarded the man in uniform smiling at her.

"Major William Jerrold as I'm alive. I didn't hear you. Did you materialize through that swing door? Usually it squeaks. Why did you come back?"

"Why not? I'm living here. I could do with a snack, myself. Milk in the icebox, I presume."

She watched him in incredulous silence as he filled a goblet, took a plate from a shelf, a fork from the silver drawer and straddled a stool beside her.

"This beats the airport restaurant, what?"

His question restored her voice.

"Did you say '*living* here,' Major?"

"Sure, didn't you know it? Moved my traps into Tom Trask's rooms today. Mrs. Amy has urged me to come for weeks and I understand the Admiral gave his consent. Hope you approve?"

"It's nothing in my life where you live but after the stir and excitement of officers' quarters, I'd think a homemaker's house would be boring."

"Things exciting can happen even in a homemaker's house. Wait and see."

"I'll wait. Sorry I let myself go about Suzanne. As you stood backed up against the door you looked as if the earth had cracked open and you were balancing on the edge. My temper shouldn't surprise you. You — you know that I slapped down Dianne and do my ears burn when I think of it."

"It was my mind that suddenly had cracked open."

"Anything to do with our pact?" she whispered.

"Yes and no. Sometime I'll tell you. How's the Bouvoir affair progressing?"

"Like a breeze. I'm growing quite fond of the Captain. You must have been out on a party. When you came in you were warbling, *'Oh, what a wonderful evening.'* "

"I didn't speak when I stepped into the hall."

"Maybe not, but the sentiment fairly oozed from your eyes." It was fun to tease him, he looked so thunderous. "Love is so bea-utiful, Bill."

"I've heard you say that before. I'm quite

ready to tell that I spent this evening at a night spot where the crab Newburg is something to write home about."

"And you're eating *again?*"

"I'm a growing boy. I need plenty of nourishment in agreeable company."

She suspected from his tone that Suzanne had not filled that last requirement.

"It was a snappy program," he went on. "I'll take you there, just name the day. And 'while we are on the subject,' I didn't care for your suggestion of a tender parting between Suzanne and me. I —"

"I thought I heard voices." The pantry door squeaked shut behind Amy Trask. "You, Bill. It's wonderful to know you are here to stay."

"Present me, Major. The lady in purple and pearls doesn't see me," Nan reminded gaily, glad of the interruption.

"I see you, Nancy B. I can't decide whether you are lovelier in that pale blue uniform or the greens you affect. What would you say, Bill?"

"The subject calls for serious consideration. I never indulge in snap judgment, Mrs. Amy." He lifted the mink coat from her shoulders and pushed forward a stool. "Sit here and try a sandwich. They are tops. It will be a terrific drain on your ration points to have me around if you serve midnight snacks like these."

"No sandwich, thanks. I had a bite after the theater. I'll give up a lot of things before I cut out the evening snacks. Sometimes all members of my family drift in at the same hour — it's the most heart-warming moment of my day — and we hold a talk fest of our doings. Those same doings can be vitally interesting in wartime Washington. Remember the night you arrived, Nancy B.?"

"It's photographed in technicolor on my memory. I stepped from the driving rain outside into the great, softly lighted hall. Pike took my wet coat. Patricia and Randy Bond erupted from your office. I was personally conducted to the library door. I remember that it seemed as if a hundred people standing round a fire turned to look at me. For a split second I felt like a foundling dropped on a strange doorstep."

"You looked as if you were about to turn and run. I've never seen eyes so smoky gray, so enormous, so startled. It was a case of love at first sight with me. How about you, Bill?"

"No report. I wasn't present."

"Nicely side-stepped." The smile faded from Amy Trask's eyes. "Have you seen Pat, Nancy B?"

"Yes. She had come from her four-to-eight shift at the hospital, was still in her brown-and-white jumper uniform and was hard at her homework in your office when I came in."

"She said she intended to study. I don't want to distrust my child but this is a perilous time for young girls when they have picked up the idea they can help win the war by smiling at any soldier, sailor, or marine who smiles at them."

"I don't think you need worry about Patricia, Mrs. Amy." Nan replaced the diminished supply of sandwiches in the icebox. "She has too much of you in her to hold herself cheap," she added as she carried plates and glasses to the sink. Jerrold pulled a dish towel from a rack.

"You're better than a heart tonic, Nancy B. Weren't the streets crowded tonight? People are spending like mad. This morning I priced a petit-point handbag. When the saleswoman said $135 as casually as she would have said 'A dime,' I demanded incredulously, 'Do you expect to *sell* it?' She looked at me with superb scorn. 'Sure, we had twelve come in last week. All sold but this.' That's just an example of the wild spending at the close of this year."

"It makes one shiver when one remembers that government heads are prophesying that the next will be the most crucial in the history of civilization, that it is likely to take all the money we can scrape together to back our men. You're a grand dish wiper, Major, the glasses shine," Nan approved as she replaced the goblets on the shelf.

"Bill, where did you learn to dry dishes so expertly?"

"I grew up in the family of a country lawyer, Mrs. Amy. My sister and I helped Mother with the housework. It was years later that the Pater became legal adviser to a big corporation and moved us to the city. To return to extravagant spending — I took somewhat of a flyer myself tonight — think it will keep up after Christmas?"

"As long as the goods last. Speaking of Christmas reminds me that Patricia, the Admiral and I are invited to my brother's for the holiday dinner. I've been saving gas for weeks. I thought if the rest of my family could shift for itself, I'd let the servants off early. I'll give you and Suzanne a break, Nancy B. Breakfast tray in your room. I feel as if I were letting you all down —"

"Okay with me," Bill Jerrold interrupted. "It will give me a chance to take a girl friend out to dinner. How about it, Nan?"

"Meaning *me?*"

"You and no other."

"I'd love it. Make it an evening dinner. I like to stretch out my Christmas fun."

"That settles it. There was skating on Rock Creek and the Reflecting Pool tonight. If it lasts we'll have a go at that in the afternoon. Two off your mind, Mrs. Amy."

"If the others will be as enthusiastically co-operative my conscience will be at rest."

The door swung partially open. Oliver Stiles's ruddy, round face appeared in the opening.

"Boy, I'm starved; anything left?" He entered and peered into the icebox. "Huzzas! The Trask Special."

"A glass of milk, Nolly?" Nan asked.

He shuddered theatrically.

"Oo—o-o, n-o-o-o. What's brewin' folks?" he inquired as he leaned against a white cabinet, sandwich in hand.

"I was disposing of my family for Christmas, Oliver. Think you can take care of yourself?"

"The studio will take care of me, Mrs. Amy. I'll have to work all day. That reminds me, Nan, will you go on the air for me Thursday evening before Christmas which comes on Saturday? Short wave in French?"

"I'll love it, Nolly."

"I'll let you know the exact hour later and

hand you your script the day before so you can rehearse it. Captain Bouvoir will be on that night, too. All French program."

"Sounds interesting, Nolly. I shall be glued to the radio." Mrs. Trask picked up her mink coat. "I'm going up while I'm still sufficiently awake to find the stairs. Coming, Nancy B.?"

"Yes, Mrs. Amy." Nan glanced at the wall clock. "Late for a gal who has to make that demon bus before daylight." She started for the door, went back for the green cardigan.

"Have you been wearing that, Nancy B.? Has the house been cold?"

"Warm as toast. I — I found it in your office. Perhaps I dropped it in the hall and Pike put it in his lost-and-found pound there. Good night, Nolly. Happy eating." Bill Jerrold followed her to the hall.

"Dine with me before your broadcast, will you, Nan?" he asked and stopped at the foot of the circular stairway to light a cigarette.

"Sorry. I promised the Captain that if he and I were on the same radio program, I would dine with him."

"That settles that. Good night," he said abruptly.

He needn't have been so snippy, Nan thought. Just why did I have to fall for a man who loves someone else? She pulled herself out of the spin of depression and raced up the stairs.

As she entered her room Patricia, in rose-flowered white lounge coat, was slumped in the wing chair, long, bare legs hung over the arm. Pink satin mules dangled from pink-nailed toes.

"What gives?" she demanded in a stage whisper.

"What do you mean, 'gives'?"

"Our merry widow and the green cardigan, of course. You're all shot. How come?"

"I'm not shot and I wish you wouldn't camp down in my room when I want to go to bed, Pat."

"Don't get hysterical. You didn't tell her I saw her in the hall outside this door with that green cardigan, did you? Nice gal."

"How do you know I didn't?"

"I was crouched on the top stair when she and Bill Jerrold came in. I haven't told all. Suzanne was trying on the cardigan before your mirror. What was she doing in this room? Snooping among your things? Do you sob out your soul in a diary?"

"I do *not*."

"That's a break. I'll bet she was looking for one. Phone kept ringing for her all evening. Somebody wants little Suzy and wants her quick. Perhaps she's mixed up in some dirty deal."

"Just because she leaves you and me cold doesn't justify our thinking that, Patricia."

"So, you suspect her too, New England? Be noble if it's your line. Don't you ever get so mad you want to beat anyone up?"

Nan's face grew uncomfortably warm as she remembered the ringing slap on Dianne's cheek.

"Not only have I wanted to, I've done it, Pat."

"Zowie. You're not on the angelic side after all. When you lecture me I look for little wings sprouting from your shoulders." She yawned prodigiously. "Gosh, I'm sleepy. Been memorizing my lines in 'The Merchant of Venice.'

> "The quality of mercy is not strain'd,
> It droppeth as the gentle rain from heaven
> Upon the place beneath.

"How's that?"

"You'll make a lovely Portia, Pat."

"Sure I will, but where will that get me? On the stage? In pictures? Can't you see Mother and Uncle Zeb going hysterical at the thought, to say nothing of Randy Bond, who keeps his foot in the door of my life no matter how hard I try to slam it in his face? I don't want Hollywood. I want a war job." With her hand on the door knob she grinned impishly.

"Feel a yen to place a bet?"

Eager as she was to have her room to herself Nan succumbed to the girl's charm and laughed.

"A little one. A dollar war stamp. About what?"

"That neither you nor Suzanne know that Captain Bouvoir has sub-leased a swell house across the river in which to entertain. He'll be moving in shortly. Do I win?"

"You do."

"Okay, I'll collect tomorrow. Nightie-night."

18

The smell of snow was in the night air, Nan decided, as she walked along the brilliantly lighted street crowded with gala Thursday-evening last-minute shoppers. Too many stars and too cold for it to fall tonight, though. Lucky she had worn her long black coat with the sable collar over her powder-blue jersey frock. She caught a flash in a mirrored window of the diamond eagle in the front of her black beret. It was the perfect touch. She had had qualms about using a pin so choice in a hat, then had figured that no one would suspect it wasn't rhinestones. She had gone directly from the office to dine with Captain Bouvoir, now they were on their way to the studio for the eight-thirty broadcast. Perhaps the snow would come in time for a white Christmas on Saturday. If only the weather would remain cold so that she and Bill Jerrold could skate in the afternoon, she was willing to pass up the snow.

"Why so silent, Mademoiselle Nan?"

François Bouvoir inquired. "You haven't spoken since we left the café."

"I was reveling in the beauty and glitter of the wreath-hung windows and the spicy scent of balsam from the trees outside the shops. I hope that our men in the service are seeing and smelling them in imagination tonight, and I was thinking that there is snow in the air and that I never connect it with Washington."

"There was quite a downfall a few days ago."

"And my home town and the near-by city had none. Which doesn't prove anything."

"Is your home near the coast?"

"So near that while the dim-out was in force, even a crack of light in a window after dark set us wardens to ringing bells and putting the fear of the law into careless householders. The dim-out restrictions have been lifted but sometimes I wonder if our Navy Department isn't asleep on the job."

"What do you mean by that?" He put his hand under her arm and drew her close as he asked in a low voice: "What have you heard?"

She laughed and with a pretense of shifting the brief case which held the script for her broadcast freed her arm.

"If you had asked Patricia that question in that startled voice she would have said, 'Don't get hysterical.' I have heard nothing. My remark was an excellent example of so-called arm-chair strategy and an active imagination working overtime."

"If I sounded startled at your suggestion that this country might be treated to a blitz it was because I had thought you too wise to worry over the impossible, Mademoiselle."

Nan's eyes followed a long black limousine with the Stars and Stripes and a foreign flag flying as it roared past preceded by a double-flanked police escort.

"I wonder who that visiting notable is? I didn't recognize the flag. To return to the blitz. Why do you think it impossible? Only the other day the No. 1 enemy demon declared that America was too far away to reach with bombs. I believe he was trying to throw us off guard. He has one airplane carrier left? In hiding. Where?"

"Do many Americans feel as you do?"

"Not being Dr. Gallup I haven't polled them on the subject and moreover, this is the first time I have aired my doubts. It must sound to you, a foreigner, as if I questioned the wisdom of the officials who are responsible for the defense of this country. I don't. It's just our American Way. Forget it. The

Salvation Army is playing, 'O, Little Town of Bethlehem,' under that light. Let's stop for a minute and listen. Mind if I sing to the band accompaniment?"

She didn't wait for his answer. Clear and sweet her voice rose in the music of the song.

"Yet in thy dark streets shineth
The everlasting Light;
The hopes and fears of all the years
Are met in thee tonight."

"Thank you, Miss." The man with the tambourine, already heaped with coins, spoke to Nan. "You've helped us fine."

"I'm glad." She dropped in a piece of silver. "Your music makes me want to sing."

He touched his red-banded cap, looked at Bouvoir, waited an instant, then walked away.

"We'd better go or this crowd will expect you to sing again and we'll be late to the broadcast," the Captain urged.

" 'The everlasting Light,' " Nan repeated softly as they walked on. "Never have we needed that to guide our feet as we need it now."

"Mademoiselle is becoming sentimental." His laugh was indulgent.

"Call that being sentimental? I call it being practical. We do need a light to guide us in this — this —" she remembered the Admiral's words — " 'in this time when we are groping between dark and dawn.' That's the building for which we're bound just ahead, isn't it? H Hour approaches. My pulses have broken into double-quick. Does the mere thought of the coming broadcast step up your nerves, Captain?"

"Not a step-up. I go on the air each week. I look forward to it, because I know that my father, an exile in England, is listening. *Nous sommes arrivés.*" He twirled a glass revolving door and followed as she entered the building in which the studio was located.

"Do you always speak in French on the air?"

"*Et pourquoi pas?* How else would I speak, Mademoiselle?" he asked as they stepped into the elevator.

"I hope I put my talk across. This is my first broadcast in a foreign language. You precede me. I shall listen breathlessly, as you must have learned from experience how to make your points."

"Talk to your air audience as you did to me at dinner tonight, Mademoiselle. Your diction and accent were perfect."

"It has helped me keep in practice to have you to converse with, *mon Capitaine*." The elevator clanged open. "Thank goodness Nolly is waiting for us."

Oliver Stiles slipped his hand under her arm as they stepped into the foyer. His blue eyes bulged like marbles in his round red face.

"Gosh, I began to go haywire, 'fraid you would be late, Nancy B. This way. What are you so scared about? Your eyes glow like headlights."

"It's my usual approach to anything important I have to do, Nolly. Every nerve in me begins to vibrate."

"Sure you wouldn't like a dose of spirits of ammonia? We keep it on hand for frightened females."

"Good heavens, am I as shaky as that or are you kidding me? Don't worry, I'll be calm as a summer sea when I begin to talk."

"Okay, I'll believe you, though I've been on summer seas that were plenty rough. In here."

He pulled open a heavy door. A studio on the luxurious side, for a studio, Nan thought, as she entered. White walls. Two turntables and three cabinets of records. Two telephones on a flat desk. A tall microphone. Two shorter ones on a table flanked with chairs. François Bouvoir, as if quite at home, dropped into one and opened his brief case.

"I'm doing the announcing for this program," Stiles said. "I hope you appreciate the honor, Nancy B.?"

"I do, Nolly. If I didn't know that you are one of the most popular M.C.'s on the air, that pile of letters on your desk would suggest it. Fan mail? The chalky white engineer in the control booth sprawls in his chair as if bored to extinction by the mere anticipation of our program. I hope I won't have to face that glass cage and his indifference as I talk."

"You won't. The boy isn't bored, he's had a tough break, just heard he's been classified 4F. Leaky heart. He has been crazy to fly. Didn't know he had a thing the matter with him. These days you never can tell what tragic thoughts are going on behind a face, especially when it's 'chalky.' It's best to be charitable." He drew out the chair in front of one of the mikes on the table.

"Sit here, Nancy B., opposite the Cap. Bouvoir, you follow the music, we'll test your voice first. Read a couple of lines that Jed may get the range."

The man in the control room straightened

and manipulated dials as the Captain read from a page he held. It was an education to listen to such beautiful French, Nan thought; voice and intonation were perfect.

"Have you checked on the length of your talk, Cap?" Oliver Stiles inquired when the test was finished. "Last week the announcer had to break in to sign off before you had finished, remember."

"It will take exactly ten minutes, perhaps a second less, Stiles. I've timed it twice."

"You said that last week. You have a habit of hesitating before certain words, for emphasis, I suppose it is, when you get on the air. It may add dramatic value to your talk, but it takes more time than you realize. Watch out for it tonight. Now we'll check on you, Nancy B. Read the first two lines of your script."

Her first few words were shaky but she resolutely steadied her voice.

"Okay. You'll do. Don't try to lay a page on the table when you're through with it. Slip it to the floor with your left hand. Watch the Cap and see how he does it. Five minutes to go."

He selected a record from a wall shelf and placed it on the turntable.

"We start off with the Marseillaise," he explained.

Nan watched the red hand on the wall clock. Her throat was tight. Her heart drummed. Idiot, she flayed herself, if you go haywire like this through the Captain's ten minutes you won't have a voice with which to speak. He was calm enough. He was marking his script. Was it to remind himself not to hesitate? It would be interesting to notice just which words, if any, he emphasized in that way for dramatic effect. She'd try to memorize them. The attempt would take her mind off herself.

A click at the turntable. Oliver Stiles held up his hand. The man in the control room sat erect. They were on the air.

"Allons, enfants de la patrie."

The opening words of the Marseillaise, sung by lusty male voices to a full-throated orchestral accompaniment, rang through the studio.

As she listened, deeply moved by the martial challenge, Nan remembered François Bouvoir's tribute to the women of his country.

"In France women are taking a leading part in the underground movement. No matter what her age, schoolgirl or grandmother, each has definite duties to perform in French resistance."

How many of these same women in secret places were listening to this rousing music? Would it inspire those who heard it to fight on? "Keepers of the faith." Sam's words recurred to her.

> *"Mar-chons, marchons!*
> *Qu'un sang impur*
> *Abreuve nos sillons!"*

The song ended with a clash of cymbals. Oliver Stiles made a short announcement of the program to follow without mentioning the names of the speakers and signaled to Bouvoir.

The Captain might boast that he wasn't nervous, Nan thought, but his face belied him. It was on the colorless side. Two sharp little lines appeared between his brows as he read. The hand with which he dropped the finished page to the floor wasn't quite steady. Why wouldn't he be emotionally moved when he was speaking to countrymen under the heel of the oppressor? He had a pleasing voice. The words he had chosen to express his thoughts about tragic conditions in his country were simple and easy to follow. He did hesitate occasionally, but it was worth the time for its dramatic emphasis.

The last page of the Captain's script slid to the floor and Oliver Stiles was at the tall mike. He followed a short announcement with an "Are-you-ready?" look at her. She nodded, flexed stiff lips and began to read. As the first page drifted down to join those of Bouvoir's on the floor her nervousness vanished. She read with the sense that somehow she must reach the valiant women who were listening, make them understand the sympathy and practical help that would be sent them as soon as possible. Her voice broke on the closing sentence. The broadcast was over.

"It wasn't so tough was it?" Stiles inquired.

"I loved it, Nolly. I felt as if I were faring across the ocean on silver wings." She looked down at Bouvoir who was bending over to collect the pages on the floor.

"Your script is mixed up with mine, Captain. I'll help."

She leaned over him. Stared at the portion of his neck exposed above the collar of his tunic as he bent his head. It was covered with a fuzz of yellow hair.

19

It could have been but a split second that she stood there, though it seemed a year.

"You *are* Carl Brouner. You *are* Carl Brouner!" a voice within her kept repeating. "You have dyed your hair!" Another split second and Oliver Stiles called.

"Come to the control room, Bouvoir. We want to talk to you."

"I'll pick up the scripts and put yours in your brief case, Captain," Nan offered and wondered if her voice sounded as strained as it felt.

"*Mon Dieu,* are they after me again because I hesitated before a word or two?" Bouvoir growled. "*Merci beaucoup, Mademoiselle.*"

On her knees beside the white pages, she watched him being herded into the control room. She hadn't been mistaken at the officers' dance. He was Carl Brouner. He had dyed his hair. The boy with whom she had played in Vienna was the son of a former

Austrian government official. That father was now in England. He had declared at the dance that he had never met her. He had learned her name from Patricia, had remembered their days together in Vienna, was prepared to treat her recognition as an amusing mistake.

In the light of the revelation that the man known as François Bouvoir was the boy whom she had known grown-up, many of his questions and answers during the last three weeks came back to strengthen her conviction. He had queried about her work, of activities in the Pentagon. Why the deception? Was he an enemy agent concealed in a French uniform? If so, what was he doing on this broadcast? Had the hesitations for emphasis carried a message? The facts fitted together as neatly as the scraps of a picture puzzle. Even his tribute to the women of the French underground at the Thanksgiving dinner might have been camouflage used to substantiate his loyalty to the United Nations.

Her heart pounded from excitement as she picked up one page after another of his script and made sense of the underlined words. They did form a message, a message so incredible that she doubted her own eyes. She remembered his low, eager questions on the way to the studio. "What do you mean by that? What have you heard?" No wonder he had been startled. She must get the information to Defense Headquarters, quick. Every moment counted. The three men were still in the control room. The Captain appeared angry. The other two emphatic.

Rapidly she collected and separated the two scripts. She was placing them in the brief cases when François Bouvoir returned to the studio. The face of Oliver Stiles beside him was red with annoyance.

"Okay, Captain. If you take it that way, you're through. You came to us and offered to talk on our foreign broadcast. We were mighty glad to have you; even so, we can't and won't have you going overtime."

"I told you I timed the talk. What difference does a second or two make?"

"It meant tonight that I had to sign off without handing Miss Barton the verbal orchid I had planned for her at the end. You were fine, Nancy B. You have a perfect radio voice and delivery."

"Thank you, kind sir." She dropped a little curtsey and glanced at the clock. "It's nine. Now may I go home?"

"Tired? Gosh, you look white. I believe you were scared."

"Nonsense, Nolly, it is the reflection of these walls. With the first word over the air my nervousness vanished. I thought only of the women who might be listening."

"I'm through here. We'll go somewhere for a snack, Nancy B."

"No. Thanks a million, but I have work to finish at home, Nolly." Another furtive glance at the clock. She must get away. Her best bet was to try to contact Bill Jerrold at Amy Trask's. "I'll take a taxi at the door. Good night, Nolly. I'll go on the air for you any time you need me."

It seemed hours to her excited fancy that she and Bouvoir waited for the elevator, hours more until a taxi responded to his hail. It was empty when it pulled up to the curb.

"I don't like to have you go alone, Mademoiselle," he protested. "Were it not that I have an appointment, I would insist upon accompanying you."

"Much better to go alone than if it were a share-the-ride cab. The broadcast was fun, wasn't it? Thanks for everything, *mon Capitaine*."

She looked back after the taxi started. He was a conspicuous figure in his blue uniform, standing under a light with his brief case under his arm.

"Where to, Miss?" the driver inquired.

"The nearest telephone booth."

He stopped at a glittering corner drug-store.

"Here you are, Miss."

"Could you possibly wait for me, driver?"

"Sorry, there's a big party on at the May-flower tonight an' cabs is scarce."

"All right. Leave me here."

With brief case under her arm and hand full of coins she entered the store where the aroma of coffee, bubbling in glass containers on electric plates, was denatured with the tang of cigarette smoke.

There were men and women seated at the soda bar and a line of customers behind them. The telephone booths were full. She disciplined a frenzied urge to pull out the occupant of one of them. A door slid open. She squeezed in.

"Say, what's the rush?"

She closed the door in the face of a resentful man. He stared through the glass at her with prominent, indignant eyes before he departed. She dropped a coin in the slot and dialed.

It seemed aeons before Pike answered her call.

"This is Miss Nan. I want to speak to Major Jerrold."

"Jus' a minute, Miss Nan."

She knew he was consulting the slate that hung beside the phone. In imagination she could see his black forefinger running down the white lines of writing. He had a simple but effectual method of recording the movements of the family, that saved him many steps. Why did he take so long? Was every member of the household out somewhere?

"Miss Nan — The Major, he's at a big dinner at the Mayflower this evenin' — No, he didn't leave word what time he would come home, but I reckons it will be early. He don't stay out late much. All right, I won't tell no ones you wanted him — Sure, I understand."

"Is that call for me, Pike?" As distinctly as if she herself were in the hall beside him Nan heard Suzanne Dupree's eager question. Would he tell her who had been speaking?

"No, M's Dupree, the call wasn't for you. 'Twas a gen'man, sounded like, callin' our Congressman. He rung off without tellin' his name." The click at the other end of the line indicated that Pike considered the episode closed.

"Now what?" Nan asked herself as she pushed through a triple line at the soda bar toward the door. The Mayflower? Why not?

She must talk with Bill Jerrold. He would know what should be done. The mere thought of him was like the feel of a firm hand gripping hers. Never mind his reaction when he saw her. She could explain.

Taxi after taxi dashed by as she waited. All of them full, most of them bound in the wrong direction. She had started to walk when an empty pulled up to the curb in response to her hail.

"To the Mayflower," she said and sank back on the seat with a sigh of relief. Her relaxation lasted for a moment only, before she pulled a compact from her bag and began to repair damages. It wouldn't do to appear in the hotel foyer with a shiny nose and colorless lips.

Gaily dressed women and uniformed men were entering and leaving the hotel as a liveried man swung the revolving door for her. Somewhere a string orchestra was playing "I'm Falling in Love with Someone." Change "falling" to fallen — and hard — and your feeling for Bill Jerrold is covered adequately, Nancy Barton, she reminded herself.

In the brilliantly lighted, palm-bedecked foyer, she asked at the desk to have Major William Jerrold paged, he was attending a large dinner. She was aware that three

Marine officers near stopped talking to listen to her question.

The woman on duty, with upswept hair the color of freshly minted gold, topped with a white gardenia, regarded her through half-closed, suspicious dark eyes.

"I was to meet him here a half hour ago and I'm terribly late," Nan answered the distrustful, if silent, appraisal.

An officer with a silver oak leaf on his shoulder touched his cap.

"Beg pardon, Madam, I heard you inquire for Bill Jerrold. He left fifteen minutes ago."

Nan wondered if it were true or if it were a brush-off to protect a comrade in arms from being pursued by a female of the species.

"*Merci beaucoup, Monsieur* Colonel. He was much angry, you think, because I am late?" What had possessed her to put on the French act, she asked herself, before she shrugged and added, "And can he be angry, *mon* Major! *Mais, ce n'est rien.* It is nothing. I find heem. *Bon soir, mon* Colonel." She turned away.

"I'll be damned. I'll hunt up *mon* Major too, if he knows gals like that." The words followed her. The Lieutenant Colonel had made no effort to soft-pedal his enthusiasm.

If Bill had left the hotel fifteen minutes

ago he would in all probability be at home now. In his determination to restore his health to normal he was cutting out late parties.

The Trask house was silent as a tomb as she entered. The polar bear's eyes regarded her with a glassy stare as she tip-toed across the softly lighted hall to the telephone closet. A line had been drawn through Bill Jerrold's name on the slate. It meant that he had returned. He would be in his rooms on the third floor. She looked at the list again. All the other members of the "family" were out.

From somewhere in the silent house came Westminster chimes. Quarter before ten. Three quarters of an hour had passed since she had made her breath-snatching discovery and she had done nothing about it.

The Admiral's rooms also were on the third floor, she remembered, as she fairly crept up the stairs and along the corridor to the second flight, If the information the Marine Lieutenant Colonel had given her was correct Bill had left the Mayflower only half an hour ago. He wouldn't be in bed yet. If he were he would have to get out of it pronto and listen to her.

Lucky that Mrs. Amy had shown her Tom's apartment that she might see the glorious view from an east window. She stopped before the door. Listened. No sound the other side. The soft beating she heard in her ears must be the hard pound of her heart.

She tapped lightly.

No answer.

She glanced toward the room she knew to be the Admiral's. All quiet on that front. She leaned her head close to the door.

"Bill," she whispered, "Bill."

Still no answer. She must go in.

Softly she turned the knob. Cautiously pushed open the door. Slipped in. Closed it gently behind her.

"Nan!"

She wheeled. Standing in front of the fireplace with lighter uplifted to a cigarette stood Bill Jerrold; beside him — she brushed her hand across her eyes to clear them — she wasn't dreaming — was Suzanne Dupree.

20

It seemed to Nan that years slipped by as she stood motionless while every detail of the room was photographed on her memory. Dark red walls; college pennants; group pictures; deep crimson leather chairs; a man in olive-drab lounge coat, back to the fire of dancing flames, a lighter in upraised hand, eyes burning discs of astonishment; the auburn-haired woman beside him, her thrown-back fox jacket revealing a neck white in contrast to the glittering black that framed it. Nan closed her teeth hard into her lower lip to repress a little moan of pain. She hadn't thought Bill Jerrold was like this.

"Well, see who's here! Our little Puritan, as I'm alive."

Suzanne Dupree's soft Southern drawl broke the spell of silence. Nan clutched the brief case under her arm tighter. The feel gave her courage, reminded her of her errand. Bill Jerrold flung the cigarette he had held between his lips into the fire.

"Shut up, Suzanne." He stepped forward. "What happened? Anything I can do to help?"

His frigidly polite inquiry froze Nan to an I-don't-give-a-darn-what-you-two-think defiance, whipped up mental inventiveness.

"I've had bad news from home. There is no one else in the house to advise me how to get there quickly. Otherwise, I wouldn't be here. It isn't my custom to drop in on my men friends in the evening."

"Meaning?" Suzanne's fair skin crimsoned, her green eyes glittered. "That being the case I will leave at once, Bill. The lady doubtless wishes to see you alone." Her laugh was insolently suggestive. "Perhaps bad news from home is an alibi. You were a lawyer before a pilot, Major, remember. Perhaps there are compromising letters in that brief case under —"

"Cut it."

Nan stepped aside as he seized the knob of the door.

"Out you go, Suzanne. If you know what's good for you, you'll forget these last few minutes."

"Don't be cruel, Bill. Remember the poor working woman. Think what a tidbit this episode will make for my gossip column. Miss Nancy Barton of *the* New England

Bartons drops into Major William Jerrold's room at midnight for . . ."

Nan thrust her right hand hard into the pocket of her coat. It was tingling to slap Suzanne's face, as she had Dianne's. Never again, though every drop of blood in her body registered fury.

Before she could utter the words burning on her tongue Bill Jerrold pulled open the door and pushed Suzanne into the hall. He closed it soundlessly and backed up against it.

"Why in God's name did you say that about dropping into a man's room? What d'ya mean coming here and starting a fight?" His breath came as if he had been running. "You — you little spitfire."

"From mouse to spitfire. Some jump." Nan desperately controlled a hysterical laugh. "You can't be so dumb that you think I came here just to bask in the light of your eyes, or can you, wise guy?"

"After sensing the contempt in your question, I can't. Come away from the door. Voices carry." As they reached the fireplace he asked, "Why did you come? Has something tragic really happened at home or has your half-sister broken loose again to help the Navy?"

"That was a story so Suzanne wouldn't

suspect." Breathlessly she told of her discovery at the studio. "If we could get that mustache off and show up a white scar at the left corner of his mouth, our proof would be complete."

"Is Bouvoir's script in that brief case under your arm?"

She sighed relief. He wasn't wasting a minute doubting her statement.

"No. My first plan was to take it. Then I thought if he knew I had it, he might get the idea I was suspicious of him. I memorized the words before which he hesitated — he had underlined them. When I realized what they meant, they burned themselves into my mind. He told me before we broadcast that his father in exile would be listening."

"So that's the build-up, the father passes it on."

"What next? We must do something."

"Get in touch with our boss at once. I don't dare use the phone. Bouvoir isn't working alone. Every minute counts. Slip out the front door and wait for me just outside the gate. After I'm sure you are down I'll follow. We'd better go one at a time."

She nodded. He opened the door soundlessly. In the hall she stood rigid and listened. Two flights of stairs to descend.

Down one and one to go. She stole along

the hall. The sound of a door being softly opened. She flattened against the wall and held her breath. Quiet again. That had been nerves. Plain nerves. According to Pike's slate all members of the family were out. Suzanne was in. Was she watching? As she reached the entrance hall a key rattled in the lock of the front door. The telephone closet was her best bet. If she were discovered she could say she had come in and found a call to be answered.

She dashed across the hall. Stumbled over the polar-bear head. Regained balance. The kick she administered to the obstacle relieved her tension.

In the dusky closet she listened. The door was opened and closed. Muffled footsteps. Business of opening coat-closet door. Taking down a hanger. Replacing it. Stumble over the bear head. Soft "Damn!" No sound of movement. Suppose Bill ran into whoever it was? It might prevent them from getting their information across.

"Hi!" The hail from the hall sent icy chills creeping up her spine. "Why the gum-shoe act on the stairs, Bill?"

"Afraid I'd disturb Mrs. Amy, Nolly." Bill Jerrold's voice was low but not too low to carry across the hall. "I'm off to meet a pal coming in at the airport at eleven. He's a grand guy or you wouldn't see me breaking out in the cold. So long." The front door was closed softly.

Nan held her breath. Would Oliver Stiles never move? Perhaps he had and she hadn't heard him. Dare she risk peeking from the closet? Better not. He was still there, she could hear him whistling softly the Marseillaise. What would Bill think when he found she wasn't outside?

The front door again. She never would get away.

"Hey, Nolly!" Bill Jerrold called. "There's a prowler at the garage. Beat it out the kitchen door while I cut him off in front."

Oliver Stiles forgot caution as he started for the dining room. Nan heard the squeak of the pantry door as he dashed through, saw Bill Jerrold in trench coat and cap pulled low over his eyes enter the hall.

"Where are you, Nan? Quick! Come on!"

She didn't need urging. The door closed softly behind them. They walked hurriedly along the sidewalk, empty of pedestrians now. Half of a deep gold moon was coming up in the east. The threat of snow had disappeared. Jerrold caught her arm.

"Slow up, or we will attract attention."

"I know, but every minute counts."

"We can't afford to waste any of them in the guardhouse for me — the hoosegow for you. When we get where there is more traffic we'll hail a taxi."

"Do you know where to go at this time of night?"

"Sure, I know. Hi, taxi."

The driver drew up to the curb and scowled at them from beneath bushy eyebrows. Bill Jerrold followed Nan into the cab and named a street.

"Goin' across the river to be married, ain't ye? I can spot a 'loping couple every time," the man boasted. He contorted his features into a grin that was more terrifying than the scowl with which, apparently, the Bad Fairy had endowed him at birth. "I know a parson who does a good job. Folks there call him the Marrying Minister. Reuben Hall, his name is. He's right on the street you're headin' for. That's how I knew what you was up to. White house with blue door, but I guess you're wise to that. They say the knots he ties hold, that's sayin' a lot for these divorce-while-you-wait times, ain't it?"

"Can't fool you, can we, driver?" Bill Jerrold agreed. He laid his hand over Nan's, clutching his arm in protest. "Take us there. And make it fast. I've had my orders. Off at midnight for I don't know where. A quick trip will be worth twice the regular zone charge."

"It's as good as done, Major." The man slammed the window and shut them in.

"Why did you say that, Bill?" Nan whispered as the taxi shot forward. For the first time since she left the studio she relaxed her grip on the brief case and dropped it to the seat beside her, repressed an "Ouch!" as she flexed her arm. It was stiff.

"Say what?"

"About being married."

"His suggestion was a break. If for any reason we should have been seen and he is questioned, his answer to our errand will be a red herring across our trail."

"He'll know we've deceived him when we don't go to the minister's."

"We won't give him a chance. The house with the blue door is this side of the one to which we are headed. I've passed it a number of times. I didn't tell the driver our number. When I say the word tap on the front window. Motion him to stop. Put on an act. Wrench open the door and jump out. Fire into me as if you were boiling mad, then beat it up the street like fury. When you get to a house with white pillars, sneak into the drive and hide in the shrubbery till I come along. If you're challenged by a guard insist upon being taken into the house, insist that the man tell his boss that you have come to meet me there but keep your name out of it. If anything should hold me up, give the General your information and wait for me. You'll be safe there. Get me?"

"I get you." In spite of tense anxiety she laughed. "You don't belong in the Air Force, you ought to be writing scenarios in Hollywood. But no matter what you wrote you couldn't think up anything so exciting as the things that really happen in this Year of Our Lord." She peered through the dirty glass window. "I shall be glad of the moonlight when I take to the bush. If anything happens that you can't follow, get our information across to army headquarters. Thousands of lives may depend on it. I'll take care of myself. Don't think of me. Promise."

"I promise. But what would prevent me from following. Excitement sets your imagination at high, doesn't it? You haven't asked why Suzanne Dupree was in my room, Nan?"

"Good heavens, she was there, wasn't she? I had forgotten it." She hadn't. The memory had pricked like a splinter every minute. "Even if I hadn't, it is none of my business if you entertain ladies in your rooms. It's being done, I understand — only *not* at Mrs. Amy's."

"Okay. As you're not interested I won't tell you why she came."

Nan spent the next ten minutes, checked on the illuminated figures of her wrist watch, futilely trying to think of a casual remark which would reopen the subject. He needn't have been so snippy about it. He was bending slightly forward. His profile was clear-cut against the light of the road outside. The visor of his cap shadowed his eyes. Nice clean-cut nose and stern mouth. She might have known that a man with that determined jaw and resolute chin wouldn't reopen a subject he had closed. What type of girl would he love "unprovisionally"?

"Don't be a cry-baby, gal."

His loud, impatient voice bumped her out of her reflections. Was he speaking to *her?* Then she remembered. Her act.

"I'll cry if I want to." The excitement and anger of the last few hours, the recent aching reminder that the man she loved didn't love her, had wrought her nerves to the pitch where it wasn't difficult for her to produce a sob. "I don't love you. I don't want to marry you. I've changed my mind. You're a — a dictator and I'm — I'm fed-up with dictators." Was that shrill voice really hers? "I'm getting out."

She rapped loudly on the front window. The driver pushed it open.

"Hey, what goes on?" he demanded and glanced from her face to Jerrold, who shrugged his shoulders.

"Bad case of nerves, driver. She wants to go home."

The driver swore with a nice attention to thoroughness and stopped the car.

"An' you ordered off to some hell-hole at midnight, Major. My gorry, I'd let her go." He flung open the door. "Cage is open. Fly, little birdie! Fly!"

Laughter, spurred by his melodramatic voice and gesture, rippled Nan's voice till it had the effect of tears.

"Just to show you I mean it, I *will*." She jumped out. "Happy landing," she called and slammed the door with a force that caused a shower of glass.

"Say! Come back here — you —"

The rough voice of the driver died in the distance as she raced ahead. That broken glass would complicate matters and delay Bill. She had had the choice of slamming that door or betraying the fact that she was shaking with laughter.

"Fly, little birdie! Fly!" Her feet kept time to the rhythm as the words sing-songed through her mind. She stopped and looked behind her. No sound of an engine. Bill probably had paid the driver royally for his time and broken window and sent him home.

She walked on slowly. The deep gold of the half-moon had paled to amber, the stars were so thick they made a silver-gilt ceiling. She passed the blue door. The house with the white pillars was beyond that, Bill had said. Here it was, shining like mother-of-pearl in the moonlight.

At the open gate in the stone wall she glanced back. Why didn't Bill come? There were plenty of shrubs along the drive among which to hide but they looked poky in spite of their ice-covered glitter.

She put out her left hand, gently to push the gate wider. Her brief case. Gone! She must have left it in the taxi. Would Bill see it? Her name and address were stamped on the inside. Suppose the driver turned it in with an account of the couple who had started for a minister? What publicity. She imagined the screaming headline: —

BRIDE LEAVES GROOM FLAT

or words to that effect and then her name. Thank goodness he wouldn't know Bill's.

She had better hide even if the shrubs did look menacing. There was a gap between the third and fourth. It would feel like slipping into an icebox, but it was her best bet. How the gravel creaked. A floodlight. She covered her face. She couldn't see but she could hear: —

"The redheaded girl at last. We've been waiting a long time for you to come across, Miss. Hi, buddy." The last sentence was a muffled call.

Another light flashed. Nan blinked. Her vision cleared. The steel-point eyes of the man with the bronze-mask face were boring into hers, his large mouth hung slightly open as if surprise had cast it into a new mold.

21

Bill Jerrold's eyes followed Nan Barton's fleet figure till it faded into the night, came back to the man at the wheel.

"Sorry about the window, driver. How much?"

"Five bucks countin' the fare will cover it. I guess you've had a break gettin' let out marryin' that dame." He made change for a ten-dollar bill. "I don't get many trips out here now that the military has moved out of the neighborhood."

"Moved *out?*"

"Yeah, the General give up the house yesterday. He hired it furnished. New tenant moved in today."

"Where has the General gone?"

"Search me. Want me to take you back or are you aimin' to follow the dame?"

Follow Nan? He had told her to wait five minutes, to insist upon seeing the boss, to deliver her message. Why hadn't he told her to go to the minister's house if the General was not there? Now it was up to him to turn over to the proper official the information she had discovered. If not to the man he wanted, to someone in authority. He looked toward the moon and starlit dusk into which she had disappeared. It was the safety of thousands against that of one girl, she had reminded, and he had promised. He had no choice.

"Take me to the Navy Annex and go like the devil, driver," he ordered, and stepped into the taxi and closed the door.

The man peered at him over his shoulder as the cab shot forward.

"Say, you look as if you'd just stepped out of a burnin' P38. Don't feel so bad 'bout her brush-off, buddy. There ain't no dame worth it. Anyway she's likely to change her mind again tomorrow an' want you back."

"Could be, but tomorrow will be too late. Keep your eyes ahead, not over your shoulder, driver, and burn up the road as I told you. I'm under orders. It is almost time to report."

Fifteen minutes later as he strode along the corridor toward an office he told himself that there was one chance in a thousand he would find the General. If he didn't, there would be someone to whom to pass on the information and start it on its way. He threw open the door.

"Miracles do happen!" he exclaimed as he saw the one-star boss writing at his desk.

"What's the miracle, Major?" the General growled.

"That you are here."

"It would be more of a miracle if I weren't. I've worked till three A.M. for a month." He rose hastily. "Never mind me. Why are you here looking as white and breathless as if the devil had you on the run. What's happened?"

Jerrold told of the broadcast in French. Of Nan's discovery of the fuzz of yellow hair on Bouvoir's neck, of her conviction that he was Carl Brouner, the boy with whom she had played in Vienna grown-up; of the emphasized words in his broadcast, of the father listening in England.

"If we could get the mustache off and reveal a white scar at the left corner of his mouth we'd be dead sure of our man and that's the story," he concluded.

The General fitted his fingers together with a deliberation that stretched Jerrold's nerves to the snapping point, as he observed: —

"I think even that could be managed." He seized the phone on his desk and dialed.

While waiting for the call to go through he confided: —

"I've known of the broadcasts, have had them checked. Straight as a string was the report, but my observer didn't catch on to the significance of hesitation — if he noticed it. The outcome is about what you have been looking for since the night of the officers' ball, isn't it, Major?"

"Yes. I've been sure he was the person Miss Barton thought him, that he recognized her and was being cagey. As I told you when I first reported, I have been anxious about her safety. No predicting what an enemy agent at bay might do to save his own neck. But try as I have, I couldn't pin anything on him."

He paced the floor. Where was Nan now? He must get to her. Perhaps she would remember the minister and go to him? The thought reduced his temperature several degrees.

"We've got barely twenty-four hours in which to beat 'em to it," the General declared. He spoke into the receiver.

"Yes. Yes. Where? At his home so *early?* How does he do it? Then put him on the line. Be damn quick about it." He looked up.

"They'll have me on the carpet, Major,

272

for talking rough to a sub— Yes. Yes. Listen, Colonel."

Bill Jerrold's nerves vibrated in sympathy with the tense repetition of the information he had brought. He could hear the startled voice at the other end, the give-and-take of question and answer. His part of the job was finished. How soon could he get away? The minute hand of the wall clock pointed to fifteen before eleven.

Only a little over an hour ago Suzanne Dupree had walked into his room to continue her story of her "friend" who had accepted money. To beg him to advise that same friend how to escape the trap she was sure —

A cautious tap had interrupted the story. Suzanne had caught his arm in tense fingers. Had whispered, "Don't answer." Then Nan, white-faced and breathless, had burst in. What was back of Suzanne's yarn? Her "friend" was a blind of course. She herself was in a jam. She had accepted money. Her pay for radio and newspaper work wouldn't provide a silver fox jacket and diamond wrist watch. Was she threatened with blackmail? She had been terrified. In her society reporting she had plenty of chances to pick up salable bits of information. What had Nan thought when she saw her in his room? Hang it all, what difference did it make what

she had thought then? What was she thinking now? That he had run out on her?
Where was she?

"If you'll stop that infernal pacing I could
hear better, Major."

"Sorry, sir."

He lingered at a window and looked out.
The ice in the Reflecting Pool shimmered
with stars. The Washington Monument was
a shaft pointing the way to heaven. Would
they be there tomorrow in all their beauty or
would — The click of the telephone in its
cradle snapped off the question.

"It's out of our hands now, Major." The
man at the desk mopped the sweat from his
face with a huge khaki-colored handkerchief. "When they said at first that the chief
wasn't there I thought I was in for a final
attack of heart failure."

"Will the warning get though in time?"

"Sure. It's the key defense officers on the
other end who'll have a chance to prove
what they're worth. There are only four persons who know the source of our information. Not a whisper must get through to the
Captain. I want him to keep on feeling
secure till we are ready to spring our trap. It
may take weeks to round out our evidence.
It may be a matter of days. Understand?"

"Yes, sir."

"Where are you going in such a hurry?"

"To find Nan Barton. We started out together. For fear the taxi driver might be in cahoots with someone — we couldn't afford to arouse even a shred of suspicion — I told him we were on our way to be married, then staged a quarrel. She left the cab. I had told her to beat it for the house you lived in —"

"But I *don't* live there now." The General was on his feet.

"So I learned after she had gone. I knew she couldn't get the information across to you there. It was up to me to find you. I had to choose quick. Really, I had no choice. The information *must* go through. I took a desperate chance that she would be safe. It was perhaps thousands of lives against that of one girl. If anything should happen to her —"

"Nothing will. I don't wonder you were haggard when you charged into this room." The General took a field overcoat from the closet. "My coupé is downstairs. Come on. We'll drive to the house I left yesterday and find her. We'll bring her back alive and — safe. I should have notified you of the move, but I thought you'd drop in here and I could tell you."

"I've been kept busy answering questions at the War Department."

As the car rolled ahead smoothly the General inquired: —

"Is Captain-Count François Bouvoir mixed up with any other woman, Major?"

"What do you mean, mixed up with any other woman? Nan Barton was accepting his invitations because you —"

"Take it easy. I was casting no reflections on our coworker. She has grown up as straight and true as they come. We know that the little Trask girl is a swooner at our bogus Captain's feet but even so, I'm sure she wouldn't assist him in subversive work. Seen him with any other *femme?*"

"With Mrs. Dupree, but you know that. You were having cocktails with them one Sunday afternoon at the Mayflower."

"You saw me? I kept my back turned for fear you recognize me. I didn't want Suzanne to know we had met. I knew her family years ago when she was a small girl."

"She told me that Bouvoir had been eager to meet you. Had . . ."

He stopped abruptly. Had Suzanne's suppositious "friend," Suzanne herself, taken money for bringing the two together?

"Go on," the General prodded.

"Had he an axe to grind with you?"

"Not that afternoon. I have met him several times socially. Now he greets me as an

276

old and tried friend. Probably his acquaintance with me has helped strengthen his hand. What do you know about Suzanne Dupree? If she is helping this man, my regard for her family won't protect her. This country is fighting for its life and the lives of its citizens. No time to shield a woman who may be helping the enemy. We must get every angle possible on him."

"Right, sir." Jerrold repeated Suzanne's story of the "friend" who had taken money and now feared blackmail, concluded: —

"If she is the 'friend,' as I suspect, I am sure that whatever she has sold had no subversive angle."

"Hmp! We'll have her trailed. Anything else?"

"Yes, sir."

"Go on, don't be so monosyllabic. It's like pulling an impacted wisdom tooth to extract information from you. Now let's have *all* you know about her."

Without mentioning Tom Trask by name Jerrold gave a sketchy outline of his meeting with her at her home, of her family, of her husband in the Navy, of her romantic interlude with a Marine, of the Marine's assignment to the South Pacific, of her subsequent widowhood, of his surprise when he met her in Washington.

"It's my personal opinion that a woman who has a husband overseas wading through hell, sweat and blood and is playing round here with another man is about the lowest thing in the universe and the next lowest is the man who runs round with her. A woman who would do that wouldn't stop at treason." The General scowled at the white road ahead. "You didn't mention his name."

Bill Jerrold's thoughts, which had been half on his words and half on Nan's whereabouts, snapped to attention.

"His name doesn't matter. He realized what a low trick he was playing on the absent husband and quit before the situation got out of hand."

"And she holds you responsible for the quitting? She's now living at Mrs. Trask's, she told me."

"Senator Trask and Suzanne Dupree's father were friends. When Tom Trask and I were at the Barracks near the family plantation they made us welcome. Naturally Mrs. Trask would take in the daughter."

"Naturally. There was a Trask son, you say. I'm beginning to get the lay of the land. Suzanne Dupree is a gossip columnist. She would be in the way of picking up news, wouldn't she? Here we are."

He stopped the coupé at the curb, lowered the window and indicated a house with white columns a little way up on the opposite side.

"Dark as a pocket. No sign of life, yet I know another tenant moved in at once. Let's investigate."

"Stay here, sir. I'll snoop around. Two would be one too many."

"Get going. I don't like the look of the place. It's eerie."

"It's the same place I've visited several times and you left only yesterday," Jerrold reminded as he opened the coupé door and stepped out.

"I know, but it's changed. Be careful, Major."

Careful, in bright moonlight in the District of Columbia? As he stepped between the fence post and the partially open gate without touching either, Bill Jerrold thought of the night above an airfield when the Japs had found the Allied fighters' radio wave length and a servile voice had taunted: —

"Captain, why don't you come down?"

"Sure, we'll come down you — Jap," he had yelled. He and his wing man had gone down through heavy aircraft fire, strafed two gun positions and a couple of Zeros on the ground and shot up again. And the General warned him to be careful here.

Eerie was the word for it, he agreed, as he paused in the path. The air was full of little creaks and sounds. Ice-tipped shrubs chimed as the slight breeze swayed them. A dry vine tapped with ghostly fingers against a window. A car was coming. Had the General changed his mind and decided to add himself as a re-enforcement? No. It was a taxi. Its lights illumined the open gate.

He stepped into the shrubs. They closed about him, shut him in. Through a gap he saw a man paying the driver. A man with a brief case under his arm. His face was spot-lighted by the glare of the taxi lamp. Jerrold shut his teeth hard in his lips to keep back an exclamation. Carl Brouner, alias François Bouvoir, was the passenger. He must be the new tenant who had succeeded the General. If so, he had lost no time moving in.

A shadow flitted forward to meet the man now halfway toward the house. He could hear Bouvoir's whisper: —

"Has she come?"

22

The bronze-mask man's steel-point eyes and dropped chin reduced the pace of Nan's galloping pulses to a quickstep. She was not the person he had expected. Surprise had reduced the second arrival to the same state of suspended animation: his eyes bulged like those of a fish too many hours dead. Now what? Bill Jerrold had told her to ask for the boss, but something warned her to stop, look, listen. These men were not the uniformed guards protecting an officer's house, to whom he had referred. They wore shaggy, dark topcoats with high collars pulled up about their ears.

They were emerging from their coma. Merry-pranks slithered along her veins as two pairs of eyes focused on her beret. For the first time she remembered the brooch she had fastened there this morning. The electric torches must have set the diamonds sparkling. Perhaps the men were jewel thieves, experts who appraised at a glance the value of the ornament. The brooch was worth a lot of money — it had been her mother's — she had known she was reckless when she sewed it on — they might even put her out of the way to get it. Hideous thought. Why give imagination its head for a gallop when what she needed on the job was constructive thinking? She'd better get a line on her next move. Apparently Bill was not coming. Had he discovered that their boss was not here? Had he gone to some other authority with his information? She had made him promise to do so. She cleared her throat softly.

"You may have been waiting a long time for someone to come across, but not for me, gentlemen." She had an inspiration. "Or do you mean that my boy friend is already here and waiting?"

"Say, where do you think you are, Miss?"

"It will be Mrs. in a few minutes." Could that be *her* saccharine voice, *her* self-conscious laugh? "That is, if this is the clergyman's house I was told to come to."

The man's face had regained its bronze immobility. She couldn't make out what the curious expression in his keen eyes denoted as he moved a step nearer.

"It ain't a clergyman's house an' if you know what's good for you, you'll beat it right back to where you came from."

Nan stepped from out the shelter of the shrubs with a haste that set their icy tips a-tinkle.

"Something tells me you're right, but — but — what will my boy friend think when he doesn't find me here?"

"Don't you worry about that. We'll set him straight. Bring that car of yours round to the front and take the lady where she wants to go, buddy." The second man, whose features she hadn't seen, slipped away into the shadows.

The situation sent clammy inchworms looping up her spine. She hadn't the slightest intention of getting into any sort of car with a man who, if he wasn't a criminal, was evidently in the employ of one, otherwise why the greeting "We've been waiting a long time for you to make up your mind to come across"? Whom had they expected? A woman with red hair! Could it be Suzanne? If so, with what was she coming across? Why suspect her? There were dozens of auburn-haired females in Washington.

"The car'll be here in a minute, Miss. This way."

He was eager to have her go. She shook off the hand he laid lightly on her arm.

"I'll go on my own, thank — you."

The last word trailed behind her as she dashed toward the gate. She was outside and running along the road in the direction from which she had come when she heard a car behind her. "Buddy" in pursuit? The marrying minister's house was here somewhere. The street light illuminated a name on a brass plate beside a gate: REUBEN HALL. After this, all her life she would believe in her star. It was the house of the "Marrying Minister" whose "knots" held.

As she saw the slowly approaching lights of a car she dodged into the shadow of a lilac bush near the front door and set its icy branches clashing. Was the driver looking for her? She waited till a red spark went out in the distance, then stepped into the path. A light flashed on above the bright blue door as it opened. The glow set the shrubs glittering like a frosted Christmas card.

"Husband and I have been watching you. Won't you come in?" the woman in the doorway invited. "Our name is Hall."

She might have been reading or sewing. Horn-rimmed spectacles had been pushed up till they made a bandeau for her silky white hair. Her eyes were almost as clear and blue as the door beside her. Her dove-gray frock, protected by a small, white-frilled apron, accentuated the pink-and-cream perfection of her unlined skin.

"Do come in," she urged. "Did you expect to meet someone here? I'll give you a cup of coffee while you wait." She ended the sentence with a sound which was like a bird's chirrup.

If she went in she could use the phone and try to contact Bill. If she couldn't reach him, at least she could call a taxi, Nan decided.

"You are very thoughtful. I'm cold. I would like coffee." She ran up the three steps to the door. "I — I — was told to meet a friend here and he —"

"And he's been detained?" The woman laid her hand on Nan's shoulder and drew her into the hall. "Don't worry, my dear. Now that I see you in the strong light I'm sure he'll come. No man will let *you* go if he once has had your promise. Reuben, here she is," she called as they stood on the threshold of a book-lined room, lighted by two softly shaded lamps and a smoky fire of cannel coal, all reds and ochers. Victorian. Definitely.

A man, who reminded Nan so strongly of Abraham Lincoln at his tallest and gauntest that she expected to see a black, shiny stovepipe hat in his hand, rose and bowed.

"Sally saw you dash into our yard. 'Here's another frightened bride to rescue,' she exclaimed, and started for the door. I reminded her that perhaps a girl out alone at this time of night didn't want to be rescued but she wouldn't listen and here you are."

He brushed back a heavy lock of black hair with a thin muscular hand as he regarded her with eyes which were keen behind their friendliness. Nothing to fear from him, Nan concluded.

"Now, Reub, don't cross-examine the child till she's had her coffee," his wife interposed, as she cleared a small table of books. "This man of mine was cut out for a lawyer, though if I do say it, he makes a pretty good minister. Take off your coat and sit by the fire, my dear. My, my, what a pretty dress, I love blue. That's why I had our front door painted that color. Reub laughed at me."

"I never laugh *at* you, Sally." Nan loved the timbre of Reuben Hall's voice when he spoke his wife's name. "I laughed because a friend told us that in Norway a blue door meant there was a marriageable girl in the house and we have no daughter." A faint shadow dimmed the serenity of the woman's face and was gone. "But think of the hundreds who have come in at that blue door unmarried and have gone forth with a husband, Reub. It has been almost like having daughters of our own to speed on their way with our blessing." She drew a plump hand across her eyes. "There, there, I'd better stop chattering and start the coffee."

She trotted out of the room with the long black coat over her arm. Nan's eyes followed her. For one ungrateful instant she wondered if taking the coat was a ruse to detain her.

"There's really nothing to be afraid of here." Had the tall man standing in front of the fire read her thought? "You're shivering. Won't you sit down, Miss — ?"

"I am cold." She ignored the question after that "Miss." Better not tell her name yet. She sat on the edge of a low slipper chair with carved rosewood frame, upholstered in dull blue brocade, and held her hands to the fire. She glanced at the steeple clock in the middle of the white mantel.

"I must have been walking and waiting outside over a half hour," she said, "and in spite of moon and star-glow it is a cold night."

"Did you expect someone to meet you here?"

"That — that was the arrangement — at first. We — we were coming together and then I lost my courage and — and bolted and —"

"Decided you didn't love him?"

"How did you know? Are you a master mentalist as well as a minister?"

"It's a gift." His amused response to her light touch was sympathetically understanding. "That temperamental change of heart often happens at the last minute — then I begin to talk and — well — like the Prince and Cinderella they live happily ever after."

Nan thought of Sam and Dianne.

"Not always," she differed wistfully. She watched the tongues of flame burn glowing red patches on the black soot of the chimney, heard Sam's bitter voice: "You've started something now, Dianne."

"Not always," Reuben Hall agreed gravely. "But if men and women would bring the intelligence to marriage, the determination to make it a going concern, they bring to business, there would be bigger, a whole lot bigger, percentage of fairy-story endings." He cleared his gruff voice. Sniffed.

"The aroma of coffee. Sally's put the kettle on — in this case the percolator."

A grand person. A simply grand person. If I don't watch out I'll be dumping my whole basket of problems into his lap, Nan warned herself.

"It smells delicious, but it's an imposition to keep you and Mrs. Hall up so late for a girl who — who changed her mind at the eleventh hour."

"Don't let that worry you. Sally and I are night owls. We always sit up for the midnight broadcast. We — we have a son in the South Pacific. He married before he left this country."

"I hope she was someone you liked." From the impatience with which he brushed back the drooping lock of hair she knew the girl hadn't made good.

"We tried to love her, how we tried. Our boy wanted her to live with us; she stayed three months, then returned to the job she had before she married. We were as glad to have her leave as she was to go." His thin hands clenched. "Why will a man who has been grade A in character, in his studies and his profession, suddenly go berserk over a girl who is allergic to every element that goes into homemaking?"

"But every woman isn't fitted for that job any more than every man would make a —" she hesitated — "a good minister. It isn't always the girl who fails in the partnership. Many women discover that Prince Charming isn't so completely charming out of uniform, that he heckles, that he makes home a place in which to unburden himself of the annoyances of his day, perhaps that he's a born philanderer. You see, I've caught up my sword in defense of my sex."

"You are an eloquent defender. Where did you learn so much of *genus homo?* Not from experience, I hope?"

She laughed. Curious how her knotted nerves were relaxing. Perhaps it was the cozy firelight, the homey aroma of coffee, more probably it was the subconscious surety that somehow, some way, Bill Jerrold had carried on.

"I read the ADVICE TO THE LOVELORN columns, I have a human-interest complex. That's where I get ideas."

"Was this to have been your second marriage?"

"It isn't," she started to say, "to be a marriage at all." Better wait till she was out of this mix-up before she declared that.

"I've not been married. Now that I'm getting a broad view of the capabilities a girl should bring to the partnership — *I've* never cooked — there won't even be a first."

"A first what?" Mrs. Hall inquired as she entered with a laden silver tray. Her husband took it and set it on the cleared table.

"A first marriage, Sally. I've frightened our guest with my qualifications for the per-

290

fect housekeeper. 'She can't cook,' " he added in a choked whisper and laughed.

His wife, seated at the tray-laden table, shook her head.

"As if cooking were the prime necessity. He's joking, my dear. Any intelligent woman who can read and has a mind to put to it can cook if she wants to." She held silver tongs suspended. "Sugar?"

As Nan sat before the fire and chatted with the clergyman and his wife, time dragged as if hobbled with a ball and chain. Were they wondering why she didn't go home? Why she waited for a groom who had left her, figuratively speaking, waiting at the church? Where was Bill? She had taken for granted that he would go to headquarters with the information, then divine that she had come here. Suppose his errand had been suspected and he had been kidnaped? Carl Brouner — alias François Bouvoir — wasn't working alone, of course. The thought was like a cruel hand tightening on her naked heart. She had been mad to sit here waiting. She should have gone herself.

"Here he is!" Mrs. Sally rose with a suddenness that upset the silver cream pitcher on the tray before her.

"Who?" her husband demanded and sprang to his feet.

"The groom of course, Reub. Didn't you hear a car stop? Steps on the path?" She trotted into the hall.

Nan clutched Reuben Hall's arm as she stood beside him. Suspense tightened her throat unbearably. Who was at the door? Bill or the man with the car who had been ordered to take her where she wanted to go? Or had Captain François Bouvoir suspected she had discovered he was Carl Brouner and followed her?

23

"Has she come?"

Concealed among the icy shrubs, which tinkled like an announcing bell in a shop door each time he drew a breath, Bill Jerrold stretched his hearing almost to the snapping point. Bouvoir's repeated query had been scarcely more than a whisper.

Light from the shadow's electric torch revealed his identity. He was the man who had been at the near-by table when he and Bouvoir had lunched together, who had been on the bench next to Nan that Sunday at the Tidal Basin. He was in Bouvoir's employ. What would he answer to the question, "Has she come?" He strained his ears to hear.

"No, boss. I thought for a minute the dame you told us to watch for had come across when a girl pushed open the gate and ran along the path. Nix. She was a war bride looking for the minister's house down the street where she was to meet the boy friend."

Jerrold's spirits zoomed. His sense of guilt that he had left Nan to fare for herself fell away. She had remembered the "Marrying Minister" who tied knots which held. She was safe.

"What did she look like, Dwyer?" Bouvoir had relaxed caution. His voice was clearer.

"You said the dame who was coming had red hair. Light was poor but there was enough to see that this one's was black with white gobs over each ear and a white veil. Couldn't tell about her dress."

"Thought you were a master detective. That's why I hired you. You should have observed —" The annoyed voice faded as the two men walked toward the house.

Little demons of anxiety attacked Jerrold as he waited for the front door to close. Bouvoir had told the man "Dwyer" that a redheaded girl would come. Could he have meant Nan? Not a chance. Suzanne, of course. He and she had been stepping out together. This was the explanation of her yarn about the "friend" who had innocently taken money. It was Bouvoir who was tightening the thumb-screws. The girl who had been here earlier had worn white against her *black* hair. That ruled out Nan. Where was she? he wondered anxiously as he made his cautious way to the gate.

A light flashed from an upper window and illumined the path. Someone was looking out. He flattened against an icy shrub and waited. It seemed years that the figure stood there. Then the shade was drawn and only the glow of moon and stars remained to light his way to the coupé. As he slipped into the front seat the General said: —

"We'll go up the street a way before we turn, Major. What happened?"

Jerrold told him, concluded: —

"Miss Barton was wearing something that looked like General Montgomery's beret, with a sparkling eagle in front, so it can't be she whom the man Dwyer described. That girl had white on her head, but we'd better stop at the minister's to make sure she isn't waiting there for me."

"That's little enough to do for her. We'll turn here and go back. I know the house, name Reuben Hall on a brass plate on the gate. I've noticed it each day as I passed and wondered what kind of a person he was."

"I was knocked into a cocked hat when I saw Bouvoir in that path." Jerrold glanced at the man beside him who had chuckled. "You get considerable fun out of your job in spite of its seriousness, don't you, General? You wouldn't have been surprised at the

295

identity of the tenant who succeeded you, I'll bet."

"You're right. When the genial Captain confided that he needed a house in which to entertain I palmed that one on him. Told him my orders had come to move on. That's true, but I stay till this job is finished. Now I know where to find him. Here we are. If Miss Barton is inside take her home. It won't be safe for her to be running round alone tonight. Then report immediately at my office no matter how late. That's an order, Major. We must plan our campaign. I'll wait outside."

"You're doing a lot of waiting for me tonight, sir."

"I'm not waiting for you. I'm as anxious about Nancy Barton's safety as you are. Isn't she one of my staff? Didn't I get her into this mess? The door is opening. Beat —"

Jerrold didn't wait for the next word. He sprinted along the path, up the steps. If Nan was not — The blue door opened.

"She's here. Waiting for you. Come in." The plump, rosy-cheeked woman beaming at him seemed sure that the girl inside was the one for whom he had come. Suppose she were not? Suppose this one had black hair?

As he stopped on the threshold of a book-lined room for a split second the faces of the tall man and the girl whose white-knuckled fingers clenched his arm blurred in the dancing firelight, then a husky voice demanded: —

"Bill! Bill, did you find —"

"Now that I've found *you,* I've accomplished *everything* I started out to do this evening," he answered and knew by the way Nan's fingers relaxed that she understood he had steered the information she had given him into the right channel.

"Everything but the marriage, soldier." The plump woman made a sound like a bird's chirrup. "And Reub can manage that in a jiffy. I'll call our maid for a second witness."

"Not so fast, Sally. Not so fast." Reuben Hall smiled at Jerrold standing just inside the door. "My wife is incurably romantic. She has forgotten that our guest said she changed her mind and ran away because she didn't want to marry."

"I don't know why not." Sally Hall's eyes twinkled. "Anyone so good-looking — can have me."

Bill Jerrold returned her smile with interest.

"Thanks for helping me out, Mrs. Sally. How about it, Nan? Changed your mind?

Shall we put it through?"

"Put *what* through?" His eyes warned her. She swallowed hard. "Oh — oh, *that?* No. No. Not tonight — Bill. I don't — I just can't make up my mind tonight. You will forgive me, won't you?"

Of course the wistful appeal in her eyes was an act, but she was fifty times more alluring than Suzanne Dupree could ever be with all her tricks.

"Sure, I'll forgive you. I don't want a wife who doesn't want me. Where's your coat? I'll take you home."

"I'll get it." Tears of disappointment glittered in Sally Hall's eyes as she turned away.

"Thank you for your kindness, Mr. Hall," Nan said. "I shall remember this evening all my life —" Her laugh was shaky. "I'll begin at once to learn to cook."

"Good. But there are other qualities to be brought to the marriage partnership and one of them is to keep a steady course, not to be blown off it by indecision. Remember, it isn't the storm that counts, it's the way you set your sails to meet it."

"You mean because I changed my mind about marrying? Sometime I'll come back and tell you why. May I, Bill?" she asked as he held the coat Sally Hall had brought.

"Sure, and I'll come with you." Above her head his eyes met those of the man in front of the fire, before they looked down at her. "Who knows, by that time you may have changed your mind again, Nan. Ready?"

Seated between the General and Jerrold in the coupé, she told of her adventure from the time she had jumped from the taxi. An occasional grunt of understanding was the elder man's only comment. The younger kept an unbroken silence. She concluded: —

"As Bill intimated that the information I discovered has gone to the proper authorities, I think we can write *Finis* to this adventure. We have our man."

"No." The General snapped the correction. "You both understand, don't you, that not a word of the real reason of this night's trip must come out until I give the word? If worst comes to worst, let them think you're married. Otherwise, we may lose the cagey Captain."

"Okay, sir, but it can't possibly come to that. No one knows we went out together. If any of the members of Mrs. Trask's family see us come in, we've been to a late movie, that's all. There's a taxi ahead. Drop us here and we'll pick it up."

In the road they watched the red tail light

of the General's car dim and go out in the distance.

"There was something about the higher-up's 'If worst comes to worst, let them think you're married,' that gives me the creeps," Nan whispered as a taxi pulled up to the curb.

"Hop in!" Bill gave the address and followed her into the cab. From the driver's radio came a low-toned, throaty voice singing "When You're Away, Dear."

"*I* could write a song with that title," Nan declared fervently. "The things I thought when you were away, Bill, would fill an opera score."

"I had a few thoughts myself. I suffered the tortures of the damned wondering if you were safe, blaming myself for having left you."

"But I made you promise —"

"I know. Forget it. Each time the evening's adventure recurs to you push it forcibly from your mind, otherwise you may unintentionally reveal what you discovered; may give a hint to those backing Bouvoir's broadcast that their scheme has been uncovered. Who do you think followed the General as a tenant in that house with the white pillars? That same François Bouvoir."

"Bill! Are you sure?"

"Sure as shootin'. He drove up in a taxi, spoke to the man who spoke to you and went in. When I reported that to the General he said he knew it. He not only knew it, but suggested the house to the Captain so he would know where to locate him."

"Pat told me that François Bouvoir had leased a 'swell house across the river in which to entertain.' It gives me the shivers to think how near I came to being his first guest." She drew a deep sigh. "This day has been years long. Running for the bus this morning seems the hang-over of a hectic dream."

"The strain and excitement of the last few hours are beginning to let you down. Close your eyes and relax. You've had quite an evening all told." He slipped his arm around her. "As I told you, my shoulder is pretty darn comfy. Try it?"

Her head dropped against him. The feel of his coat against her cheek gave her a blissful sense of security. Why not when she loved him so achingly?

"Fits as if it had been born to rest there, doesn't it?" he asked softly.

"Perfect. Curious, now that we've forwarded that information — I — feel — as — if —" Her lids felt as if weighted. She made a futile effort to lift them.

"Wake up, sleepy. We're not far from the house." A voice and a slight shake roused her. It took a minute for her to orient herself. Where was she? Something under her head was throbbing steadily. She looked up. Bill Jerrold's eyes were smiling into hers. Had she been sleeping against his shoulder? She sat erect quickly and adjusted her beret, which had slipped over her left ear.

"Did you say we were near the house?" she asked. "I — I must have dropped off."

"I'll say you dropped off. You slept like a kitten. We'd better decide on our story. We've been to a late movie. What say to HOLY MATRIMONY, WITH MONTY WOOLLEY?" There was light enough to reveal his grin. "That fits in with this night's adventure, doesn't it?"

"It does. Reuben Hall gave me a new angle on the married state tonight." She laughed. "No woman has a right to assume it till she can cook well. Feed the beast is evidently one of his precepts for a happy — Bill, look! The house is lighted from top to bottom. What can have happened?"

"Tom has come! I'll bet Tom has come. What a break for his mother." His voice was rough with emotion. "Wait for me, driver. I'll be right out. I want you to take me across the bridge again."

Nan had a curious sense of expectancy as they raced to the house. She had a feeling that just around the corner lay another adventure.

In his excitement Jerrold let the front door slam. From the library came a crash of chords.

"The Wedding March. Tom's brought home a bride, Nan. Whoopee! I knew he'd get over the Suzanne brainstorm. Come on." Jerrold seized her aim.

As they stood on the threshold Nan's nerves tightened, her heart stopped. Neither Tom Trask nor a bride was in the room, only Amy Trask, the Admiral, Pat in pink and Suzanne at the piano in glittering black. She brought the Wedding March to a close with a crash and rose.

Amy Trask came forward with outstretched hands.

"My dears, my dears, why didn't you tell me?" she said.

"Tell you? Tell you —" Nan felt the pressure of warning fingers on her arm.

"What's it all about? What do you mean?" It was Bill Jerrold's surprised voice, it was Bill who was carrying on.

"You shouldn't leave evidence behind you with your name inside, honey." Suzanne's green eyes glittered as she held up a brief case. Her voice dripped sweetness as she explained: —

"A taxi driver brought it. Said it was left in his cab by a couple who were on the way to be married. That the man was a Major ordered overseas. Then we knew you were the happy groom, Bill."

24

Nan felt as if she had been caught up by a cyclone, whirled head over heels and crashed to her feet. Married! She and Bill. Why hadn't he denied it at once? "If worst comes to worst let them think you're married," the General had said. The situation was fantastic, but not as fantastic as some that might follow if the persons looking at them believed they were.

She dashed her hand across her eyes to clear them. The last few minutes had not been a nightmare, they had been real. Dancing shadows from the orange-and-scarlet flames in the fireplace were blowing shadow-patterns on the backs of books against the wall, the warmth of the room drew the scent of balsam from the tall Christmas tree with its glittering balls, between the windows, the Admiral's "Hr-rump!" was real, so were the tears in Mrs. Amy's violet eyes.

"And what a taxi driver knows, the world knows." Bill Jerrold's voice also was real.

"We didn't tell you, Mrs. Amy, because we didn't know ourselves until a few hours ago. I'm leaving on an assignment at once. The taxi is waiting for me." Relief made Nan slightly lightheaded. She could hug him for that. She should have known she could trust him to get the situation under control.

"Bill! Bill! Are you going back to —" Amy Trask steadied her voice. "Forgive me. I know better than to ask that question. The taxi is waiting? Why are we standing here? You must want to say good-by to your —"

He laid his arm across Nan's shoulders.

"Nan and I said our good-bys before we came in, Mrs. Amy. But, she might see me to the door. Good night, everybody."

"Good luck, Bill!"

Nan wondered if the chorus of husky voices made him feel as guilty as they made her? As he went out she followed and partially closed the door behind her.

"Bill Jerrold rides again." Her flippancy was a cloak to hide her panic at the thought of being left to carry on the marriage farce alone. "Where are you going?" she whispered.

"General's orders. This is your chance to escape questions, Make a dash for your room — they'll think you are overcome with emotion and will let you alone tonight." He bent his head and kissed her quickly on the lips.

"That's in case anyone is spying. Camouflage," he explained lightly.

Honk! Honk! Honk!

"The driver's telling me. Good Lord, I must go and I want —"

Honk! Honk! *Honk!*

"Good night — dearest."

She watched him run down the path, waited till the taxi started before she closed the door.

His husky "dearest" echoed through her mind, his kiss, light as it had been, burned on her lips as she ran up the stairs. "Camouflage." After all they had been through together tonight, one would suppose, even if he loved another girl, he would kiss her because he wanted to, not for effect.

Good heavens, now what, she wondered as she entered her room and saw Patricia standing before the mantel.

"Pat — please — I can't, I just *can't* talk with anyone now." The catch in her throat was not an act, it was the memory of the last few hours barging back like blood rushing through veins after the circulation had been shut off for a time.

"It'll be a lot better for you to talk; you

can't fool me, Nan Barton. What's it all about? Give. You're not married, are you? Zowie, I wish you could have seen your face when the Dupree *femme* held up that brief case. You looked as if you'd been bopped. Bill Jerrold didn't blink a lash, though. You can't baffle him. Come clean. Give me the lowdown. I won't blab. I promise." She crossed her throat. "I know you think I'm just a kid but when I make a promise I keep it."

"No report, Pat. Stay here if you want to, but I've been on the move every minute since I ran for the bus this morning. I feel as limp and shabby as a rag doll that's lost her stuffing. A shower will set me up."

"I heard you and my Captain broadcast. It was a knockout. What's happened since? I know there's a mystery. I shall stay here and wear you down till you tell me."

Nan pulled off her beret.

"Then make yourself useful. Rip this diamond brooch off my hat, will you?"

"Diamonds! Real? Heck, Nan, you haven't worn that all day? You might have been murdered for it!"

"You're telling me." Nan shivered as she remembered the eyes of the two men who had stared at her as she shrank against the icy shrubs. "I thought of that, too, but a trifle late," she admitted as she opened the bathroom door.

"If you are married where's the wedding ring?" Pat flung the triumphant query after her. "Better think that over before I turn that sixty-four-dollar question over to the green-eyed Suzanne. She'll smear you, good and plenty. Can't you see what she would do with it?"

"Your threats don't frighten me, Pat," Nan warned and closed the door between them.

As she glowed under a hot spray and shivered under an icy one, she wondered if she dared tell Pat the truth, that there had been no marriage. The girl had a quick and facile imagination; she might help out in a ticklish situation; it would be like walking a tightrope to maintain the balance between truth and fiction. How long would the deception have to be kept up? Pat was right, Suzanne Dupree would be on the watch to trip her. Bill wouldn't be here to help. Where was he going? "General's orders," he had said. Back into active service? Her heart dropped like an elevator out of control. Silly, of course not. His absence was part of the build-up to trap the man the General had called "the cagey Captain."

She couldn't tell Pat any of that or what

the broadcast had revealed: Pat might say something to the man she knew as Captain François Bouvoir that would arouse his suspicion.

How much would she dare tell her? She knotted the sash of her white terry bathrobe about her waist. Could she trust her to keep a promise? She could and would. She reached that conclusion as she entered her room.

Patricia turned from the dressing-table mirror and held up the diamond brooch she had unpinned from her shoulder.

"This eagle's a beaut. I haven't seen you wear it before."

"I've put away till Victory most relics of a social past."

"The shower set you on top of the world, didn't it? For a person who claimed to be a blushing bride you were doubling as a little gob of gloom when you came into this room. You're a knock-out with your red hair twisted in that curly top-knot." Pat sniffed. "What's the perfume?"

"White violets. BATH CRYSTALS WITH A LASTING FRAGRANCE. That's a quote from the bottle in case you care."

"I'll say it's lasting. Do you trade? Going to loosen up and tell the truth?"

Nan sat on the green-covered couch at the foot of the bed.

"Come here." As Patricia dropped down beside her, she asked in a low voice: —

"You know there is a war on, don't you?"

She felt the tightening of the girl's muscles.

"I've heard rumors to that effect."

"All right, then. Bill and I are not married, but, because of — of — well a suspicious situation, a higher-up has ordered us to pretend to be."

"Spy?" The word was a mere whisper.

"That is what we are trying to discover."

"It's Suzanne! I'll bet a hat it's Suzanne. She's always having mysterious calls on the phone. Pike made me swear not to tell —"

"I thought you kept your promises."

Patricia's face reddened to the lovely arched brows.

"I do. Honest, I do. Only that caught me by surprise and —"

"If you are surprised into admission of what I've just told you, lives may be lost, Patricia."

"I won't be, honest Nan I won't, if I have to lock myself in my room to avoid people." She rose. "I know where I can find a wedding ring. I'll give it to you at breakfast. I bought one at the Five and Ten. I know what you've opened your mouth to say. Don't go haywire. I've never used it. Never

311

intended to." She turned as she reached the door. "I'm — I'm terribly proud you trusted me, Nan, I feel as if I really had a war job." Her voice was suspiciously choked for a person of her self-proclaimed sophistication. "Someday — perhaps I'll trust you, too."

Nan regarded the door she had closed behind her with puzzled eyes. What had Pat meant by that cryptic remark?

The question kept popping up between appointments the next morning — the business of the War Department didn't stop because it was the day before Christmas — intruded at the song fest at noon in the center court of the Pentagon, where the employees and the A.A.F. band from Bolling Field made the welkin ring. At least, it helped to keep her from wondering if Captain François Bouvoir (to the world; Carl Brouner to her) had been taken into custody. When he was, would he suspect that she had helped uncover his treachery? *Helped* was the word. Credit belonged to Bill Jerrold. Hadn't he suspected that the Captain would bear watching the first time they met?

Bill had told her to push all thought of last night's experience from her mind. Not so easy when the memory kept swooping back like a searing flame, catching at her breath, submerging her spirit in a black cloud of premonition. The Captain wouldn't let himself be taken easily. He was a fighter. Years ago, when he was a small boy playing tennis, he would refuse to admit defeat. The memory set her heart thumping heavily. "I'm frightened," she told herself. "I'm frightened for — for Bill."

As she entered her office after lunch she felt in the frilled pocket of her navy crepe frock for the ring she had found under her breakfast plate. A product of the Five and Ten indubitably. She wouldn't need that until she went home tonight. Why go home? Why return to the Trask house till the High Sign was given that the bogus marriage could be explained? That was a thought. By official edict all government offices would close at three-thirty this afternoon. She would stay at the Pentagon until late, go home, sneak up to her room, pack a bag and go somewhere even if she had to spend the night in the Women's Waiting Room at the Union Station. She had made no date for the evening, hoping that Bill would ask her to dine and hear the carols. No possibility of that. He was incommunicado for the present.

She answered the ring of the telephone on

313

her desk. She could see the dim reflection of her face, her silver beads and the white frills at her neck in the polished mahogany surface as she listened.

"Ken!" She glanced over her shoulder. Had Colonel Long heard her surprised exclamation? It had been loud enough to carry through stone walls.

"No," she answered his hesitant question. "No hard feelings now about that hurry-up call to the Mitchells. The present is too full to spend time on the past. . . . No, I haven't." It had been a mistake to admit she had no engagement for the evening. "Dine with you and go on to the Army and Navy Club's Christmas-eve celebration? Give me a minute. I'm not a fast thinker at the phone."

A solution to her present problem? Ken couldn't have heard about the alleged marriage. She could spend a few carefree hours with him, or could she? Had he come to Washington to ask her to marry him again? Was this another "conspiracy"?

"Is Dianne with you, Ken? You needn't swear to convince me she isn't. I'll go. No. *Don't* come to the house. Every minute of the afternoon is filled. I know the offices close early, but I have last-minute shopping to do. I shall have to rush dressing. . . . Meet you where we danced the last time you were in Washington? I'll be there. What Major? Oh, *that* one. Gone. His orders came yesterday. . . . Did it? Perhaps I was. I'm not now. I'm all excited at the prospect of such a grand party. . . . *Not* good-by, Ken. *Au revoir.*"

She cradled the phone. Ken had said that her voice sounded homesick when she answered his call. He couldn't know that she had been in the midst of plans to escape her present happy home till she was free to tell the truth about Bill and herself. Was she plunging into more trouble to go out with her one-time fiancé? If the chilly prickle in her veins — to which she was becoming uncomfortably accustomed — was a reliable portent, she was. Only time would tell.

Doubts as to the wisdom of her acceptance pricked again as she walked along deserted ramps and entered an almost empty bus under the concourse at the Pentagon. From the window she looked at the sky as they crossed the bridge. Cloudy. Too bad if it snowed. Tomorrow would be the first holiday in months for countless government workers. The weather would not affect her now that Bill had had to call off the plans for their celebration. Breakfast tray in her room, Mrs. Amy had promised. Heavenly luxury. After that a long, lazy day at home, opening the stack of intriguing silver-and red-wrapped packages that had come by mail, reading and writing. She would lock her door and refuse to answer, no matter who knocked. Where was Bill? Was he as disappointed as she that their Christmas party had to be canceled?

She glanced at her watch. The bus crawled. No outdoor lights this season, but the shops were brilliant. Carol singers at almost every corner. Colorful as an animated Christmas poster. If only all the boys in service were at home to enjoy it. At home in a world at peace.

A clock chimed the half-hour as she soundlessly entered the Trask house. Six-thirty. She had agreed to meet Ken at eight. She made a careful detour of the polar-bear head and wrinkled her nose defiantly at the glass eyes. Their glitter always gave her the curious feeling that they were warily on the watch.

In the telephone closet she wrote *"Out. Dinner and reception"* against her name on Pike's slate. With intense satisfaction she noted that an engagement was registered beside each name. Even the Admiral was celebrating: *"Dinner at the Navy Club."*

Her lucky night. No one to put her

through the third degree, she exulted, as she ran up the stairs, instinctively avoiding the treads which she had learned from experience squeaked.

She opened her door and locked it quickly behind her. So far so good. She drew a ragged breath of relief and turned. Suzanne Dupree stood in front of the mantel.

"So the bride came back," she drawled.

25

Backed against the door Nan regarded the woman challenging her with maliciously triumphant green eyes. Why was Suzanne here? Captain François Bouvoir had taken her out a lot and —

"The redheaded girl at last!"

The words echoed through her mind like a voice on a phonograph record. The record clicked. "We've been waiting a long time for you to come across, Miss."

The man with the bronze-mask face and piercing black eyes had said that before he had really seen the person standing against the icy shrubs. Was the woman in front of the fireplace the "girl" for whom the two men had been waiting? François Bouvoir was the tenant of that house. Was she helping in his subversive work? It was evident that she was suspicious of the story of the marriage. If she communicated her doubts to him, the General and Bill Jerrold might lose their man. Just one answer to that: she herself mustn't let Suzanne Dupree out of her sight. Allowing that the suspicion that she was involved with the alleged Frenchman was crazy, what harm could it do to act on that premise? It was an old rule to get in the first lick of accusation. She arranged her beaver coat on a hanger — silly, why did her hands shake? — crossed to the dressing table, removed her white *calot* with its navy veil, fluffed her hair before the mirror and turned.

"Why shouldn't I come back?" she asked lightly. "*I'm* not the one who should run away." She dropped to the bench in front of the dressing table and began to buff her nails. In spite of her absorbed attention to her fingers she felt Suzanne's impulsive step forward.

"Are you insinuating that *I* am?"

Were the green eyes frightened? Nan tossed the buffer to the dressing table, rose and thrust her not too steady hands hard into the frilled pockets of her frock. Why did every nerve in her have to vibrate in moments of excitement?

"You must be a mind-reader. You haven't liked me from the moment I entered this house, have you, Suzanne? In spite of that, I'm giving you a break. I'm not insinuating, I'm *telling* you, when I say you'd better beat it and beat it quick — unless you crave being brought before a grand jury and tried for treason. There's a lot of that being done now."

Even in the room lighted softly by lamps and a fitful fire the pallor of the woman's shocked face was apparent.

"Has that heel double— ?" She cleared the hoarseness from her throat and substituted a credible attempt at a laugh. "What's all the melodrama about, Nancy Barton — I forgot, it's Mrs. William Jerrold — or is it? I presume the happy groom has satisfactorily explained his affair with a married —"

"Absolutely. You'd be surprised how much I know; even why you were in his room last night." That was sheer bravado, She didn't know why the woman regarding her scornfully had been in Bill's room, she knew nothing of his romantic past, but she would stake her life that there had been no dishonorable love affair in it.

"Did he tell you why I was there?"

"Page him. He always tells the truth."

"Trusting type, aren't you, honey? How charming."

The hateful innuendo in the taunt steeled Nan's determination to find out to what extent, if any, Suzanne Dupree was involved with Captain François Bouvoir.

"Sure I'm trusting, to a degree. But I'm not trusting you, Suzanne. You'd better stop fencing and listen. At any moment now, someone may knock on the door and you'll hear a voice say, 'Open in the name of the law.' They'll be after *you* to explain some of your dates."

A catholic taste in motion pictures helped in a mental emergency, Nan reminded herself, and swallowed a nervous chuckle. That threat of the law had bubbled to the surface from the subconscious limbo of forgotten movies.

"I still don't know what this is all about," Suzanne Dupree declared contemptuously, but the hand in which she held a lighter was unsteady. She removed the cigarette she had placed between her lips and flung it into the fire behind her.

"Time is flying and the F.B.I. work fast in this town, Suzanne. It is suspected — that's putting it lightly — that you have been giving aid to the enemy, that —"

"I haven't. I *have not.*" The last trace of her assurance had vanished. "I can prove it."

"Believe me, you'll have a chance —" Nan glanced at her wrist watch — "in just about one hour. In that same hour I must shower, dress and meet a date. As I'm no lightning-change artist, it will help if you will depart, pronto." The slam of the front door was faintly audible.

"Who — who's that?"

Nan shrugged and removed the silver studs from her ears.

"F.B.I. ahead of time, perhaps. Could be. Beat it, I must dress."

"Nan." Suzanne Dupree clutched her arm. "I'm beginning to realize that I've been a credulous fool, but nothing worse, I swear. If I'm dragged into court, even if I'm proved innocent, I'll be through as far as my job is concerned. You've *got* to help me. I've *got* to get away."

"Where can you go?"

"That's easy. Home — for Christmas."

"*Tonight?* To the plantation? How will you get there?"

"I know a pilot who leaves at nine. He promised to take my gifts to the family. He'll do *anything* for me." Even in her distress Suzanne preened. "If I can get to the airport without being stopped . . ."

If she can get to the airport and make that plane she won't have a minute in which to warn François Bouvoir, supposing I'm right and she is working with him, Nan figured. To see that she doesn't have a minute, that she boards that plane, is my job. Take it easy, gal. Go slow, she warned herself.

"It's nothing in my life, what you do. If you think you can get away, okay, Suzanne. I may be arrested for allowing you to go, but I'll take the chance. It will save Mrs. Amy a lot of unpleasant notoriety if you are out of this house when the authorities pounce." That last was an inspired suggestion. "On your way, I must dress for my date."

"I *can't* do it alone! I *can't,* you've got to help me."

"Why me?" Nan removed the silver beads. "You've hated me from the time I arrived in this house and haven't hesitated to show it. Besides that, you snooped in this room the night you borrowed my green cardigan. I presume that was tied up with your 'credulous-fool' activities?"

"It wasn't, really it wasn't. You and Bill Jerrold have been going out together. I thought he might have told you things about me, things I didn't want known, that you might have written in a diary."

"Pat was right. She suspected you were prowling round here for something like that. You admit it and then say I've *got* to help you. Your nerve is colossal. Nothing doing and I *mean* nothing doing."

"I didn't intend any harm about the diary, I didn't really hate you, hon— honey. I—I was jealous. Before you came Mrs. Amy talked hours on end about your beauty, told us you were a social headliner and accomplished to the nth degree. Your brother-in-law had given you a grand build-up to her. I was having things my way here. I didn't want interference. Help me to make that plane. I have a rich marriage practically in the bag — If a breath of scandal touches me —"

"You should have thought of that before you mixed into subversive —" Nan reached for the zipper in the back of her frock. Suzanne caught her arm.

"Don't take your dress off, *don't*. If I have done anything subversive I did not know it, I swear I didn't. Do you think I've forgotten that my husband was killed in this horrible war? That I would knowingly help the enemy?" She snatched up the white *calot* with its dark blue veil and crushed it on Nan's head. "Quick! You've got to help me get off."

"Oh, all right." Nan adjusted the hat. "What do I do first?"

"Come to my room. Help me pack my bags. I'll need two. Then we'll slip out the back way and hail a taxi."

"*We?* You don't expect me to go to the airport with you?" Considering that she

324

wouldn't leave Suzanne under pain of death till she had boarded that plane, Nan considered her protest a histrionic masterpiece.

"You must. I can't go alone. Don't let me down, honey."

Glycerine tears, Nan thought, as two big drops rolled down Suzanne's cheeks.

"Beauty in distress. You win, Suzanne. I'll help." She caught her jacket from the hanger, tucked her bag under her arm. "We haven't a minute to lose. Let's go."

There were miracles. She had just seen one come to pass, Nan decided, as she stood at the gate and watched Suzanne cross to the great silver ship escorted on one side by the pilot, on the other by another admiring male, a Carolina neighbor returning home. They had packed, slipped out of the house, secured an empty taxi and arrived at the airport at five minutes before nine to find that one reservation had been canceled a few moments before.

The five minutes had seemed an eternity. Suppose that in some way Suzanne had communicated with François Bouvoir? Suppose he were to appear?

Running steps behind her. Someone late for the plane? She didn't dare turn to look. The gate rolled shut. The plane slowly taxied forward on the long concrete runway.

Took on speed. It was a shining shape in the distance when it rose on great silver wings.

Nan released her breath in a long unsteady sigh. She hadn't realized she had been holding it. *Where do I go from here?* she thought and turned. All the blood in her body seemed to crowd back into her heart. The man who had flashed a light on her as she backed against icy shrubs — was it only last night? — stood behind her. He touched his hat.

"Late by half a minute, I'd say, wouldn't you, Miss?"

His casual question confirmed her suspicion that Suzanne had been the person he had expected to see last night. Was he trailing her? Had he been tipped off that she was taking the plane?

"I'd say that you are more than half a minute late, a whole lot more," she said and rapidly walked away.

Considering what she suspected, her reply had been reckless, she admitted as she hailed a taxi to take her home. Why was the man with steel points for eyes constantly appearing on her horizon? The cab picked up speed. One might think she was a person to be watched instead of Suzanne. Would he follow her?

As she opened the front door of the Trask

house she flexed her neck. It was stiff from the work-out she had given it by turning her head every few moments to peer out the back window of the cab, to see if she were being followed.

"I began to think I'd have to set the Shore Patrol on your trail," an angry voice declared as she entered the hall.

She blinked at Kenneth Rand incredulously. Why was he here? For the first time in hours she remembered that she had a date to dine with him.

"I'm sorry, Ken, terribly sorry. A — a girl friend had to catch a plane for home — didn't know she was going till the last minute. She was so flustered. I had to help her pack her bags and get to the airport. I didn't have a chance to telephone —"

"Don't be so breathless, sweet." He caught her close. "I forgive you. You know I love —"

"So you've found her," a husky voice exclaimed.

Nan jerked herself free from the arms which had tightened about her and stared at Bill Jerrold, backed against the front door. His eyes below the visor of his cap blazed with anger in a face drained of color. His hands were thrust hard into the pockets of his trench coat.

"I — I thought you'd g-gone." She could have bitten out her tongue for assisting at the frightened stammer.

"That's evident." He tucked his cap under his left arm and took a step forward. "*Your* lieutenant came here half an hour ago with a frantic report that you were missing — he'd been waiting for an hour for you to keep a date with him. Got Pike so worked up he phoned me. Since then I've been trying to contact you." He ran a finger under his collar as if suddenly it had tightened. "Where have you been?"

Nan resented his harsh question — after last night he ought to know she had been trying to help. Resented the sarcasm in "*Your* lieutenant." One might think he was her husband really and entitled to an explanation.

"What's the big idea standing Nan up like that, Major?" Ken Rand ruffled like a turkey cock preparing for the fray. "What's it to you, anyway? I'm the guy she let down. If I've forgiven her —"

"There's something in what you say, *Mister* Rand." Bill Jerrold replaced his cap at a snappy angle. "It was evident you had reached the kiss and make-up stage when I barged in. Sorry. Let the good work go on. Roger!"

Kenneth Rand looked at the door which had been opened and closed with extreme care and grinned at Nan.

"Bright fella to know when he's not wanted. Come here. The Major was right. I was about to kiss you."

She backed away from his outstretched arms. She must get rid of him before the other members of the family came in.

"No, Ken. I'm sorry I had to walk out on our date — you might have had a grand time with another girl — but I don't want you to kiss me again — ever."

"Why not?"

"Because I don't love you and never will. Please go. It's too late for our party now. I've had a terrific day. I'm too all in to talk. Good night." She backed toward the stairs. He caught her hand.

"Have you gone nuts over Jerrold? If you haven't, why didn't you stop him when he stood you up? Cocky guy. I've never seen a Major who wasn't. Are you in love with him? Come clean."

She freed her hand and backed up three stairs.

"I'm not in love with anyone, Ken, and do not intend to be until this horrible war is over. Now, will you go?"

"Okay. Okay. I heard you the first time."

He picked up his long blue coat from the chest under the stairs, slipped into it, adjusted his white muffler and with gold-braided cap in hand looked up at her.

"You needn't go any higher. You've had your last chance at me. I don't intend to touch you. So long."

She held her breath as he opened the front door. Suppose Mrs. Amy or the Admiral or Pat came in as he went out and spoke of the marriage? Why didn't he go? Why had he stopped?

"Oh, Nan." He had lowered his voice to a hoarse, theatrical whisper. "I'm going. It isn't *au revoir* this time, it's *good-by*."

26

Christmas morning. In her pale blue house coat, Nan stood at the open window of her bedroom looking out at the storm, at a world without color, a world so still she could hear her own heartbeat. As snow goes it was rather a gay snow, swirling in fantastic patterns, blowing in little white clouds from the skeleton branches of trees, turning shrouded shrubs into crenelated castles and laying spotless damask tablecloths on the four squares which in a few months would be green lawns.

She glanced at the crystal-and-gilt clock on the mantel. Eleven. No wonder she had slept late. She had been awake till dawn living over the events of the last forty-eight hours, wondering if the warning the General sent had been received in time? If the man known as François Bouvoir was in custody? If Suzanne really had helped the Axis agent?

What a day yesterday had been. It had

had nothing on the day before. That had been even more hectic, ending as it had in the admission of a marriage when there hadn't been one. So far, with the exception of Suzanne, she had escaped meeting anyone who had heard it. Would Suzanne mention it in her gossip column? Not likely. She had been suspicious of Bill's explanation and she was meticulous about making sure that her newspaper and radio statements were facts. She wouldn't dare come out with it now.

The episode with Ken Rand had been unfortunate — she shouldn't have accepted his invitation. It had provided one bright spot, it had revealed the fact that Bill Jerrold had not been ordered into active service. That aching anxiety could be canceled. He had been furious when he entered the hall and saw her in Ken's arms. Had his anger been because he loved her? Why fool herself? Long ago he had declared that he was "unprovisionally" in love. She had shrugged off Suzanne's statement that he had had an affair with a married woman, but how did she herself know he hadn't? Because she couldn't love a man who would was the answer.

She closed the window. Opened the door in answer to a knock and smiled at Pike, clothed in immaculate white, as he entered with a laden tray on his outspread left hand and a florist's box in the other. A folded newspaper protruded from the right pocket of his coat.

"Breakfast in my room! Luxury with a capital L, Pike. Set it here." She indicated a small cleared table in front of the low, fat chair covered in striped cotton. "Are the flowers for me?"

"For you an' no other, Miss Nan. I waited for you to ring for your breakfast before I brought 'em up. My, my, they sure am lovely," he crooned, as she lifted a cellophane box from the pasteboard covering. The transparent sides revealed a mammoth bunch of violets. She read the card.

To wear on our Christmas celebration.
I'll have a real present for you then.
BILL

He must have ordered the violets before the epochal evening of the broadcast. Little he had thought then that there would be no Christmas celebration for them together.

"Hopes I brought what you like, Miss Nan." Pike's voice switched her attention back to the present. He lifted a silver cover.

"You have. The bacon smells de—licious.

Two dropped eggs on toast! Perfect. You remembered that I liked my orange sliced and lots of cream for my coffee." She drew an envelope from her pocket. "Merry Christmas, Pike."

"Thank you, Miss Nan, I sure do thank you." He thrust it in the breast pocket of his jacket. "I likes to get breakfast for someone who eats. There's M's Suzanne now, won't take nothin' but orange juice an' black coffee. She's sleepin' late this mornin'. She didn't answer when I knocked an' —"

"Good heavens, she isn't here. She has gone home, Pike. I went to the airport with her." Nan sank into the fat chair. "I — I meant to leave a note for Mrs. Amy but when I came in —"

"That sailor man was waitin' for you, wasn't he? He sure started a rumpus last evenin'." Pike laid a napkin across her knees. "Does you want your orange first or will I pour your coffee?" Obviously he was eager for conversation.

"The orange. What do you mean by rumpus, Pike? What did the Lieutenant do?"

"He came stampin' in an' said you was to meet him for dinner and he'd waited an' waited an' —"

"Did anyone come in, any of the family, I

mean, while he was here?"

"No, Miss Nan. They was all out. I told him to sit down in the office an' I'd phone roun' to some places I thought you might be at."

"Did you? I'm ready for coffee, Pike."

He lifted the silver pot and poured a steaming, dark amber stream into a large gold-banded cup. Its delicate aroma filled the air.

"I just phoned the Major, Miss Nan." He added cream to the coffee.

"That's enough, Pike. How did you know where to contact Major Jerrold?"

"Does you remember the first time he came to breakfast? He gave me a phone number then an' said as how if at any time you seemed to be in trouble I was to try to get in touch with him an' keep on tryin' till I gets him."

"But that was weeks ago, Pike. I had only met him the night before. Why should he care what happened to me?"

"I didn't know his reasons, Miss Nan, but I liked him first, 'cause M's Amy liked him fine. Then I likes him for myself."

"You are very fond of Mrs. Amy, aren't you, Pike?"

"I reckon that ain't quite strong enough a word, Miss Nan. M's Amy, she's an angel jus' straight from heaven. I'se been in the family since Master Tom was seven — bringin' him up wasn't no trouble — but, Miss Pat, she's different. I'se done the best I could with *her*, too, but she has me worried."

"Why are you worried about Miss Patricia?"

"She's actin' kinder secret like." He refilled her cup with hot coffee and added cream. "Yesterday afternoon she was in the garage rubbin' an' polishin' that runabout car of hers with the rumple seat. Why fo' was she doin' it? She won't use it today cause she's goin' with M's Amy an' the Admiral to her uncle's Christmas dinner in the big car."

"Someday — perhaps I'll trust you too."

Patricia's voice echoed through Nan's memory. What had she meant? Was she planning to use her runabout secretly?

"She's sure actin' suspicious," Pike went on. "I don' trust that Captain that calls her on the phone an' sends gardenias an' takes her places. I'se talked with M's Amy 'bout it, but she don't do nothin'. I don't know what I could say to Master Tom when he comes home if anything happens to her. The last thing he says to me as I carried his bags to the car when he was leavin' was

'Look after my girls, Pike. I'm countin' on you to keep 'em safe.' "

Nan's throat tightened in sympathy with the husky tenderness of his voice.

"Don't worry, Pike, Miss Patricia has too much good sense to mess up her life. What's happened to that snappy Second Lieutenant she was battling with in the hall the night I arrived? I haven't seen him here since Thanksgiving."

"You mean Mr. Randy Bond? His family used to live in the next house before his ma and pa broke up. Those two's been fightin' like that since they was little chil'en. He's a mighty fine boy, right smart, too, Miss Nan. Miss Pat says he's bossy." He chuckled. "I reckon he is, but that's the way a man should ought to be, lookin' after his womenkind."

Nan remembered a young white face, a young hoarse voice declaring: —

"I refuse to be a decoy any longer. And mark this, Smartypants, if I come across you necking with that French officer I'll give him a swift kick in the teeth." Indubitably a man who would "look after his womenkind," was Randy Bond.

"I reckon I'se talked to you too long, Miss Nan." Pike set the cover in place over the empty silver platter. "But I sure feels better for tellin' you my family worries. Thanks for listenin'."

"I've been interested, Pike. I love Mrs. Amy and Miss Patricia. You may take the tray. It was a delicious breakfast and thank you."

"I'll jus' fix up your fire before I goes." He put on a log, did things with tongs and poker till blue- and green-tipped scarlet flames shot up the chimney. "That's better. Nothin' lak a fire, Miss Nan, to keep folks comp'ny." He drew the newspaper from his pocket.

"Here's the mornin' paper. I hopes you has a happy Christmas. You'se goin' somewhere to dinner, isn't you?"

"Of course, Pike." No sense in telling him that her date with the Major was off. It would be like him to feel that he must give up his holiday and get her something to eat. "Meanwhile I'll have a long, happy day opening my presents, reading and doing nothing. I'll put this on my door." She hung a card DO NOT DISTURB in large letters on the outside knob. The butler chuckled and lifted the tray.

"That's sure tellin' 'em, Miss Nan. But I reckons you won't be troubled with callers. Paper says this snow'll turn to rain befo' night. M's Amy, the Admiral an' Miss Pat has gone to church before they goes to M's

Amy's brother's house, an' the two gentlemen won't be home all day. When we colored folks gets off you'll have the house all to yourself. I reckon they had a scare on the Coast last night. Paper's full of it. It says the King of England's goin' to speak, too."

A scare on the Coast! Hadn't the warning gone through or had it been too late? Nan clutched the newspaper. If only Pike would go.

"Thanks for everything. Run along and have a grand time, Pike."

Almost before the door closed she was curled up in the wing chair by the window. She unfolded the newspaper. There it was, in great black headlines.

EAST ON ALERT FOR YULE RAID

KEY DEFENSE OF STATES CALLED

A report that a sneak air attack might be attempted by the enemy on Christmas day alerted all military and civilian-defense agencies along the Atlantic Coast, the Eastern Defense Command revealed in two announcements late Christmas eve.

Then farther on: —

The warning on which the alert was based came from a well-authenticated source.

Nan read to the end of the long column, drew a ragged breath of relief and dropped the paper into her lap. "Came from a well-authenticated source." She'd say it had. Hot from the griddle. The warning had arrived in time, thank God. With her head tipped back against the chair, she closed her eyes and relived the tense moments in the studio when she had discovered the significance of the underlined words on the script from which François Bouvoir had broadcast. Translated they summed up to: —

Go ahead. Precautions relaxed. Strike as planned.

A message which would flash across the ocean with lightning speed, which his listening father would relay as quickly. Had he seen this announcement? Did he know that the entire Eastern Coast was on the alert? Would he remember her greeting at the officers' dance, "Carl!," her outstretched hands? Would he trace the warning to her? What would happen if he did?

Suppose the question did send a ripple

along her veins? Whatever happened to her would be but a drop in the bucket to the tragedy which might have occurred if she hadn't been lucky enough to sense that "Go ahead" message so cleverly inserted in the broadcast. That sort of thinking helped her morale but — suppose François Bouvoir — Carl Brouner really — were to come here after he saw that headline? Foolish thinking. Wasn't he being watched every minute?

She picked up the paper. At what time was the King to speak? She would open her presents, listen to him, then dress and go out, it didn't make any difference where. The prospect of Christmas day alone in this great ark of a house was getting her down.

Opening the gaily covered packages banished her depression. Her friends must think she lived in a shopless wilderness: their gifts ran to gay accessories, the colors selected with nice attention to avoid conflict with her auburn hair.

She crooned with delight when she opened the huge box from Dianne and Sam. The sheer silver lamé with its long sleeves and deep V neck had an amber rose and a pale yellow one at the waist. A broad silver bracelet was set with a huge Spanish topaz; there were outsize earrings and a ring to match.

Her conscience nipped sharply. Sam had said twice that Dianne missed her. She hadn't written to her sister since the night she had put on the shrew act and slapped her face. It was up to her either to write an appreciative letter or return the present. The letter had it. She would christen that adorable frock New Year's Eve. Would Bill be back by that time to take her out, or would he celebrate with the girl he loved?

Dressed in her gray wool frock she tuned in for the King. Snuggled in a corner of the green couch, hugging her knees, she listened. First came the solemn boom of Big Ben. Then a nice English voice announced: "His Majesty the King."

"Once again from our home in England the Queen and I send our Christmas greetings and good wishes to each one of you all the world over."

Eyes on the fire, Nan listened as the cultured, slightly halting voice went on in its message to sick and wounded, to subjects in the security of their homes; giving thanks to the Allies; praising Allied unity; citing hope for the future in closing: —

"No experience can be too strange

342

and no task too formidable, if a man can link it up with what he knows and loves."

She turned off the radio and sat motionless, steeped in wonder at the marvel which could bring a voice from across the ocean into the room with her.

Later she was roused from her absorption in the thrilling climax of a story by a sound like an explosion.

The blitz! At last! Wheels crunching on hard snow. Must have been a backfire she had heard. A car was going out the garage drive. Curious. Pike had said there was no one in the house. Also, he had said that Pat had been polishing her runabout yesterday. Was she in that car?

She ran to the window. The weatherman had been right. Snow had turned to sleet. The roads would be a glare of ice. Whose car had she heard? Even Pat wouldn't be so reckless as to drive in this storm. Perhaps one of the family had come in while she was listening to the radio — there might be a message on Pike's slate. Why not run down and look? She snapped on the light of a lamp. She hadn't realized the room was so dark.

She opened her door. The DO NOT

DISTURB card swung on the knob. Evidently someone had taken seriously the warning she had hung there as a joke, for on the floor lay a note. She picked it up, tore open the envelope. The message inside had been hastily scribbled.

Dear Nan:
When you told me your secret I said someday I'd trust you, too. I'm off to celebrate with my Captain at his house. Remember I told you he had taken one? He's giving a party just for me. Isn't it thrilling?

PAT

For one panicky instant her heart stopped. Pat at François Bouvoir's house when at any moment he might be arrested? Was it really a party? Why hadn't her mother known of it? She wouldn't put it past him to have the young girl as a lone guest. If that was his plan he would be terribly surprised when another appeared.

She crushed on a black sou'wester cloche. Fastened white overshoes. Belted a matching storm coat. Stuffed bills into her black bag. Tucked beige pigskin gloves into a pocket. Started for the hall. Dashed back for the violets. Ran down the stairs pinning the flowers to her belt.

As she reached the hall the telephone rang. It rang again and again, reverberating harshly through the still house. Ominous sound. It chilled her blood. She touched a button and the great chandelier blazed into light.

Has Pat crashed on the icy road? Is someone trying to contact her mother? she asked herself in the terrified instant before she answered the call.

27

"Mrs. —" Nan steadied her voice. "Mrs. Trask's residence."

"I want Patricia. Is she there?"

A man. A young one, a fiercely angry one and, glory be, *not* reporting an accident or he wouldn't have demanded Pat.

"No. This is Nan Barton speaking."

"Randy Bond this end. Where is Pat?"

"She went to dinner at her uncle's —"

"She isn't there. I phoned. Bet I've scared them nutty. They paged her all over the house. No dice. Her mother said that at the last minute Pat decided she wouldn't go to dinner in the limousine, took her own run-about. She must have left her uncle's in that. It isn't in the garage. The roads are a glare of ice. What do you suppose that dope is up to?" The boy's voice was hoarse with anxiety.

"I know where to find her. Have you a car?"

"Sure, of sorts — but it's a gosh-awful day

to drive one. Tell me where that brat is. I'll get her — and how. You better not risk it."

"She left a note to tell me where she was going. She must have come home and changed her costume after she left her uncle's. I heard a car in the drive. I was just starting out to pick up a taxi to join her when you rang. Hurry. Hur—" A click. Randy Bond had rung off. He was losing no time.

She paced the hall as she waited. Once she caught the glitter in the glass eyes of the polar bear. Sinister thing. It gave her the creeps.

She paused and glanced at the phone. Ought she to try to contact Bill Jerrold? No. She might interrupt at a crucial moment. She and Randy Bond must see this through alone.

The grind and groan of a brake. A car stopping? She had the front door open as the boy in trench coat and field cap with a gold bar slid and slipped along the path. He caught her as she skated off the lowest step. His grip on her arm stopped the circulation. Sleet stung her face.

"I told you it was a fierce day. I haven't chains on my jalopy. You'd better stay at home, Miss Barton."

"I'm going. Don't waste time. Pat has

gone to have tea with —"

"That smooth Captain? Who else would tempt her out in a storm like this? The dope. She's nuts about him. Hold tight when you get in. Everything is ice-coated."

Nan slid into the seat. The sky had darkened. Randy Bond turned on the headlights of the small car. The glow made driving more difficult. The defroster on the windshield swung rhythmically back and forth. Judging by the squeaks the jalopy had contracted arthritis in all its joints. He had been right when he had said it was a car "of sorts."

"I'll wring that kid's neck when I get hold of her for putting on a crazy act like this," he raged.

How typically male. The boy was frightened for the girl he loved and growled for relief.

"She's probably doing a little serious thinking herself, at this moment, Randy. She's driving a car, also, remember."

"Do you think I'm not seeing that runabout skidding like this? That I'm not expecting every minute to see it piled up against a tree?" He carefully maneuvered the car back to the middle of the road. "She shouldn't be allowed a license."

"She's seventeen." Nan raised her voice

to make her words audible above the noisy motor.

"And thinks she knows all the answers."

If it eased his anxiety to rage at Pat, better let the good work go on.

"Very fond of her aren't y-you?" she asked and hoped that the catch in her voice hadn't betrayed the fact that the sudden slide to the side of the road has set her heart thumping like an Indian war drum.

"That was a humdinger. I thought we were all set for the fence. Sure, I'm fond of her. She's been the only girl for me since we were kids together."

"Perhaps she feels too sure — of you." The skidding wheels had stopped her voice for an instant.

"It isn't that. She's picked up some cock-eyed idea. Says I'm not romantic because I won't stand for a hurry-up war marriage." The light was dim but not too dim to reveal the surge of crimson under his fair skin. "She's just a spoiled kid who thinks she's mature enough to marry. She isn't the only one. The woods are full of 'em. My father and mother were divorced when I was fifteen. When I marry it will be for keeps. I don't intend to have my kids juggled from one parent to another as I was. I'm off tomorrow. She's likely to fall for someone while I'm away. Okay, she'll be free."

His hurt young voice, his tightened lips, set tears thick in Nan's eyes. Heartbreak and tragedy everywhere and so little one could do to help. She laid her hand lightly on his knee.

"Pat is really a grand person. I believe you'll find her waiting for you when you come back, that she has kept you only in her heart while you were absent, Randy."

"Thanks. Sorry I broke down and told all." He sniffed. "Your violets are broadcasting fragrance like nobody's business. What's Pat's idea playing round with this French guy?"

"She is flattered that a man of the world, a cosmopolite, should pay her attention."

"Yeah! You've said it. I caught him kissing her hand. I started to pin his ears back, remembered my uniform and beat it. Do women *really* like that sort of stuff?"

"I can speak for myself only, Randy. I don't. It means no more to a foreigner than a handshake to you or me."

"Could be, but I'm not so sure in Pat's case." He cautiously manipulated the wheel till the car was back in the middle of the road. "Boy o boy that was a close call. Why doesn't the Street Department get a move on and sand this highway?" He gave her a quick look. "You're kind of white but you haven't yelped once."

She smiled with a confidence she was far from feeling.

"That's because I have such faith in the driver. Perhaps — perhaps we'd better not talk. This road needs your undivided attention."

"There's something in what you say," he agreed. "We're in luck that we haven't met other cars."

Only the scrape of wheels on the slippery road, the splash of sleet against glass, the crack of branches under their load of ice, the boy's quickly drawn breath, broke the silence as they drove on. After countless and what seemed to Nan miraculous escapes from an overturn at the roadside and hours, which really were minutes, peering through the windshield she exclaimed: —

"There it is. On the right. The house with white pillars. The runabout is at the curb and whole — thank heaven."

"Hey, don't get so excited." He skillfully drew up his car behind Pat's. "The sidewalk and path have been graveled. That's a break. Frenchy must have been expecting company and boy is he going to get it! Come on."

He couldn't know that her excitement was not because of relief that Pat had arrived safely, but because of the uncertainty of what might occur before they could get her out of the house. The General had said he would make no move to arrest François Bouvoir till he had his accomplices lined up, but suppose he already had them and the F.B.I. appeared? It could mean at the least unpleasant notoriety for the girl. Pat must make her exit as speedily as possible.

"Come on. Come on! What you waiting for?" Randy Bond prodded as he stood beside the car.

"Just a minute. Let's go very military and plan our campaign. Take Pat home in this car. It's your chance for a heart-to-heart with her before you go away tomorrow. I will drive her runabout back."

"You've gone haywire. You can't drive in a storm like this."

"If I had joined the Red Cross for overseas service as I wanted to I would be driving over tougher roads than this, wouldn't I? Come on."

Halfway up the path she stopped to warn: —

"Don't fight with Pat. Just say that you had to see her and *don't* on any account — I quote — give Frenchy a swift kick in the teeth."

His chuckle indicated that his nerves, tensed by the drive, had unknotted to a degree.

"I'll be a perfect little gentleman. Here we go," he said and thumbed the bell.

A colored man in white opened the door.

"Captain Bouvoir?" Nan inquired and stepped past him into the hall. Randy Bond followed close at her heels.

"I — I reckon the Captain isn't expectin' you, Miss?"

Were his great black eyes bulging from surprise or fright?

"Not expecting us?" Nan paused in the act of pulling off a glove. "Isn't this the date of the cocktail party? Randy, have we made this nightmare trip on the wrong day?"

"Boy, I've got the card of invitation here somewhere." He fumbled in the pocket of his trench coat. "I —"

"What's the trouble, George?" François Bouvoir asked from a doorway at the right. His eyes widened with incredulity and narrowed.

"Mademoiselle Barton and Lieutenant Bond! To what do I owe this pleasure? It must be that you are here to wish me a Merry Christmas, yes? Is it the custom of the country? Come in. George, take Mademoiselle's coat."

"I'll keep it."

As Nan entered the room, Patricia was standing in front of the fire. Her brown eyes

353

were enormous, her cheeks almost as red as her soft beret, which matched her thin wool frock. Did her excitement presage an outbreak of anger?

"Nan! Oh, Nan, I — I hoped you'd come." There was a sound in her throat like a heart being swallowed. "Hi, Randy!"

"Hi, yourself. When we found the going was bad, Nan and I had the heebie jeebies to think of you driving home alone. So here we are."

"I should not have allowed Chérie to drive home alone, Lieutenant," Bouvoir countered smoothly.

"Oh yeah?" Randy Bond caught Nan's warning eyes and tempered his voice. "Now we can save you the trouble. I'm taking 'Chérie' and Miss Barton is driving Pat's runabout. An icy road is our meat, isn't it, Nan?" He caught up Patricia's fur coat from the back of a chair. "Get into this and make it fast, dope."

"Captain," the colored man spoke from the threshold, "you're wanted on the phone an' quick."

"Don't go till I come back," Bouvoir said and hurriedly left the room.

Patricia buttoned her jacket with quick, nervous fingers.

"I never was so glad to see anyone in my

life as I was to see you, Nan, when you came in that door," she whispered. "I honestly thought there was to be a party and when I found I was the only one here —"

"Did that heel get fresh with you?" Randy Bond demanded.

"He did not, bright boy. I wasn't glad Nan came because I was *afraid* of him. I just knew I'd made myself terribly cheap by coming — and believe it or not, I hated myself and — and I guess you will too after this — Randy."

The break in her voice, the appeal in her eyes, sent a wave of red to the boy's white face.

"What I think of you, brat, will keep. Come on, let's get going before Frenchy comes. We're off, Captain," he announced jauntily as Bouvoir stepped into the room in a long blue coat with his cap under his arm. "Going out yourself, looks like."

"I have had what you Americans say is a hurry-up call to the city. Will you give me a seat in your car, Mademoiselle Barton?"

The muscles of Nan's body tensed. Why this sudden decision? His face was colorless. Its lines had sharpened. Had the telephone message summoned him?

"Must you go, Captain? The roads are dangerous. Can't your errand wait for tomorrow?"

355

"No. If you can face the danger, Mademoiselle, surely I can. Even if I hadn't been ordered to sit in on a conference I wouldn't let you go alone." He motioned toward the low table laden with glasses. "You see, I prepared for other guests. Chérie was the only one who dared venture out. Won't you have something to drink before you go?"

"Thanks, no." Patricia and Randy Bond were already in the hall. "I hope it won't make you nervous if I drive, Captain?" Nan drew on her gloves. "Having just come over the road I know every skid!"

"I have more faith in your skill than in my own. I place myself in your hands, Mademoiselle."

In the hall he spoke to the colored man who held open the door.

"I shan't be back tonight, George."

"Yes, sir, yes, boss." George looked out at the street. "It sure is powerful bad going, sir."

Randy Bond and Patricia were already in the jalopy when the Captain opened the door of Pat's runabout.

"We'll drive slowly," the boy called. "Follow as close as you can. Then we'll be on hand to pick up each other's pieces in case of a crash." After which cheery suggestion the jalopy lurched forward with a snort.

The violets fell from Nan's belt as she slipped into the seat behind the wheel. She pushed them gently on the floor toward the door. She would pick them up later. She waited until Randy's car was a safe distance ahead before she started the runabout. From the corners of her eyes she threw a longing glance at the Reuben Hall house as she passed. Every window was wreath-hung. She could smell the smoke of cannel coal, could visualize the homey living room with Sally and Reub. What wouldn't she give to be there with them?

"Why that profound sigh, Mademoiselle?" Bouvoir inquired. "Is the strain of driving too much for you?"

"No. *No.* Oh! I — I thought Randy's jalopy was going over that time. He's straightened it out. Would you mind not talking? I must concentrate on the road."

The mist had lifted when they reached the bridge. The Monument was visible through a thin haze. Suddenly a great red sun broke through and balanced on the horizon like a mammoth crimson golf ball poised on a tee. Every ice-tinseled twig on the trees was a tiny flame from the reflection, every stalk by the roadside was an icy spear, blood-tipped. The air had a crisp, washed-clean quality. The entire western sky burst into color.

357

Rosy cloud-peaks melted slowly, steadily like mounds of pink ice cream.

"The roads have been sanded, thank goodness." Nan's tense nerves and muscles relaxed with a suddenness that made her lightheaded.

"Prenez garde!" Bouvoir warned sharply. "We almost hit the rail of the bridge."

"I know, everything is under control again, Captain." Her voice reflected her relief. "Here we are, safe on the other side. Where shall I leave you? I'm not sufficiently noble even with these awful roads sanded to go out of my way for you."

"You'll not leave me. We go on together until I say 'Stop, Mademoiselle.' "

28

Bill Jerrold dropped the newspaper he had been reading to the General's desk.

"We got our warning through in time. Bouvoir must have seen these headlines. EAST ON ALERT FOR YULE RAID. I wonder if he suspects how his message leaked out."

"I hope not, Major. You are sure that Miss Barton is spending the day at the Trask house?"

"So Pike reported when he phoned just before he left for his holiday."

"I don't like the idea of her being there alone. I hope to have the situation under control before dark and you can join her."

"Yes, sir."

Standing at a window Jerrold stared out at a sleet-encased world. Nan wouldn't need him. Doubtless the Navy would take over in his place.

"Lousy afternoon to be handed on Christmas day. If our job of waiting before we land Bouvoir till all the lines are safely in your hands hadn't busted up a skating date this sleet storm would have done the trick." He visualized the two figures in close embrace he had seen in the Trask hall. "I guess it was washed up anyway."

"A date with Miss Barton, I presume?"

"Yes, sir. Even if I hadn't seen — that is, after my admission of the marriage in the Trask living room my course was charted. Orders to shove off, pronto, were my excuse for immediate departure. I had to choose quick between leaving Nan to face the deluge alone or a more embarrassing situation."

"Right. You proved again that you are a soldier schooled in the strategy of quick decision and action. Leaving the brief case in the taxi with her name in it certainly balled things up for her. You took a chance of undoing what your take-off had accomplished when you returned to the Trask house last evening."

"How did you know I was there, sir?"

"It didn't need a Sherlock Holmes to make that deduction. You answered a phone call at this desk. Exclaimed, 'An hour ago? Has had no word from her? Okay, Pike, I'm on the job.' You banged the phone into the cradle, flung a curt 'I'll be back' over your shoulder and charged out of this office.

Pike is butler at Mrs. Trask's, isn't he?"

"You're the original Sees-All-Knows-All, sir. Nan Barton was to meet a friend at a night spot. He waited an hour after the time agreed upon, then went to the Trask house to check on her and stirred up Pike, who reported to me. After phoning to every place, even Girl Town, where I thought she might be with Gladys Grant, I beat it to the Trask house to check with the Lieutenant as to exactly where and when she was to meet him and interrupted a tender reunion of two loving hearts in the hall."

"Well, well, that was something." Bill Jerrold hotly resented the General's chuckle. "Highly embarrassing for you, Major. Did you find out why Miss Barton didn't keep the date with the Lieutenant?"

"No, sir. After a few fitting words to express my opinion of the situation I departed."

"You might have given the girl who has helped us a chance to explain, Major." The General touched a button on his desk. "That would be only fair to her."

The door to an inner room opened. The man who entered was the person whose face had reminded Nan of a bronze mask, whom Bouvoir had called Dwyer.

"You move in a mysterious way your

wonders to perform, General," Bill Jerrold said.

"There are times when I can't let my right hand — you, in this particular case, Major — know how my left is manipulating. My favorite sleuth, Walt Gustin, Major Jerrold."

The immobility of the detective's face broke into a likeable grin.

"Now that the truth may be told I'm sure proud to know you, Major. I saw red for a minute the other night when it looked as if it were on the cards for me to knock out the General's No. 1 aide."

"You mean the night I hid among those icy shrubs? Gives me the shivers — not malarial — to think of it. Didn't know you saw me."

"Sure. I saw you gum-shoe along the path. I'd had an acute attack of willies a short time before when Miss Barton started to hide in those same bushes. I was on the watch for another dame." He grinned reminiscently. "She's game. When I growled, 'Where do you think you are, Miss?' she came back, sugar-sweet, 'It will be Mrs. in a few minutes.' I take my job as all in the day's work but her sporting blood got under my skin." He rubbed his right hand across his eyes as if the haze of anxiety still lingered.

"I'd got to get her out of the way before Bouvoir, for whom I was ostensibly working, or the woman we were expecting, came. She didn't wait for me. She took herself off and to an A-1 place, the General told me later."

"Who was the woman you were expecting, Gustin?"

"Just a minute, Major," the General intervened. "I want you to hear why Miss Barton kept the party of the first part of the 'tender reunion' waiting last evening."

"If you'd gone through the hell I lived through when I thought Bouvoir might have kidnaped her, your voice wouldn't be so amused, sir."

"Right, Major. Give us the works, Gustin."

"I'll answer the Major's question first, General. The woman I was looking for was Mrs. Suzanne Dupree."

Even though he had expected to hear that name, Bill Jerrold winced. The certainty hurt. He considered her a total loss as wife and daughter, a poacher on other women's man power, but he had liked and admired her parents. A treasonable act of hers would be a blow over the heart for them.

"At ease, Major," the General ordered. "You're tense as a G string." As Jerrold dropped into a chair across the desk from him, he prompted: —

"Cut out the slow motion and speed up the picture, Walt. Sit down while you tell the story. In a chair, *not* on my desk."

"Yes, sir." Seated, Walt Gustin drew a notebook from the breast of his blue serge coat.

"You put me on this case, General, when Major Jerrold reported that Miss Barton had mistaken a French officer for a boy — Carl — she'd played with in Vienna years before; and the Captain denied being the person she thought him; and the Major had a hunch that Bouvoir was the Austrian, that if he were in this country under an assumed name he was up to no good and wouldn't stop at putting the girl out of the way when he was convinced he hadn't fooled her. Right so far, Major?"

"It smacks of Hollywood as you put it, but that's right."

"My job was to tie up with Bouvoir — remember the day at the Pentagon, Major, when I sat at the next table to you and the Captain?"

"Yes."

"He and I had made a deal that morning. He said he suspected he was being shadowed by an anti-French Committee agent and wanted me to take over a watchdog job. Said I had been recommended by a friend."

"Your Machiavellian hand again, sir?" Jerrold inquired.

"Don't interrupt, Major, we haven't time to waste," the General reminded. "Go on, Walt."

"I had been instructed by our boss here to keep an eye on Miss Barton, too. Remember that afternoon at the Jefferson Memorial, Major, when —"

"I remember each time I have seen you. Where does Suzanne Dupree come into the story?"

"She was in it when I took over. Used to meet Bouvoir for cocktails and dinner at the night spots. I figured she was looking for write-ups for her column, but I couldn't make out why he was with her so much. She's a humdinger as to looks and can turn on the charm, but the more I saw of Bouvoir the more I realized he wasn't falling for any dame, he was after upper-bracket contacts. Then, one day, when I was waiting for him, I heard him say as he and Mrs. Dupree came out of the Mayflower Bar: —

" 'Because of your family connections you have cards to many of the social functions here, given by the Cabinet members and Army and Navy heads, Suzanne. Each time you arrange to take me with you will be money in your pocket. To enlarge my social circle is one of my duties. My countrymen who are in Washington want to make themselves what you call 'solid' with the Americans, who can be the most powerful friends in the world.' "

That explained Suzanne's "friend" who had been taking money and was in a jam, Jerrold thought, before he asked: —

"Did she believe he was an accredited official of the French office here, Gustin?"

"I'm sure she did, Major. He was. He'd fooled 'em all. We have lines out to discover when he and his father first became agents for the Axis. When Bouvoir told me that Mrs. Dupree was coming to the house to plan a social campaign for him, that he had engaged her as a Public Relations Counsel, that we were to be on the watch for her night before last, he had me guessing. If he was the person we thought him, I didn't believe the woman knew it, though I was sure she had collected a lot of dough for the invitations she had secured for him. She didn't come that night."

"Evidently she came to my rooms to sound me out first," Bill Jerrold said. "From her excitement and the few words she had a chance to say before we were interrupted, I deduced that she had become suspicious of Bouvoir. She was frightened. I left the house soon after. When I returned she was in the Trask living room. She couldn't have met Bouvoir at his house. She may have contacted him yesterday."

"She didn't. I put a man on his tail and devoted my time to shadowing her, even to the airport last night."

"The airport! Where has she gone?"

"We've been round Robin Hood's barn getting to it, but that's what I called Gustin in to tell you. Make it snappy, Walt," the General commanded. "We may have a call at any minute to pick up our man."

"There isn't much more to say, sir. Miss Barton was there to see Mrs. Dupree off. That's why she didn't keep her date with the Lieutenant. I dope it out that knowing how palsy-walsy the Dupree woman and the Frenchman were, Miss Barton figured that she might in some way warn him. So, frightened her out of the picture. I could be wrong. Check with the young lady, Major; if I'm okay, let me know." Gustin reached for the phone. "Shall I answer the call, sir?"

The General nodded and sat forward in his chair. Jerrold's nerves tensed. Was this it?

"Yep, Gustin speaking. Say it again. He went out with Miss Barton?" He moved away from Bill Jerrold's outthrust hand.

"Take it easy, Major. Go on, George. Why was she there? . . . Yes. . . . Yes. . . . Yes. . . . Yes. . . . Which car did they go in? . . . You couldn't tell? How long have they been gone? . . . Okay." He clamped down the telephone. He was standing, as were the General and Bill Jerrold. Before they could speak he explained: —

"It's our man at Bouvoir's house, General. Miss Patricia Trask went to Bouvoir's, She had been there but a short time when Miss Barton and —"

"Where is Nan now?" Jerrold's face was drained of color, his voice hoarse.

"Let's get the rest of the story, Major. Did George say why she went to the Captain's house, Walt?" the General demanded.

"He heard her say the roads were so bad that she and the Lieutenant had come for the girl. Just before the two youngsters left together —"

"Together! Didn't Miss Barton go with them?"

"She had planned to drive the Trask car home alone, Major. Just before they started, Bouvoir had a phone call. When he came back he was corpse-white — that's according to George — and told Miss Barton that he had had a call and would go along with her."

"He'd been tipped off." The General dropped to his chair, caught up the phone and dialed. "Know the number of the Trask girl's car, Major?"

"No, sir. How long have they been gone, Gustin? Are you sure that Bouvoir and Miss Barton were in the runabout?" Jerrold was pulling on his trench coat.

"George wasn't sure. He said they all went out together, then he had to answer the phone. They left twenty minutes ago. George has been all this time getting in touch with us. The sleet has brought down some lines."

"Take my car, Major." The General clapped his hand over the receiver. "Walt, go with him. You may be ahead of them and able to cut them off after they cross the bridge. I'll get the number of the runabout and send out scouts." He spoke into the phone. "Connect me with him, quick."

"Shall I take the wheel, Major?" Walt Gustin inquired when, after what seemed hours of delay, the General's coupé was located.

"No. We'll stop at the Washington end of the bridge. We ought to be ahead of them, though we've wasted time getting this car. Keep your eye peeled for a jalopy or a run-about with a rumble seat. We don't know which we are after. Here we go."

He drove cautiously, forcing his terror for Nan's safety into the background, keeping his eyes ahead while Gustin kept watch through the rear window. Even under its sprinkling of sand the road was turned into a glittering highway by the headlights. The glow from a great red sun turned bordering trees and shrubs into daz-zling beauty.

At the Washington entrance to the bridge he stopped to watch a jalopy turn back and approach.

"That them?" Gustin asked eagerly.

"Maybe. We don't know —"

"Hi!" a man called above a lowered window. "Have you seen a runabout — Gee whizz, it's you, Major Jerrold."

"Where is Nan Barton?"

"Gosh, we don't know. That's why Pat and I turned round." Jerrold could see the white face of the girl peering over the lad's shoulder.

"When did you see her last?"

"She was following us close. After we crossed the bridge we looked back and she was turning the wrong way. I yelled but this motor was so noisy she couldn't hear, I guess. Captain Bouvoir was with her. They headed south, away from the city."

29

"Together! You and I go on together! What do you mean, Captain, by that 'Stand and deliver' voice?" With her heart knocking in her throat, Nan's laughing question was a triumph of will over fright.

His eyes were those of a trapped animal, desperate, murderous, as they stabbed into hers. Her breath caught. He knew that the message in his broadcast had been discovered. Had the phone call he answered been a warning to escape?

"Turn south," he ordered.

Suppose she kept straight on? She would try to signal Randy.

"Don't touch that horn." Something hard pressed against her right side.

"Turn. Drive on."

She drove slowly. One expedient after another for delivering the man beside her into the arms of the law flashed through her mind to be rejected as impractical. If only she could contact Bill Jerrold. That was out.

The situation was up to her.

The lights of a car directly behind shone on the windshield. Had Randy Bond seen her turn south, imagined something might be wrong and followed? Could she signal to him? Her heart thumped so hard it seemed as if the tense man beside her, crouched forward, must hear it, must feel the vibration of her body. Her teeth were clamped into her lower lip, her hands within her gloves were cold and clammy.

With a warning *Honk! Honk!* the car behind, a sedan, maneuvered cautiously abreast. It wasn't Randy. It might be someone who would help. Could she get an SOS across to the driver?

"Don't speak," a low voice warned. Whatever it was digging into her side increased its pressure. The rear light of the car that had passed dimmed into a red star and blinked out. Definitely no help from that.

The road, set in a dazzling, flame-tipped icy border, stretched ahead endlessly long, free of traffic, whitened by the glare of the headlights of the runabout. Now what? Cut out panic and do some constructive thinking. She fought for control. The thump, thump of her heart sounded loud as the stalking thud, thud, of a prehistoric monster.

"Drive faster!" the man beside her commanded.

"On this i-icy road? Y-you're crazy," she replied, with a valiant attempt at flippancy which had an excited gulp in the middle of it.

He answered something under his breath and stared ahead as if with all his power he were urging the runabout forward. If only she could make him drop the automatic jabbing into her side — if it were an automatic. It would be in a movie and all her information as to a melodramatic situation like the present had been gleaned from the screen. Perhaps if she could incite him to talk he would relax his hold and she could grab it. A cockeyed possibility, but even that was better than driving on and on, with her muscles tied in tight knots and her heart doing stunts.

Lights reflected on the mirror above the windshield again. Another car following? It was coming slowly. No help there, or was there? The air in the runabout was heavy with the scent of violets. Flash! If she could push them out to the road in some way they might help. Possibility, not probability, but anything was worth trying.

She located the bunch with her foot. Swiftly opened the door and pushed it out.

"Don't jump! Shut that door." The pressure on her side increased. She closed it with a bang.

"I hadn't the slightest intention of jumping, *mon Capitaine*. I'm not tired of life. I wanted air. This runabout is getting uncomfortably hot. I'd rather take my chances in a crash than be smothered."

Chatter wouldn't get her anywhere. Evidently the driver of the car behind had no intention of passing. It had stopped. Would it turn back? The buck had been passed to her again. If only she had let Bill know she was going after Pat. Perhaps some of the General's staff were already at the Captain's house, had discovered that he had gone and started after him. Joyful thought. The wings of her spirit which hope had unfolded closed again. How could they know in which direction to follow?

She cleared her tight throat in preparation for a remark which might lead to conversation. Something dug into her side. Indignation burned up caution.

"Stop jabbing me with that automatic — if it is an automatic," she protested loudly in the hope that the driver of the car behind, which was following again, might hear and step on the gas. "I've seen too many movies to make that break." She turned for an instant to look at the man beside her, crouched like an animal about to spring.

"Speaking of movies, what *is* this all about, *mon Capitaine?*" She was proud of her laugh. "You had me so rattled with your theatrical 'Turn south. Drive on' I thought for a minute you were doubling for one of the escaping German prisoners."

"You are putting on quite an act yourself, Mademoiselle." He maintained his tense regard of the glittering white road ahead, the pressure on her side. "You have been suspicious of me since the evening you called me 'Carl.' *You* picked words from my broadcast. *You* sent that warning. *Tiens!* You will get yours for that, as you Americans say."

Her heart stopped and galloped on. Was he planning to shoot her and take over the runabout? That thought helped. The car behind still followed, the reflected lights made fiery patterns on the windshield. Curious how close it trailed them.

Trailed! Trailed! Perhaps it wasn't curious. Perhaps the person or persons in it were a part of the Axis intelligence system to which François Bouvoir belonged — they might be following to rescue him at the right moment. Could she block their move? The sound track of memory went into action. She heard Bill Jerrold's voice: —

"You'll measure up all right if ever the test comes, the time when there is only one way to go. Ahead. You'll be on your own. You will know there is no one to help, know that you've *got* to make good — or else."

This was it. She was on her own, all right. No one to help. The man beside her mustn't know she suspected that the car following would attempt to rescue him, or that she was determined to circumvent it.

"You get more and more incomprehensible, Captain. *I* 'picked words.' *I* 'sent a warning.' One minute I feel like a heroine of a melodrama, then I tell myself I'm still a prosaic translator-secretary."

"You can skip the humor, Mademoiselle. Concentrate on driving. The road has been well sanded. It is no longer dangerous." His eyes flashed to the windshield, which still reflected the lights of the car behind. "Faster! Faster!"

"The road may be sanded, but it is tricky. Caution is an old New England custom, Captain. I won't drive faster." Just where would that defy get her? If she didn't talk she would scream.

"Turn in there." He pointed with his free hand to a side street.

"No. It isn't sanded. It's a glare of ice. We —"

He caught the wheel. Whirled it with a force that wrenched her right wrist. The runabout turned with a suddenness that brought a yell from the driver behind, the screech of brakes, the wail of a siren. The police. Had the General sent them?

"Now you've done it, Captain," she shouted to make her voice heard above the tumult. "Those are cruising police. They'll land us both in jail for reckless speed."

"Faster."

As the runabout raced into the dimly lighted street she strained her eyes to see what lay ahead. Looked back. The car which had barely escaped collision was following cautiously. It was up to her now to make sure they had their man. It might mean the end for her. Why think of that? She had been eager to help her country. "You've got to make good — or else." Bill's voice again.

With a little prayer for courage to take whatever came, she jerked the emergency brake. The wheels screamed. The runabout skidded crazily. Crashed into a tree with a jolt that threw them against the windshield. A thud. The automatic? She pushed open the door beside her. Jumped. Would he follow? He was out the other side.

"Far's you go, Captain," a voice announced. "It was fun while it lasted, wasn't it?"

Nan stared incredulously at the man with a strangle-hold on the throat of her late passenger. Bill! Bill Jerrold! Had he dropped from a chute? Her world did a wing-over-wing. Steadied. The two struggling men were illumined by the prowl car headlights. Had he been with them? Why —

"Bill! Look out!" she warned wildly. The Captain had wriggled a knife from its sheath. Before he could use it Jerrold sent him crashing to the ground.

"Take over, Sergeant," he said to the burly, red-faced officer looking down at the motionless figure on the ground. "I'll get in touch with the F.B.I. I wouldn't have caught him if you hadn't picked me up. You made better time than I could."

"You fellas that come out of this war sure can put across a kayo when you get mad, Major. Guess you were a commando, weren't you? Hi, Joe!"

In response to the call a man stepped from the prowl car. He was as thin and gaunt as the sergeant was round and ruddy.

"Help me dump this guy into our car. He's passed out cold. You and the dame come along, Major. She'll have a little explaining to do why she was helping this fella you were after escape."

"I! *Helping!*" The hard pressure of a hand on her arm cut off Nan's voice. Bill Jerrold shook his head. His lips formed the words: —

"Not now."

Standing beside him on the icy road she watched the limp figure of the onetime Captain François Bouvoir being lifted into the prowl car. What would happen to him now? For the first time she became aware of pain under her left eye. Must have bruised it when her face banged against the windshield. She started to lift her right hand to investigate the damage, dropped it quickly.

"What's the matter? Hurt?" Jerrold demanded.

"Did I say 'Ooch'? Nothing but my imagination grabbing the bit in its teeth. I — I thought of what might have happened if you hadn't arrived in time."

"Stop thinking. We did. At first we weren't sure we were following the right car — the license plate was so coated with ice the police couldn't make out if it was the number of the runabout they'd been ordered to find. When we saw the bunch of violets in the road, that tied it. I had sent you violets to wear today. Other cruising police are looking for the jalopy."

"Sure the car is usable?" the Sergeant called. "It took a lot of punishment against that tree. I thought we'd be collecting junk."

Jerrold shook the wheels, tested the motor.

"One of the headlights smashed. Everything else under control. Don't wait. We'll follow. Come on, Nan." He held out his hand.

Instinctively she moved hers to meet it. Sharp pain stabbed at her wrist. The car lights and his head jumbled in a fantastic pattern. Through her dazed mind echoed Sam's fierce voice. "You've started something now, Dianne." There had been a mouse and a girl and a telegram. Sam! Was he here? Had everything that happened today followed the ball Di had started rolling, roll—ing, roll— She caught at Jerrold's sleeve.

"Ken! The world is going round and —"

Something closed tight about her. Something pressed hard on her lips. She was aware of the sudden passion of her response, of a whispered: —

"Dearest! Dearest!" before she drifted into a soft, smothering dusk.

30

Gladys Grant's dimples flashed as she looked at Nancy Barton, seated opposite her at lunch in a Pentagon cafeteria the last day of the year.

"You may hand it to me for tact, Nan. I've seen you several times this week and haven't once remarked that your left cheek, almost as black as the top to the beige skirt you're wearing, suggested a sock in the eye, and that your right wrist was bandaged. Now that both are almost back to normal would it be out of order if I inquired 'How come?' "

"You missed the high spot, Glad. You should have seen me the Monday after Christmas when I reported for work. My left eye, set in a broad mourning band, was partially closed; my right wrist was strapped. Colonel Long took one look at me and shouted with laughter. 'Great Scott, what happened?' he demanded. 'Oh, I've been getting round,' I tossed off debonairly. That sent him into another paroxysm."

"I call laughing at you darned ungrateful."

"Fortunately I had Sunday off in which to pull myself together. I was fit to work next day, if a trifle hard on the eyes. The Colonel apologized handsomely, offered me the week off and heroically swallowed a chuckle each time I entered the office."

"Are you telling how you acquired these souvenirs of a gay past?"

Nan considered her answer. Each day she had searched the papers expecting to see an account of the arrest of Captain François Bouvoir, but not a word had she found. Was Glad leading up to something she had heard about him?

"Did I speak out of turn?" The question spiked reflection.

"No. Christmas afternoon I decided to go social, borrowed Pat Trask's runabout and skidded to a tea. You may remember that the morning snow was afternoon sleet. Coming home the car spun into a terrifying act. I lost my head. Jerked the emergency brake. The car smacked against the bosom of a giant oak with the force of a runaway locomotive."

"The light touch. I get it. I shouldn't have asked the question. You driving alone in that storm! Tell that to the Marines. And that reminds me, I presume you know that Major Jerrold is in the hospital."

"Glad! I didn't." Relief rolled over Nan in a glowing tide. Now she knew why she hadn't heard from him during the past interminable week. "Is he very ill, Glad?"

"*No.* Light touch of malaria, but they made him keep quiet. The doctor reported that the chill had been occasioned by excitement and was our Major furious! 'Does that mean I'm to have one of these infernal attacks at every crisis in my life?' he raged. The M.D. is used to Leathernecks. He grinned. 'You'll outgrow them as you get older, Major.' Which patronizing reply made our hero madder. 'Isn't twenty-nine old enough?' he demanded. He was dismissed yesterday. I'm glad he's okay again. Bill Jerrold is in a class by himself. He's not only tops as a fighter. He's tops as a man."

Dismissed yesterday. No word to her. Why should he want to see her? The headman-in-her-life arrangement had been a ruse to follow up François Bouvoir. Now that the Nazi agent was in custody, Bill was free to return to his "unprovisional" love, wasn't he?

"Celebrating tonight, Nan?"

"No. I've kept up the office work, which has been heavier than usual, and reported for my Nurses' Aide evenings. With my face and wrist painfully stiff, it hasn't been easy. All members of the Trask family will be out welcoming the New Year and it will be my chance at heavenly quiet. Perhaps the emphasis on coming Invasion this past week has cast its shadow over my spirit. I can't rise to the idea of a night club with its horns and grotesque caps and racket when I think of what is ahead for our men fighting and for those who love them. To be honest, I haven't been invited."

"What's happened to the French Captain who's been rushing you? Is he dating the Trask infant?"

"Pat has been away during the holiday vacation. The Captain has found someone he likes better, doubtless. What goes for you, Glad?"

"Representative Ralph Carew has invited me to do the night spots with him. He's getting human. I didn't have to suggest it." She rose. "Time's up. Happy New Year."

Sam Mitchell was waiting in Nan's office when she reached it. He caught her hands, eagerly extended, in a hard grip.

"I was afraid I'd have to leave before you came, Nancy B."

"Sam! Aren't you staying over for tonight?"

"No. Flew here on business. Going back on an afternoon train. Not a plane seat to be had. What happened to your eye? Skin round it looks kind of yellow."

"Nothing much. Don't waste our precious minutes together talking about me, Sammy. How's business?"

"Running on greased wheels."

"Grand. How — how's Di?"

"Fine and busy — too busy for the tame cats she's always had about the house. Life in my happy home is a darned lot smoother. That's what you want to know, isn't it? Your Christmas letter made your sister very happy." He glanced at the wall clock. "Time to shove off. Take care of yourself. Hope the New Year comes in trailing clouds of glory for you, Nancy B. Good-by."

Nan thought of Sam's hope for her as she sat before the mirror in her room in the early evening dressing for dinner. There was only one person who could come dragging clouds of glory for her and he hadn't cared enough to let her know where he was. She answered a knock.

"Come in. Pat! When did you get back? I've missed you terribly."

"Sez you."

There was a change in her, Nan thought, as the girl slowly crossed the room. Nothing she could put a finger on. The round neck and cap sleeves of her pink frock set off her white throat and slender arms, the bubbles of pink and silver sequins at her ears were immensely becoming if completely out of character with her youthful costume. She leaned against the wall beside the dressing table.

"Did you mean it?" she asked. "Mean that you are glad to see me?"

"Why *shouldn't* I be?"

"Because I got you into such an awful mess, that's why. Zowie, Nan, I won't forget Christmas night till I pass out for good. Bill Jerrold's face when Randy yelled that you and Captain Bouvoir had turned the wrong way; the prowl car following us to this door. Mother and Uncle Zeb in the library waiting for us, their faces ghastly white from anxiety about me. Cops asking where you were. Later Bill Jerrold's eyes burning like headlights as he stalked into the living room with you limp as a ragdoll in his arms. I thought you were dead. That I'd killed you." She struggled with a harsh sob.

"Pat *dear,* I was far from dead. I was aware of everything that happened after your car skidded into a tree until I moved my wrist, then the pain knocked me out. It was nothing but a sprain and a slight concussion. I was at work Monday."

"You wouldn't have been out in that fierce storm if I hadn't gone to Captain Bouvoir's. I hope I never see him again. That afternoon in his house I kept thinking of Red Ridinghood and the Wolf. It wasn't anything he did, it was just something inside me being ashamed I was there. I spilled the whole thing to Mother. I'll hand it to her for not saying 'I told you so.' Randy's right. I have been a know-it-all brat. That doesn't mean that I'm going back into mental rompers, that I don't intend to work out my own problems. The Army declares that a boy of seventeen or eighteen isn't a juvenile. He's old enough to fight for his country. Why shouldn't a girl that age be considered adult?"

Nan laughed.

" 'Don't get hysterical' — that's a quote, in case you care. Of course you'll 'work out your own problems' — who else?"

"You're a sweet kid, New England." Had it been anyone but Pat speaking, Nan would have suspected tears in the roughened voice. "I'm not going drippy, but it's only fair to tell you you've kept me on the beam since you came. You've listened to my views on life and love as if I were a grownup and had the same right to my opinions you have to yours. If I told them to Mother I shocked her. That'll give you a rough idea of what I've been up against."

Nan slipped the silver gauze frock over her head.

"When you remember some of those opinions, can you wonder, Pat? Your mother — like millions of other women — is passionately determined to do her part to help make the world to which her son will return a world which will measure up to a victory for right living on the home front, equal to the victory for which our men are making terrific sacrifices on the battlefields. She was troubled about your friendship with Captain Bouvoir. You'll admit she was right?"

"Sure she was right. I didn't tell her about his invitation for Christmas because I knew she wouldn't let me go. Cross my throat, I did think there would be others there. Let's forget it." Pat sniffed. "You smell like a perfume ad. 'Is he dark and fierce and a Devil Dog? Wear flower scents to melt his tense reserve?'" She giggled. "That stuff you're wearing would melt a Stone Ager. Whose eyes are you aiming to knock out in that snazzy outfit? Those topaz ear studs pick up the color of your hair."

Pat was back in character. Probably never

again would she open her heart as she had tonight, but having seen into its depths Nan had no fear for her.

"I'm dining with my best friend."

"The Captain?"

"No. I haven't seen him since Christmas."

"Bill Jerrold?"

"*No.* With myself. Dressing for dinner is one of my top spirit-lifters. This frock was a Christmas present from Di and Sam. I haven't had a minute before to try it on. Pike is to serve my dinner before the fire in the library. This 'snazzy outfit' is in honor of a gal named Barton."

"Heck, no romantic lead. What a lousy New Year's eve. Where's Bill Jerrold?"

Nan became absorbed in fastening the silver bracelet.

"I wouldn't know. Taking his latest heart-beat out, doubtless. What's your program?"

"I'm doing some swanky night spots with Randy."

"Randy! I thought he'd gone."

"Orders changed at the last minute. That's the Army. It will be a great night. Even the old-time Capitalists will be on the move to welcome this New Year. Gosh, I hope the next January first will see Tom home — safe. Who's knocking?" She opened the door.

"The Major's waitin' for Miss Nan," Pike announced.

"What — what — Major?"

"Major Jerrold, Miss Nan. He's come to have dinner with youse. Wasn't you expectin' him?"

"Sure she was expecting him. She'll be right down. Scram, Pike." Pat closed the door. "Holding out on me, weren't you?"

"Cross my throat I didn't know he was coming, Pat. Your mother must have invited him."

"Okay. Okay. Get a hustle on. Here's your silver bag."

"Will I do?" Nan turned slowly like a model.

"Do! With your hair shining like red gold and your eyes blazing like kleig lights? Get along with you." She swooped and kissed Nan warmly on the lips. "Thanks for listenin' to my sob stuff, New England."

He was standing in the hall as she went slowly down the stairs. The light from the crystal chandelier picked up the gold insignia on his tunic, shone in his eyes as he looked up.

"I'm a week late to keep our dinner date," he said as casually as if the events of that night just a week ago never had happened. "You knew I'd come, didn't you?"

"No. I thought now that François Bouvoir was out of the way — our — our wacky arrangement would end."

"Oh, that's ended all right. Now —"

"Dinner is ready in the library, Miss Nan. Sure is good to see you back, Major." Pike's eyes and teeth gleamed in his dark face as he drew out Nan's chair at the small round table not too near the fire. He placed a tiny silver girl with bouffant skirts beside her plate.

"Here's the bell. When you's ready for your next course, ring, Miss Nan. I'll hear it."

Because there was something in Bill Jerrold's eyes she couldn't meet, because she could think of nothing else to say, Nan touched the delicately broiled grapefruit on her plate.

"This isn't a man's dish. Mrs. Amy knows I love it and thinking I was to dine alone —"

"Mrs. Amy knew you were not to dine alone. I've had her on the phone every day this week to check on you. Couldn't come myself. Busy licking a slight chill. She said after your shake-up you shouldn't go into a crowd tonight. Remembering your face when I brought you into this room a week ago, that went double with me."

"Did you tell her that the marriage story

was a bluff? She seemed to know it."

"As soon as I knew that Bouvoir — Brouner really — was in custody I explained to Mrs. Amy that it was a yarn in the line of duty. She admitted that after the first shock she and the Admiral suspected it was a military expedient and hadn't mentioned it."

"What happened to the Captain? I haven't seen a reference to him in the papers."

"Wait till after Pike serves the next course and I'll tell you."

She couldn't have told what she ate, she knew only that Bill exclaimed, "Swell duckling." That she helped herself automatically from the two silver dishes Pike offered.

After the butler left the room Jerrold told what the General and Gustin had discovered and that they found the white scar at the corner of the Captain's mouth.

"The night he broadcast on the program with you was the first time he had sent information over the air. The hesitation on the previous occasion was practice stuff. His other scripts were straight goods. Oliver Stiles never will know that his station was used by a Nazi agent. Part of Bouvoir's job was to contact men in the know, sound them out on our foreign policy and report to his boss. They found many letters in German among his papers."

"Then he did bring that letter to Colonel Long's office to find out if I believed him to be Carl Brouner. I didn't, but each time I went out with him I was plagued by the thought: 'I know I met you before the officers' dance. Where?' Why has there been nothing in the papers about him?"

"Hush-hush stuff. Members of a French group requested that there be no publicity, that he be turned over to them. It took some diplomacy — we could have held him on several counts — but they got him. The accomplice who phoned a warning to him Christmas afternoon from a pay station was taken into custody quietly when he stepped from the booth."

"Will Suzanne be involved?"

"No. She took money for introductions. Nothing else. A short announcement will appear that Captain Count François Bouvoir has been transferred. His punishment will remain a secret. Exit the Captain. Enter Lieutenant (j.g.) Rand. Still like him a lot, don't you?"

"I do *not*. You are referring to the tender scene you interrupted Christmas eve, I presume."

"Then you don't remember calling me

'Ken' before you collapsed after the smash-up?"

"If I did, it was because I was in a daze with sharp, broken scraps of memory of a crucial day in my life all mixed up: Ken's wire announcing his marriage, Di's anger at me, Sam's fierce 'You've started something now, Dianne,' and my smarting conviction that I had been a mouse."

"You a mouse!" His laugh was tender. "I have something to tell you, but your eyes are so fiery I'm scared stiff."

"Only one way to go. Ahead. That's your combat prescription for fear, Major. He didn't — but suppose Ken did kiss me? You kiss the girl with whom you're unprovisionally in love, don't you?"

"I haven't as yet made a practice of it." As she met his laughing eyes her heart bailed out and took her defiance with it. "I've kissed her twice. Want to hear the romantic details?"

"After dessert you may spend a long, happy evening talking about her. It's part of my hostess training to listen to a soldier's raves."

Pike had carried out the small table, returned to freshen the fire and departed before Bill pulled a chair facing her as she sat in one corner of the sofa.

"Here we go for a heart-to-heart. Once upon a time I looked up into hazel eyes fringed in long, sooty lashes. That's the precise moment I fell in love."

"But you said —"

"That day in your office that I was unprovisionally in love? Sure I did. I was, with a dream girl. Military tactics. You wouldn't have consented to the arrangement if I had told you that I was sure you were my dream walking, would you?" There was no laughter in his voice and eyes, he was in lordly earnest.

"I — I wouldn't have believed it."

He rose and pulled her up into his arms, kissed her gently, then his mouth crushed demandingly on her lips.

"Believe it now?"

She looked up at him in response to his husky whisper.

"I believe it, Major."

It was some minutes later when he produced the ring and slipped it on her finger.

"Will it qualify as 'splashy'?" he asked.

"It's perfect. That gorgeous diamond, the emeralds and baguettes, are breath-taking. I love it."

"Would I be considered commercial if I asked for a payment on account?"

She kissed him.

"You're improving with practice. Not so chilly. Ready for some news?"

"You haven't been ordered to the Pacific?"

He gently pinched her cheek.

"That brings back the color. I'm ordered to a Marine training base and will I be glad to get my teeth into real work again. The General and I shove off in a week. How about marrying me before I go?"

"Bill! I would in a minute, but how can I leave my job?"

"I'm not asking you to leave it until your boss finds someone to take your place — if he plays fair and doesn't take too long. You can take it up with him tomorrow. He owes you a vacation after this last week. Marry me Tuesday and we can have a few days together before I go. You'll find plenty of ways in which to help win the war at the base. How about it?"

"It sounds like heaven, Bill."

"That's co-operation, that gets us somewhere. What say if we take Pat's runabout — I asked permission to use it — and drive to the Halls' tonight to make a date for our wedding with Reub and Sally?"

"Major, you have the most marvelous ideas."

"Got a lot more up my sleeve — you'll be

surprised!" He put his arms about her and drew her close.

"Would you be happier to be married at your sister's home, dearest? It could be arranged."

Head against his shoulder, she thought, if I go back I'll be swept along in the tide of Di's management. I won't have a word to say about my own wedding.

"You're a dear to suggest it, Bill, but, I'd rather be on my own. Just you and I and Reub and Sally — and Sam. I'll phone him in the morning. Perhaps he'll come."

"You won't have to tell him I love you. I told him the night I flew north to rescue you from the Navy. Get a long, warm coat to cover your gorgeousness while I bring round the car."

At the foot of the stairway she put her arm about his neck, kissed him with passionate fervor, whispered: —

"I love you, Bill." Head tipped back, she asked gaily: "How'm I doin'? Still chilly?"

His eyes widened with amazement and laughter.

"Definitely *not* chilly. Lady, you're doin' fine. I'll take that up with you later. Better get your coat while the going's good, *Miss* Barton."

His turbulent eyes, his husky warning, set

her pulses quick-stepping.

"*Mister* Jerrold, it's as good as done," she declared breathlessly. A streak of silver up the stairs and she was out of sight.

About the Author

Emilie Loring grew up in Boston in an atmosphere of writing and dramatics. Both her father and her brother were playwrights, so it is small wonder Mrs. Loring's own novels are filled with a strong sense of drama and with the romance and mystery that give unfailing pleasure to so many thousands of readers.